Dear Mystery Reader:

Toussaint, Montana. Deep in the heart of Big Sky country, sometime-deputy sheriff and cattle-brand inspector Gabriel Du Pré lives and works. Part Metis Indian and 100% intuitive sleuth, you've never met anyone quite like him. In Peter Bowen's fifth DEAD LETTER offering, THUNDER HORSE, Du Pré is in the middle of a battle between progress and preservation, and of course, murder.

All is well under the Big Sky until plans to turn a picturesque spring into a commercial trout farm go awry. In the midst of digging the ponds, an earthquake strikes and uncovers ancient fossils. Fossils of the Horn People, a group about whom so little is known that finding their bones is an archaeologists' dream. Combine that find with rumors of a T-Rex skeleton and you've hit an archaeological jackpot. That is, until archaeologist Robert Palmer turns up dead. On a quest for answers, Du Pré, with a little help from an Indian guru, his best friend, and a local professor, must pull out all of his sleuthing stops before it's too late to save not only the priceless fossils, but a few innocent people, too.

Bowen's Montana is the perfect destination for all mystery lovers. Once you've finished reading THUNDER HORSE, I'm sure you'll agree.

Yours in crime,

Joe Veltre
Associate Editor

Other titles from St. Martin's **Dead Letter** Mysteries

THE REVIEWERS RAVE ABOUT PETER BOWEN'S MONTANA MYSTERIES

"Peter Bowen writes mysteries that are truly mysterious— informed by Western legend, steeped in Indian superstition, peopled with characters who communicate by reading one another's minds . . . [A] mesmerizing series."
—*The New York Times Book Review*

"Marvelous . . . Du Pré is a striking character."
—*Portland Oregonian*

NOTCHES

"A haunting tale, punched out in arresting rhythms of speech powerful as a tribal drumbeat."   —*Entertainment Weekly*

"Beautiful portraits of the land itself, of Du Pré's Metis heritage, and especially of his fiddling and his music."
—*The Washington Post Book World*

"[An] absorbing tale of vengeance . . . Bowen excels at depicting the liminal, shifting worlds his characters inhabit."
—*Publishers Weekly*

"Du Pré manhunts in a way that puts to good use his creator's considerable knowledge of native lore . . . Bowen writes a provocative, involving adventure."   —*Kirkus*

COYOTE WIND

"Fiddler, father, widower, cowboy, and lover, Du Pré has the soul of a poet, the eye of a wise man, and the heart of a comic . . . Mr. Bowen has taken the anti-hero of Hemingway and Hammett and brought him up to date."
—*The New York Times Book Review*

"The best of Tony Hillerman meets Zane Grey, but with an original and compelling voice that readers won't soon forget."
—Ridley Pearson, author of
The Angle Maker and *No Witnesses*

SPECIMEN SONG

"Bowen tells his story in short, perfectly crafted sentences . . . The dialogue, the relationships, the Montana landscape, and, most of all, the quirky and memorable characters are matchlessly drawn."   —*Denver Post*

"Powerfully poetic . . . the rewards are great . . . One of the most unusual characters working the fictional homicidal beat."
—*Booklist*

WOLF, NO WOLF

"Ruthlessly funny . . . Bowen plays his language the way Du Pré plays his violin: plaintive, humorous, wild, the sounds of the sentences as meaningful as the story."
—*The Washington Post Book World*

"There are few characters with the strength of Gabriel Du Pré. They have names like Nero Wolfe, Lew Archer, and Jim Chee. Which is to say Peter Bowen has created a crime-fiction classic."   —David McCumber, author of *Playing Off the Rail*

"Bowen's work is an intriguing blend—it can be dark, but it's also comic . . . Original and compelling."
—*Rocky Mountain News*

"Bowen has a wonderful ear . . . Du Pré is likable for his intelligence, his poetry, his humor."   —*Bloomsbury Review*

THUNDER HORSE

PETER BOWEN

St. Martin's Paperbacks

THUNDER HORSE

Library of Congress Catalog Card Number: 97-49628

ISBN: 0-312-96887-6

Printed in the United States of America

St. Martin's Press hardcover edition/April 1998
St. Martin's Paperbacks edition/March 1999

10 9 8 7 6 5 4 3 2 1

For Saint Boo

✦ CHAPTER 1 ✦

I thought that Le Doux Springs was on state land," said Du Pré.

Bart had a map spread out on the dining table. He was drinking tea from a glass in a silver holder with a handle like a beer mug.

"Everybody did," said Bart. "But the survey was wrong and the original homestead took in the springs. So they've got it."

Du Pré looked out the window toward the Wolf Mountains.

Long time ago we come down here, hunt the buffalo, camp at Le Doux Springs. Lots of them wild plums there, for the pemmican. Women, they pick the plums while we go hunt them buffalo, drive them into a corral, kill them, butcher them out.

I know twelve songs got Le Doux Springs in them. God damn.

The water came up out of the ground in a meadow, three large pools fifty feet apart, thousands and thousands of gallons a minute. Snows melted long ago up in the Wolfs and flowing underground a long way till they came up.

Beautiful place, big meadow with a lot of water, flowers, thick grass, the creek cut down through the silt left by beaver dams twelve feet thick. Walls of soil and the creek cut through to the yellow clay that got wet and then wouldn't let any water through it.

Clean water, very cold. Lot of watercress. Little brook trout

1

in the weeds, darting out to grab food. Catch dozens in an hour. Fry them up, eat them bones and all.

"So," said Bart, "they own the water and they want to shunt it into some big ponds. Really big ponds. Me, I get to dig those ponds."

"Shit," said Du Pré. "This is not right."

The family that owned the ranch had hung on, even set up to handle a few dudes. But the parents died and the kids didn't want to live there and so the ranch had been sold.

To a Japanese company that was going to raise fish with the cool clear clean water. Pen-raised trout.

"I tried to buy the place when I found out it was for sale," said Bart. "I offered them twice what it's worth. No dice. They aren't raising trout for market there, I can tell you that. What they paid for it they can't make it back doing that."

"OK," said Du Pré. He took out his tobacco pouch and he rolled a smoke. He lit it.

"It's going to be a resort," said Bart. "There's a couple others in the Rockies. They raise giant trout for Japanese fly fishermen to catch and get mounted and ship home."

"In these ponds," said Du Pré.

"Which I am going to dig," said Bart.

"OK," said Du Pré.

It was late March and the wind was raw and the land looked barren and dead.

"The West is gone, Du Pré," said Bart. "It'll be a theme park. This is the only thing in the Wolfs now. You want to see utter destruction, go look at a ski hill. That's the *end*."

Du Pré nodded.

Long damn way from where we were. Long damn way.

"You drive my Rover tomorrow?" said Bart. "Maybe help me set up?"

Du Pré nodded.

"We go and make a joke out of Le Doux Springs," said Du Pré, "I help you you bet."

"Thing that I don't get," said Bart, "is that there isn't anything else around here. Nothing. No big airport. No town bigger than Cooper. Eastern Montana, a whole lot of nothing. No restaurants, no ski hill, no golf course."

"Yah," said Du Pré, "maybe we build a golf course, out back here."

"You aren't getting it," said Bart. He sighed. He put his glass of tea down.

"Golf course," said Du Pré.

"There isn't any reason for them to be building this resort here," said Bart. "None of it makes any sense. So, I want to know why they are building it anyway."

"I meet you, the bar," said Du Pré. "I maybe have a drink, we talk about your golf course here."

Bootheels on the deck outside. Booger Tom. The old cowboy opened the door and he stepped in, shivering. He was wearing a Hudson's Bay Company blanket coat that had once been cream with black stripes. The coat was patched and no longer cream-colored. A dark and rubbled gray with black stripes.

"Damn wind," said Booger Tom.

Du Pré shrugged.

Next he will say only a stupid son of a bitch will live here, Montana.

"Only a stupid son of a bitch would live here in Montana," said Booger Tom.

"Yes," said Bart and Du Pré.

Booger Tom stomped over to the table and he looked down at the map.

"Le Doux Springs," said Tom. "Heard there was some Nip company gonna dig it up and make trout ponds."

"I am going to dig it up," said Bart, "for the Nip company."

"We could put a golf course out back here," said Booger Tom, "have the caddies all dressed like sheepherders. You know, a little class."

"We were going to the bar," said Bart.

"So was I," said Booger Tom. "I hate to drink alone."

Bart and Du Pré and Tom went out and they got into Bart's Rover. Du Pré's old police cruiser was in Toussaint, getting some belts changed and new tires put on.

"A golf course," said Booger Tom. "We could have a bunch of cutting horses, too."

"Christ," said Bart.

He drove down the road that wound along the bench toward Toussaint.

A bald eagle sat on a deer carcass, so stuffed with meat it couldn't fly. It flapped its wings and tried to take off.

"Downright noble," said Booger Tom. "I like a country has that for the national bird."

The eagle ran a few feet flapping its wings and it fell on its face.

"Makes ya proud to be an American," said Bart. "Really does."

"Golf course," said Booger Tom. "Jesus."

A coyote ran up out of a draw.

Bart slammed on the brakes and Du Pré jumped out, grabbing the rifle clipped to the back of the front seat. He swung the gun up to his shoulder and aimed and fired and the coyote leaped up and fell. It flopped a minute and then it lay still.

Du Pré stepped through the fence and he walked quickly over to the coyote. He stood looking at it a moment and then he poked the open yellow eye with the end of the gun barrel.

"Good shot," said Bart.

Du Pré felt the coyote's belly.

"She just have pups," he said. "They die, too."

Du Pré dragged the carcass up toward the road. The underfur was already slipping and the pelt was worthless.

Shoot you two weeks ago, I keep your hide.

Bart helped Du Pré hang the coyote on the fence.

"This do any good?" said Bart.

Du Pré shrugged. He'd been hanging coyotes on fences all his life.

They got back in the Rover.

"God damn," said Booger Tom, squinting off across the road, "there's another one."

Du Pré scrambled out again. The coyote was three hundred yards away, dodging in and out of patches of sagebrush. Du Pré looked through the telescopic sight awhile. He dropped the gun from his shoulder.

"Lost him," he said.

Bart and Booger Tom and Du Pré stared hard.

A flicker of movement, once, between a sagebrush and a flat yellow-gray rock.

Du Pré put the crosshairs on the rock and he swung them slowly to the right.

The coyote was behind the sagebrush. Du Pré aimed at where the coyote's chest should be and he squeezed the trigger.

He put the crosshairs back on the rock and he swung them to the right again.

Nothing.

Du Pré opened the bolt of the rifle and he handed it to Bart and he crawled through the barbed-wire fence and Bart gave him the gun and Du Pré walked up the sloping hill toward the rock. He racked another shell into the chamber and he checked the safety.

Bart followed, jogging a little to catch up.

Du Pré got to the rock and he went through the sagebrush. Spatters of blood, new and red, on the ground.

Du Pré followed the blood trail.

The coyote lay fifty yards away, on its stomach, head between its paws. The wind ruffled the yellow-brown fur.

Du Pré waited. The coyote didn't move.

He aimed carefully and fired once more. The coyote jumped when the bullet hit and then it stretched out and went limp.

They walked back down to the fenceline and Bart went through and Du Pré handed him the rifle.

"Get him?" said Booger Tom.

"Yah," said Du Pré.

"Don't get two shots like that very much," said Booger Tom.

Du Pré nodded.

No, you don't.

❖ CHAPTER 2 ❖

Susan Klein looked up briefly from a book when Du Pré and Bart and Booger Tom came in. She finished whatever chapter she was reading, her lips moving, savoring the words. She closed the book and moved off to the kitchen and the grill hissed as the patties of meat landed on it.

She came back out.

"I want a grilled cheese sandwich," said Bart.

"Life," said Susan Klein, "has disappointments."

She drew a beer for Booger Tom and a ginger ale for Bart and she filled a tall glass with ice and poured it half full of bourbon for Du Pré. She topped off the glass with water. She put the drinks in front of them and she went back to the kitchen.

"A golf course," said Booger Tom. "Damn, why didn't I think of it before?"

"Yah," said Du Pré, "the cutting horses can eat that grass short around them holes they knock the balls into."

"Fuck you both," said Bart.

The police scanner above the cash register crackled and Susan Klein came out and listened to the dispatcher's voice and the officers checking in. Nothing much going on.

"You hear about the storm?" said Susan Klein, looking at Du Pré.

Du Pré shrugged.

"Freak storm out of the Arctic," she said. "Be here tonight, maybe three feet of snow. A lot of warm wet air coming up from the south."

"Good," said Bart, "we can't move the equipment tomorrow."

Susan Klein came out of the kitchen with three platters of cheeseburgers and fries. She slid them in front of each man.

"I want a grilled cheese sandwich," said Bart.

"Eat your cheeseburger, you guinea prick," said Susan Klein. "Some news about the snow, eh?"

March. The worst blizzards of the year were in March. Not every year, or very often, but when they came they came hard. Deer and elk died because they were weak from the winter. Cattle were calving and it made new calves prone to pneumonia.

This is the dead time, Du Pré thought, when the animals die and the grass is not up yet and it is getting warmer and there is mud. I don't like March.

"Le Doux Springs," said Booger Tom. "I used to camp there. Get down on them creekbanks and there's lots of buffalo bones. Burned ones. Lots of spear points and scrapers."

Maybe twenty miles from the big buffalo jump, Du Pré thought, good place to camp. Run a few hundred buffalo over the cliff there it stink pretty good a few days. Stink for a long time.

"Du Pré," said Bart, "let's move the stuff now. Right now. It gets muddy it'll be hell moving Popsicle."

Du Pré nodded.

They finished their burgers and drinks and they went out and got in the Rover and headed back to Bart's ranch, up on the benchlands that lapped against the Wolf Mountains.

Bart fired up the big Peterbilt tractor that pulled the lowboy trailer his dragline, Popsicle, sat on. The trailer had twenty tires on it. The dragline weighed thirty tons.

8

Du Pré started the diesel dump truck that pulled the back-hoe on its trailer.

Booger Tom sat on the hood of the Rover, drinking out of a plastic flask and smoking a cigar he'd grabbed on the way out of the bar.

Du Pré left first, driving down to the county road and turning right to head west. The dump truck was new and it drove easily. He got it up to fifty on the gravel road and when he looked back Booger Tom was there and Bart had yet to wallow down and make the turn. The road had a big turnout directly across from Bart's gate so he could swing out onto the road.

Du Pré got his tobacco pouch out and he rolled a smoke and wished that he'd brought his flask, which was in his cruiser back in Toussaint.

He slowed and braked and stopped.

Booger Tom drove up and he handed the plastic flask he had been drinking from out of the window. Du Pré had a snort. He looked at Booger Tom.

"Keep it," said the old cowboy, "there's a roadhouse a half hour up. I'll stop. You keep going. We won't get back until midnight anyway."

Booger Tom drove past and Du Pré started the big dump truck up to speed. There were more dials on the dashboard than Du Pré cared to know about.

He drove for ten miles and then turned onto a good two-lane blacktop road which wound around and caught the highway that went northwest of the Wolf Mountains.

Du Pré held it to sixty-five. The backhoe jumped a little too much if he was going any faster.

I am in my damn cruiser I come up this road a hundred and ten, Du Pré thought, this pretty good road.

Du Pré looked off northwest and he saw a black line on the horizon, faint as a crayon streak and far away.

Damn Alberta Clipper.

There was a box of tapes on the seat. Du Pré held up some and he found a Balfa Brothers tape and he jammed it into the deck and listened to the Cajun music.

Du Pré drove. The light was good but it would be dark in a couple of hours.

I hope we got that damn dragline parked the right place before it is dark, Du Pré thought, not much fun to move it in the night, there.

Good fiddling that.

Du Pré hummed along with the music. He had some whiskey.

The roadhouse lights shone up ahead on the right. Just a log saloon with a big parking lot, a place to drink and eat, one gas pump out front and inside a few staples on shelves in a room off the main area.

Du Pré pulled past the roadhouse and he parked the big dump truck out of the way near the fence, so he wouldn't have to turn going out onto the road.

He dropped to the ground from the step on the fender and he walked toward the roadhouse. Bart's Rover was parked out front.

There were half a dozen pickups rowed in front.

Du Pré pushed the solid plank door and he went in.

Some ranch couples sat at the bar drinking and a couple of cowboys were shooting pool. Booger Tom was down at the end of the bar, a new bottle of whisky sitting in front of him. He had a drink, one with ice.

Du Pré ordered a double ditch from the young woman behind the bar and he rolled a cigarette and lit it.

"Figure half an hour 'fore he catches up," said Booger Tom. "That rig is a bastard on the gravel."

The jukebox was set low and a country tune wailed.

They finished their drinks and went out and Du Pré pulled out on the highway and looked in the rearview mirror and there was Bart, the yellow running lights on top of the cab of the Peterbilt winked a couple of times.

Du Pré got up to sixty-five and held it there, and the Rover shot past, waddling a little. Booger Tom did not like or understand power steering and Du Pré grinned.

Air pretty blue in that Rover, there.

He turned off east on the road to Le Doux Springs. The road was badly potholed and one spot had water standing over the road. Du Pré inched through it, but the roadbed was sound underneath. He drove on and when he got to the gate that led up to the springs he stopped and waited until he could see Bart turn off the highway five miles away.

The ranch road was even worse, the new owners hadn't done any work on it and the old ones probably couldn't afford to.

Du Pré topped a hill and he looked down and saw the little valley that ran back to the mountain and the buildings. They were empty and deserted, not a soul in the house or bunkhouse or barns or sheds. The windmill's vane was broken and the wheel jigged from side to side.

Booger Tom had opened the gate that crossed the road that led up to the springs a half mile away. Du Pré pulled through and he got down, leaving the big diesel running.

"Damn shame," said Booger Tom, "they sold the damn stock, too. Not a fresh cow turd, or a horse apple. Wonder how long the place has sat empty?"

Du Pré shook his head.

They smoked and waited and then Bart's huge tractor-trailer ground up over the hill and moved down toward the ranch.

Bart drove through the gate and up into the pasture and he pulled the huge tractor-trailer around in a wide circle and parked it. The dragline could crawl the last two hundred yards on its steel tracks.

The light was failing.

Du Pré pulled the dump truck and backhoe far out of the way and he shut off the engine and locked the cab up and walked back to the Rover, which Booger Tom had driven up close.

They went back past the deserted ranch. The original cabin was in the backyard of the main house.

"Homesteaded in eighteen eighty-one," said Bart.

Du Pré looked at the ranch house.

Children once play there, he thought.

In the little corral, there must have been ponies.

✤ CHAPTER 3 ✤

Hey Du Pré," said Madelaine, "we stay in bed a few days now, eh?"

They were sitting in the Toussaint Bar looking out at the snow swirling down. Big fat wet flakes. There was a half foot on the ground and the snow had just begun fifteen minutes ago.

"Yah," said Du Pré, "nobody do very much, this."

"Damn Japanese," said Madelaine. "My old auntie, she tell me when I was little that she camp there, pick them plums while the men hunt the buffalo. Gabriel Dumont, he lead the people. The springs are good water all the time."

Du Pré nodded.

"We dance maybe." She got up and grabbed Du Pré by the collar and pulled him to his feet, laughing. She went to the jukebox and she put in money and a Métis tune began. They danced the clog steps on the scarred pine floor.

A few ranchers applauded.

"Du Pré!" one said. "Get your fiddle! I got my guitar!"

Du Pré went on dancing. He liked the rancher, but he wasn't a very good guitar player. The man's brother played bass. Not well either. But they were neighbors.

Du Pré smiled at Madelaine. She winked at him.

He went out to his old cruiser and he opened the trunk and unwrapped the blanket around the fiddle case, an old one, rawhide like a parfleche, porcupine quills sewn into the top in stars.

13

He went back in and tuned with the two men and they began to play, just a little dragging on the beat. Some of the other people got up and they began to dance.

They played for twenty minutes or so and a lot more people came in, Susan Klein had called there and here and told whoever answered that Du Pré was making a little music. Though it was snowing hard it wasn't cold and people drove in or walked from town and they stomped the snow from their boots outside and they came in and ordered drinks and danced or just sat and listened.

Bart and Booger Tom came and they sat at the bar clear toward the back and they ate steaks. They would talk in low voices. Du Pré and the two ranchers weren't using a sound system.

Du Pré ripped off a stair of notes and ended the song and he nodded to the ranchers.

Madelaine had been dancing by herself and she glowed with the exercise. Her pretty skin was flushed and her eyes danced.

"You buy me some pink wine, sailor?" she said.

Du Pré put his fiddle in the case.

There was a tinkling sound and Du Pré swung round to look at it. The bottles back of the bar were dancing and the wagon-wheel chandeliers were shimmering and the electricity was weakening and then getting strong again. The snow slid off the steel roof and whumped to the ground.

Chairs that were empty danced on the floor.

Earthquake.

Du Pré and Madelaine stood together for thirty seconds or so. There was a fading sound of tinkling glass and something fell off and broke on the floor. The lights went out for a moment and then they came back on.

"Not too bad," said Madelaine.

Du Pré shrugged.

The newspapers had said there were hundreds of little earthquakes under the Wolf Mountains every year. Almost all of them were very mild, so weak that they couldn't be felt at all. But once or twice a year the ground shook hard enough to shake things off bookshelves and make the hanging lights dance.

Long time ago, before Du Pré was born, when his father Catfoot was a child a big quake had hit. Catfoot said there was a sound like a giant train passing. He had been walking in the sagebrush and the ground split right in front of him, opening like a mouth and then snapping shut. Some cattle and horses just disappeared and never were found.

"I grab that sagebrush," Catfoot had said, "so damn hard it still got finger marks in it."

Everybody was quiet and then they all laughed nervously.

"Damn ground moves," one of the ranchers who had been playing with Du Pré said, "all bets are off. Shee-it."

Everyone laughed louder.

Du Pré got a drink and he and Madelaine went to Booger Tom and Bart. The old cowboy was poking Bart in the chest and making a point.

"I never been successful," said Booger Tom. "I know you wanted to lose money on the damn horses and I made money. If you had to make money, I'd lose money. I wear my hat on my ass. Boots on my ears."

"Christ," said Bart.

"You guys," said Madelaine, "this argument it is boring, hear it all of the time. Why don't you—"

The building lurched violently and the lights went out and glass crashed on the floor. It lurched again.

A huge sound came from far away very rapidly, a giant sound like a great train passing.

15

People screamed. There were yells.

—God damn!

—Oh!

—Henry!

Something crashed down and there were some groans.

The bar was pitch black inside and all the mercury vapor lamps on tall poles in the town were out and the snow was falling down and it was suddenly very, very silent.

"I was the one that farted," said Booger Tom. "Couldn't help myself."

Madelaine lit her cigarette lighter. The flame gave off a feeble yellow light.

—Help . . . .

Bart and Booger Tom were still sitting on the bar stools. Du Pré was down on one knee, Madelaine on both.

A small flashlight flicked on and then another. The ranchers carried them in their shirt pockets.

One of the wagon wheel chandeliers had come down on a couple. The man was sitting dazed, blood running down his forehead. The woman was folded over and the heavy wheel was still on her. A couple men lifted it off and she slid down to the floor. Her head thumped.

Du Pré lit his lighter and he leaned over the bar and saw Susan Klein holding on to the stainless steel tubing at the wait station. The mirror in the old carved barback had shattered.

"You OK?" said Du Pré.

Susan was clutching the tubing with both hands hard. Her eyes were screwed shut.

"I'm cut bad," she said.

Bart and Du Pré kicked their way through the tipped-over stools.

Du Pré swung up on the bar and he looked down.

The bottles were on the floor, some broken, some not.

A heavy piece of the mirror had fallen against Susan's Achilles tendons. Blood welled from the cuts and flooded over the broken mirror and dripped on the floor.

Du Pré swung over. The mirror piece was wedged against the shelves in back.

Du Pré looked for a moment.

"Bart," said Du Pré, "You grab her shoulders good, hold on."

Bart reached over the bar and gripped Susan's shoulders with his huge hands. He nodded at Du Pré.

Du Pré tapped the glass hard with the bottom of a heavy tumbler.

It cracked and broke and Susan slumped.

Du Pré slid the glass away.

Clear to the bone.

"Lift her up," said Du Pré. "We got to get the bleeding stopped."

Bart lifted Susan, who was not a small woman, slowly and gently up and he laid her facedown sliding on the bartop.

Du Pré grabbed the pressure points above her knees on the inside.

The wound was awful. The Achilles tendons had been sliced through and the muscles of the calves were bunched up high and quivering with nothing to restrain them.

Madelaine packed the wounds with ice.

Susan moaned.

Du Pré knelt and he looked carefully at the blood on the mirror and he lifted up the broken pieces and checked the floor.

"She did not lose too much," he said.

Madelaine was wrapping her jacket around Susan. Bart took off his heavy wool coat and he put it on her.

The woman who had been hit by the wagon wheel was sitting up and vomiting on the floor.

"I'll jerk the seats out of the Rover," said Bart. "We have to get these two to the hospital."

Du Pré nodded. Cooper was twenty miles away and it had a small hospital.

Bart picked his way through the people and he heaved on the jammed front door and tore it open and he went out.

There was faint light from the snowy street. The snow was a foot and a half deep.

"I got some sleeping bags in my truck," said a rancher. He went out after Bart.

"What we got for a stretcher?" said Madelaine.

Susan moaned and stirred.

"Damn," she said.

Madelaine stroked her hair.

"You going to be all right," said Madelaine.

"Yes," said Susan.

Bart came back in.

"Let's go," he said.

He picked Susan up gently and carried her to the door, Madelaine holding her head.

The woman who had been hit by the wagon wheel walked out, her arm on the shoulder of her husband.

Bart had flung the seats from the Rover into the street. The bags had been unzipped and rolled out.

Madelaine got in and Du Pré and Bart slid Susan in face-down.

"Give me bunch of snow," said Madelaine.

Du Pré grabbed a bucket near the back doors of the Rover and he packed it with the thick heavy snow.

They got in and Bart drove off.

✦ CHAPTER 4 ✦

Du Pré looked down from the window of the little airplane at the crew of power company workers straightening a line of poles that the earthquake had tipped off plumb.

A jagged tear in the earth ran south of the Wolf Mountains, ending almost at the east end of the range and curving around the west end and zagging north to end against a faulted range of hills that faded out into the Great Plains.

There hadn't been a lot of damage. There weren't that many buildings in the county, or the one next to it, or the one next to that. The tallest building in a hundred miles was the three-story courthouse in Cooper, and it had been abandoned twenty years before because the population had dropped so low the building was too big for the county employees. Their numbers had dropped three-fourths from the 1920s.

Buster Dunn, one of the deputies, flew the plane. He'd been a pilot in the military, spotter aircraft.

"Nobody killed, thank God," yelled Buster over the plane's racket.

Susan Klein was in the hospital in Billings. She had had surgery twice on her cut Achilles tendons and Benny expected her home in a week.

"Wearing casts for months," said Benny, "it ain't gonna put her in a good mood."

The little hospital in Cooper had patched Susan up and as

soon as a helicopter could get through she'd been flown out. Some of the nerves in her feet had been cut.

Du Pré stared down at the slash the earthquake had made. In places the earth had risen and dropped so twenty-foot walls of earth and stones sat exposed.

"Man on the television said the Wolfs are a foot and a half taller," said Buster Dunn. "Jumped up just like that."

Buster turned north at the west end of the Wolfs and followed the earthquake line to the end and he turned and headed back. Du Pré pointed toward Le Doux Springs and Buster flew that way. They could see the giant green dragline that Bart called Popsicle sitting on its trailer and the backhoe, with Bart at the controls, cutting a hole in the ground for some reason.

"I'm gonna head back," yelled Buster. "I got work to do."

They landed near Toussaint in a few minutes, the big soft tires sending up sprays of ice and water from the grass airstrip.

Buster swung the plane around toward the circular hard-stand he parked it on. Du Pré jumped out and grabbed a wing when Buster had the little plane about where he wanted it. They ran cables to eyes and tied the plane down thoroughly.

Du Pré got in his old cruiser and he wallowed through the pools of slush and mud to the road and up on it and he turned right and went to the Toussaint Bar.

Madelaine was behind the bar, pulling a beer for a rancher.

"Du Pré!" she said. "It is good to see you. One more time you go up in that fool machine you don't die!"

Madelaine hated flying. She hated the thought of flying.

Du Pré slid up on the barstool and he waited while Madelaine made him a tall drink. He rolled a smoke and lit it and he looked at the hole where the mirror had been. A new one had been ordered but it wouldn't be here for a week.

Benny was replacing panes in the sixteen-light windows that had broken or cracked.

What the earthquake had done mostly was ruin the wax seals under toilets. Almost all of the toilets within fifty miles of the earthquake scar had to be unbolted and lifted up and new wax rings put down.

Du Pré looked down at a ripple that went across the old pine floor of the bar. It was new, where the floor joists had bent. The nails had been pulled partway out but the earthquake didn't drive them back in.

God damn, thought Du Pré, it gets a little drier, me, I will be under this fucking floor with Benny, pounding on things while them brown recluse spiders crawl over me.

Du Pré hated small enclosed places.

But Benny Klein was his friend.

"So what you see from up there Du Pré?" said Madelaine.

"Earth ripped apart," said Du Pré, "maybe eighty miles long, that."

"I got a new spring out to my place wasn't there before," said the rancher sitting a few stools down, "which is good. On the other hand, my damn trout pond disappeared, fish and all. My granddad said there was a hell of an earthquake back in seventeen. Didn't do much but knock down a few bobwire fences. But he damn sure remembered it. Sounded like the biggest damn freight train world ever saw."

Du Pré nodded.

"Lourdes she call," said Madelaine, "said to give you her love. She likes that Chicago, you know, likes that school. Bart is a nice man."

Madelaine's youngest daughter was in a private Catholic girls' school in Chicago.

"I tell her watch out for muggers, she say after them nuns muggers aren't much. Hee."

21

Madelaine laughed. Her rich black hair had locks of silver in it. She was wearing some of her turquoise and silver jewelry, old pieces handmade a long time ago. She had a very good eye.

"Your kids pretty well gone," said Du Pré. "You got a good job, keep you out of trouble."

"No shit," said Madelaine. "Poor Susan she will be in them casts for months, there, physical therapy, she is not going to stand here cripple herself for life. We got me and two others and we are worn out doing the work she used to do by herself."

"Yes," said Benny Klein, the sheriff, "scary, ain't it. She was only in here fourteen hours a day on the slow ones. If I worked as hard as my wife, I'd die."

"You guys are pussies," said Madelaine. "Women been working three times hard as men since God screwed people up the first time."

Father Van Den Heuvel, the big clumsy Jesuit who had the little church in Toussaint, fumbled through the front door. His long black wool overcoat was misbuttoned and he was bleeding from his left hand.

Only man I ever know, thought Du Pré, knock himself cold shutting his head in the door of his car.

Bunch of times.

Saw him try to chop wood once. Jesus.

Father Van Den Heuvel looked dimly through his badly steamed glasses.

"Du Pré," snapped Madelaine, "you go and help he or he fall against the stove."

Du Pré got up and he went to the priest and took him by the arm and steered him past the big barrel stove, hot, a kettle of water boiling on top.

"Thank you," murmured the big priest, "I think." He sat on

a bar stool. He kept losing his balance, his wool coat was bunched under him and it slipped on the leather seat.

The night of the earthquake the bell in his little church tolled all night, every time there was an aftershock.

Du Pré helped Father Van Den Heuvel with his coat. He hung the long black woolen on the staghorn rack bolted to a fencepost stuck at the end of the partition that led back to the johns.

"Snow is melting," said the big priest.

Madelaine looked grimly at the wet trail he had left across the floor. He wore size sixteen shoes and his galoshes had brought in a lot of slush. He had somehow managed to fill them walking from his car into the bar.

"Church attendance is up a lot," he said brightly. "Nothing like a natural disaster to make my flock want to hedge their bets."

Du Pré laughed. Father Van Den Heuvel was not terribly committed to literal interpretations of the Bible and he thought most Church doctrines were, as he put it, "unhelpful."

"My car is stuck," said the priest.

"You get that car, stuck, an inch of dust," said Du Pré. "Where is it?"

"Down the street a little," said Father Van Den Heuvel.

Du Pré grinned and he nodded. He would go get in it and drive it out of wherever it was stuck easily. If the priest tried it, the car would sink another inch every time he pressed the accelerator.

The telephone rang and Madelaine went to get it. She talked for a moment and then she walked back along the bar carrying the cordless plastic box. She handed it to Du Pré.

"Gabriel?" It was Bart.

"Yah."

"I think you better come on out here."

"Uh?" said Du Pré.

"I found some skeletons," said Bart, his voice sinking to a whisper.

"Christ," said Du Pré, "now them ranchers are murderers? What are you telling me."

Bart laughed.

"No," he said, "not these ranchers. I found some old skeletons. The earthquake lifted up a chunk of earth near the springs and there they are, right in the wall. I just noticed it. I walked up to the springs to see how they were after the quake."

"Skeletons," said Du Pré. "Got some Indian burial?"

"Must be," said Bart. "You know any Indians that buried their dead all covered with red dust? Red ocher, maybe, though it seems even brighter than that."

"No," said Du Pré, "me, I don't know that."

"Well," said Bart, "maybe Benetsee does. Is he around?"

"I go see," said Du Pré.

"I think you'd better," said Bart.

❧ CHAPTER 5 ❧

Du Pré floundered up the rutted drive to Benetsee's old cabin. Water shot up when the wheels dropped into the deep holes wallowed into the clay. Dirty snow sat melting in piles.

Smoke from the old metal chimney.

Du Pré shut off the engine of his old cruiser and he got out and stared at the cabin's front door.

Paint. It had been *painted.*

Turquoise.

He squelched through the mud and rotting snow and up the steps and he noticed the boards on the porch floor were new. Usually when he came he stepped carefully so he didn't fall through the rotted old planks.

Du Pré looked at the door. It fit. Someone had rehung it and put new stops on the jambs.

It opened.

Pelon, the young man who had just appeared a couple years before, Benetsee's student, stood there grinning.

"Nice paint that eh?" he said. He had a gold front tooth and his hair was wrapped with marten skins, his feet were in brightly beaded moccasins.

Nez Percé work, Du Pré thought.

Pretty nice. Pelon, he used to be a computer programmer, wore suits, short hair. Big paycheck.

"Come in," said Pelon.

Du Pré stepped inside and he looked around and his eyebrows shot up.

The place was clean. The papers and books and pipes and whistles and bone-handled knives and pots and pans were on shelves. New shelves.

"Benetsee he is dead, yes?" said Du Pré.

"Oh, no," laughed Pelon, "he is out, the lodge. Sweat since dawn. He be out now, said you would be coming."

Du Pré nodded. Benetsee knew things he could not possibly know. Riddles. Weather. Answers to riddles. Old songs. *Really* old songs.

Du Pré looked out the little window at the back of the cabin. It had always been covered by hides and grass stuffed between. Now the frame had glass in it.

Steam curled out of the door of the sweat lodge, a mess of old sleeping bags and tarps and tenting thrown over a willow frame.

Benetsee crawled out of the lodge on his hands and knees, naked but for a huge pair of boxer shorts, paisley ones. They hung past his old knobby knees when he stood up, like a skirt.

Bart's old shorts, Du Pré thought, Bart, him weigh two-fifty, more, Benetsee he weigh maybe ninety-five pounds.

Du Pré laughed. So did Pelon.

Benetsee went behind some clothes hanging on a line and the shorts fell to the ground and Du Pré laughed and smoked a cigarette and the old man came back out from behind the wash. He was dressed in his old stained black iron cloth pants and moccasins and a thick red check shirt and he had wrapped his head with a blue kerchief. He shuffled around the side of the cabin and he came in the front door.

Benetsee looked at Du Pré and he grinned.

"Pret' nice door," he said, looking at the new paint. "Pelon, he get tired, praying. Paint things, fix things, must be some hurry, have me die, yes."

They all laughed.

"I am thirsty," said Benetsee, "Need a smoke. Wonder if there is a young man, has manners here anywhere."

Du Pré laughed again and he went out his old cruiser and he got a jug of screwtop wine from the trunk and a package of tobacco.

He slid and slipped back up the steps and he scraped the mud off best he could on a steel strip stuck in a chunk of firewood.

Inside, he opened the wine and he filled the jar Benetsee held out.

The old man drank a pint of cheap wine in one long swallow. He held out the jar again, Du Pré poured.

"Ah," said Benetsee, "that is ver' good."

Du Pré rolled the old man a thick smoke and he lit it and handed it to him.

Benetsee sucked down the thick tobacco smolder and he closed his eyes and he nodded and rocked a little, sitting in an old chair once shaky but now wired together.

"Bart he find some them Horned Star People," said Benetsee. "Got red all on their bones, long time gone."

Du Pré nodded. He waited.

Benetsee belched.

"Long time gone," said Benetsee.

Pelon poured hot water into a cup, from the kettle on the woodstove.

Chaparral tea. Good for kidneys.

Benetsee had more wine. He kept his eyes closed. He rocked back and forth a little.

Du Pré waited.

Benetsee began to sing, a high keening ululation, eerie, fey. His eyes flew open.

"Long time gone," he said, "very long time. He find them bones deep I bet."

"Earthquake shove them up," said Du Pré. "They are by them Le Doux Springs."

"Got red powder all over, them," said Benetsee. "Look close you find little pieces, walrus ivory."

Jesus, thought Du Pré, thousands of miles from any damn walrus.

"Who them Horned Star People?" said Du Pré.

Benetsee shrugged.

"People, long time," the old man said. His face creased, he grinned, old black teeth with brown roots. "People coming down that Great North Trail long time, long long time."

Du Pré nodded.

"They make these little necklace things," said Benetsee, "them ivory pieces. Got a star on them, got horns on the star, horns like them old cattle. Used to be buffalo had horns like that, long time gone."

Du Pré looked at his hands.

Sure there were, he thought, ten thousand years ago there were those longhorn buffalo. Horns go six, eight feet, tip to tip. They are bigger than the buffalo we got now, and them buffalo we got now plenty big enough, them. Weigh a damn ton, more.

"Bart wonder maybe you come look," said Du Pré.

"Yah," said Benetsee, "I never see them Horned Star People, Pelon him don't either, we come. You got wine, we come. Tobacco."

"Old bastard," said Du Pré.

"Yah," said Benetsee, "tell you things, them Horned Star People, maybe you are surprised they tell you."

Benetsee shrugged into his old leather jacket and Pelon put on a new down coat Bart had given him. They went out to Du Pré's cruiser and got in and Gabriel started the car up and he backed and filled till he could point it back down the rutted drive. They floundered out to the county road and lurched up onto the firm gravel and Du Pré floored it.

Pools of water stood in the flats of the plains. Wet cattle stood looking mournful.

"Du Pré!" said Benetsee, from the backseat. "You got a damn glass in here, huh?"

Du Pré sighed. He slowed and stopped and he got out and opened the trunk of the cruiser and he grabbed two battered tin cups, the enamel chipped. Blue and white. Cowboy china.

He handed them to Benetsee. The old man sloshed wine into one and he handed it to Pelon.

Du Pré rolled three cigarettes. He lit Benetsee's and Pelon's and his own and then he handed them around and got in.

"We maybe go now," said Du Pré. "Go and look at what Bart find, yes?"

"I know what Bart find," said Benetsee.

"Old fart," said Du Pré.

"Hee," said Benetsee, "I piss Du Pré off all his life. You tell Pelon about the deer, huh?"

Du Pré laughed.

When he was ten Catfoot had taken him hunting, first time, hunting deer, make some meat in the fall. They got up early and went out to a place where the deer crossed after coming down from the hills to a creek for water just before dawn.

Catfoot and Du Pré waited sitting on a log up on a little

ridge and pretty soon Catfoot touched Du Pré on the shoulder and jerked his head toward the trail.

There was a huge buck standing there, very still, head raised, and looking right at Du Pré.

Du Pré was ten and he was very excited and he tried to aim right but he was shaking so bad he could not. Finally he took a deep breath and held the sights as still as he could and he pulled the trigger.

The .30-30 boomed and Du Pré went over backward, he was a small child and he wasn't holding the gun tight to his shoulder so it kicked him instead of pushing him.

HIT ME IN ASS HIT ME IN ASS!!!!! someone screamed.

Du Pré scrambled up and he looked toward the voice and there wasn't anyone there. No deer either.

Du Pré looked at his father, Catfoot, but Catfoot just looked back at him, not saying anything.

HIT ME IN ASS HIT ME IN ASS!!!!!

"You hit that deer," said Catfoot, "Not a ver' good shot though."

They waited twenty minutes for the deer to lie down and stiffen up and then Catfoot and Du Pré followed the blood trail.

The trail led down into a coulee.

Benetsee was there, sitting on a rock.

The deer was lying in front of him, a pool of blood spread out from the slash across its throat.

"How you like my fine big fat deer?" Benetsee had said.

Du Pré looked at the old man, confused.

Catfoot started to gut the deer. He motioned to Du Pré to come and look.

There was a bullet hole in one haunch.

Not a bad wound at all.

The deer had run down into cover, in the coulee.

Where it met Benetsee.

Du Pré and his father went hunting the next day.

"See," said Catfoot, "real good hunter there, that old man, he don't need no rifle, he hunt them deer with a knife."

Du Pré looked at his father.

"He sing good, that Benetsee," said Catfoot.

✤ CHAPTER 6 ✤

Du Pré looked at the skeletons, packed in about a foot-wide layer. Several of them.

Bart had two skulls sitting on a square blue plastic tarp, just below the cutbank ten feet high the earthquake had made in seconds.

Bright red powder dusted the skeletons, the skulls, skeined the yellow earth between layers of gravels.

Benetsee was standing away, praying, his fingers dribbling tobacco.

Du Pré's tobacco.

"Really something, isn't it?" said Bart. His broad face smiled, he looked a little sad, a little bemused.

"Them Japanese know?" said Du Pré.

Bart shook his head.

"I think this is real important," he said. "If I call them then they may order me to cover this over or something. I wouldn't do it. I don't know what the law is, or how archaeologists can get the right to dig here properly. I called Foote. He'll try to buy the site here. Try pretty hard. And he may. The springs are dry, and that was the water for the ponds."

Le Doux Springs dry, Du Pré thought. Now that is some damn thing.

He walked over to the conelike holes in the grass. Water

stood in the bottom, but it wasn't bubbling up fast and cold. Just sat there.

Now that water run under the earth. Run around the mountains maybe and turn north.

Red River.

Du Pré laughed.

He walked back to where Bart and his digging machines were. And old Benetsee praying, Pelon standing quietly behind the old man.

"There's something else," said Bart. "You know I majored in anthropology in college. I was even sober enough of the time to learn a little. I still remember a few things. Look at these skulls, Gabriel. What do you see?"

Bart picked up one gently. It had no jawbone. The teeth had fallen out. Red ocher filled the sutures of the skull, red zigzag lines.

"Very long skulls," said Bart. "I think they may be Caucasian."

"Ah!" said Du Pré. He laughed.

"Yes," said Bart, "that would indeed be funny. I think there was another skeleton found . . . Washington? . . . Ten thousand years old."

"Hum," said Du Pré, "these peoples they come a long time ago, I guess. Can't tell, Benetsee say they have these walrus ivory amulets, got a horned star on them."

Bart went to the wall and he peered at it and he took out his pocketknife and he dug a little and caught something that fell. He spat on it. He rubbed it with his fingers.

Du Pré walked over.

Bart was holding a dark yellow lozenge that had a layer of mineral stain on it, and splotches of the vermilion powder. He scraped carefully with his knife.

A many-pointed star with long horns appeared.

"Like this?" said Bart. His voice was awed.

Bart's cell phone chirred in his pocket. He took it out and unfolded the mouthpiece.

"Bart . . ." he said. He listened.

"It's a major archaeological site," he said. "Big stuff. If they won't sell now, tell them you'll have to inform the press."

Bart listened.

"If necessary," he said, "do just that. I . . . OK, OK . . . thanks. Yeah, he's right here."

Bart handed the little telephone to Du Pré. Du Pré put it to his ear.

"Gabriel," said Lawyer Foote, "I trust you can keep Bart from punching out the present owners."

"They are not here," said Du Pré.

"They are very obdurate about not selling," said Foote, "which is very strange. This whole business is very strange. There is absolutely no reason for them to build such a trout pond there. The Wolfs are remote, air connections are nonexistent. There's something else going on."

"Yah," said Du Pré.

"Could the Métis possibly claim the site as a burial ground?" said Foote.

"We don't be here ten thousand years," said Du Pré, "maybe five hundred, not this far west."

"I think," said Foote, "that it would be best if you and Bart pull those skeletons out of there and get them away. There is a big goddamned fight coming, I can see that."

"OK," said Du Pré.

"Let me talk to Bart again," said Foote.

Du Pré handed the telephone back to Bart.

Benetsee was still praying. Pelon was standing, hands folded. Du Pré had to piss. He did.

"I hate to," said Bart, "it screws up the site. I suppose we could try to lift out the whole layer."

Bart turned away. He spoke a few more minutes. He folded the cell phone back up and he put it in his pocket.

"How are you at grave robbing?" he said.

Du Pré shrugged.

"I'm going to cut down on each side of that," said Bart, pointing, "and then try to get the burial out in one chunk. Then we will hide it. Says Mr. Foote."

"OK," said Du Pré.

"We'd better hurry," said Bart, "I got this feeling."

He went to the backhoe and he started it. Black diesel fumes belched from the stack and the rain cap flapped. He lurched over to the cutbank and he extended the bucket and he began to chew down straight on one side of the reddened bones. The gravelly soil was soft and easy to cut. The bones were seven or eight feet down under the layers of rock the mountains had shed and the waters had moved.

Du Pré stood smoking. He looked at the burial, a foot thick and seven feet long. He wondered how far back it went.

Du Pré started the dump truck and he backed it over to where Bart could lift the bones and drop them into the bed.

Bart waved at Du Pré.

Du Pré walked over and jumped up on the step on the rear of the backhoe.

"Drop the tailgate off. . . ." Bart yelled over the roar of the engine. "Maybe I can set this down easy!"

Du Pré nodded and he jumped down and went to the dump truck and got a heavy hammer and a big punch and he knocked the pins out of the hinges and he dumped the slab of steel off. The tailgate stood in the mud for a moment and then slowly fell over.

Bart was cutting the overburden off the top of the yellow-red compressed earth that held the bones. Du Pré waited, holding a shovel, and when Bart swung the bucket away he stepped up in the hole in the cutbank and he shoved the blade of the shovel under the gravels and he cleaned out the last layer over the jackstrawed bones.

Du Pré squinted. Another amulet. He reached down and picked it up. He slipped it in his pocket.

Bart came up with a hoe and he scraped the last little bits of gravel away from the yellow earth. Bart reached down and he picked up a chunk and he twisted it in his hands. The yellow soil had a lot of clay in it and it was like a very, very stiff dough.

The burial pocket was about three feet across by seven, and had been dug in the gravels. The yellow earth came from someplace else.

Fairly common in cuts the creeks made in the plains. Du Pré had seen bands of it all his life, in the walls of coulees and gullies, or any place the waters had cut down through the soils.

"I think I can chivvy it out," said Bart.

Du Pré nodded. He got down out of the cut and he stood off to one side.

Bart very carefully stabbed the gravels around the yellow patch with the long tines on the backhoe bucket. He cleared out scoops of gravel from each side and then he jammed the bucket down and he twitched it, the engine of the backhoe racing to pump up the hydraulic pressure that powered the bucket.

The yellow slab came free and slid forward. Bart pulled it out till it barely touched the ground.

He switched ends and he shoved the front-end loader bucket under it.

He tilted the bucket back and the mass of yellow earth and bones tipped up.

Bart put it gently as he could in the back of the dump truck.

Du Pré had put a chain on the tailgate of the dump bed. Bart lifted it up with the backhole bucket and set it on the bed and Du Pré pounded the pins back in. He crawled over the sides of the bed and to the ground and he patched the gate.

Bart was obliterating the cut he had made, scraping the gravels out so that it looked more like it had happened when the earthquake hit.

Benetsee was standing at Du Pré's elbow.

"You got that ivory, your pocket," the old man said.

Du Pré nodded. He took it out.

Benetsee spat on it. He rubbed it on his black greasy pants.

"Long time gone," he said. "Now we go hide these bones, huh?"

Du Pré shrugged.

Bart shut off the backhoe after he pulled it a hundred yards away.

Du Pré looked at Benetsee.

"You move that truck," said the old man. He pointed to the ground.

Du Pré looked down.

Water was percolating up out of the muddy tracks Bart had left.

It was flowing, faster and faster.

Le Doux Springs, rising once again.

❧ CHAPTER 7 ❧

W here you get all that yellow mud on you?" said Madelaine. She was standing behind the bar, slicing limes into eighths.

"Le Doux Springs," said Du Pré. "Them skeletons was in it."

"Funny mud," said Madelaine.

"It is loess," said Du Pré. "The wind it push it down here from up north. Out in Washington they got it two hundred feet deep."

"Clean that mud a little you maybe got paint," said Madelaine.

Du Pré nodded. Madelaine made paints from muds and bark, crushed soft minerals. Benetsee used them, so did Pelon.

Us Catholic Métis, it is not far to the old ways. Been here, part of our blood, long time.

"Got mud like that west of here," said Madelaine, "find it near them buttes, the Big Dry. Each side, east of them."

Du Pré nodded.

"Le Doux Springs come up again, eh?" laughed Madelaine.

"Damn near eat Bart's backhoe," said Du Pré, "Time he drive it away it is sunk down two feet. Spring is running out of just the one place now, though."

The new Le Doux Springs was a rapidly collapsing hole twenty feet across. The earthquake had rearranged the gravels and the new spring was running two times the volume of the

38

old one. The little creek was filled to the banks and spilling out where it was flat.

"Susan be back a few days," said Madelaine. "Poor lady. Cut them tendons right through. Be in a wheelchair and casts awhile. She is the only one hurt in this, though, everybody else they get a little cut, maybe, some scared."

Du Pré sipped his whiskey.

Wonder how it is, up them Wolfs. Plenty mountain goats, sheep killed. The quake start them avalanches. Couple mountainsides come off. Have to find new trails.

"Bart is digging them holes?" said Madelaine.

Du Pré shook his head.

"Not till the man designed the trout ponds comes." said Du Pré. "The new spring is in a different place, now the drawings don't work. He is to be here tomorrow."

"Got architects for trout ponds, fat Japanese to fish in," said Madelaine. "Back to that nature, got a lot of concrete in it."

"Where you put them bones?" said Madelaine.

"Bart's," said Du Pré. "We put them in a seed bin. Ratproof, no bugs, dry. Got a nitrogen tank, keeps that air all nitrogen, kills anything tries to live in there."

"Horned Star People," said Madelaine. "Me, I never heard of them. Lots of people through here long time, I guess."

"Bart got someone who is expert coming," said Du Pré.

"Expert," said Madelaine. "That is someone from out of town, yes?"

"Yah," said Du Pré.

There was a cold mean rain falling outside, sometimes slurried with ice. The wind kept shifting quarters. The slush splatted time to time against the glass of the windows.

"Nasty day," said Madelaine.

A couple ranch hands came in, their faces red and raw looking, water running off their long yellow slickers. They looked down at the puddles and went back outside to shake off the wet.

One of them came in.

"I'm sorry, ma'am," he said. "Do you have a mop I could use?"

Madelaine went to the walkway to the cooler and she got him one. He carefully mopped up the mess. His partner came in and he put the damp slickers on pegs near the big wood-stove.

"I need this damn weather," said the hand who had mopped, "like I need another damn armpit."

Madelaine drew two beers and she poured two shots of whiskey. She set them at the stools next to Du Pré.

The hands drank gratefully.

"Calves don't come 'cept in weather like this," said one of the hands.

"Sheep," said Du Pré, "them you got to have a blizzard for."

The hands nodded.

Du Pré had known them for ten years or so. They were brothers from North Dakota, hardworking and not very bright.

One of them was still shaking from the cold.

The wind splashed a bucketful of slop against the window-panes on the north side of the bar.

"Think I'll go to college," said one of the hands.

"That's good," said the other. "Guess I will, too."

More people came in, ranchers and their families. If they had been up all night calving and had a break now a ham-burger would sure taste good.

Madelaine went out with her pad and then after she got the orders she went back to the kitchen, nodding at Du Pré to please get the drinks and watch the bar while she cooked.

Du Pré got everybody's orders, beers for the adults, pop for the kids, and he filled glasses with ice and sodas and he drew drafts and he piled them on a tray and carried them over and set them down, sometimes having to ask who had what. He got pretty much everything right, only having to dump two sodas.

The brothers each had another shot and beer. Du Pré marked it down on their tabs.

Du Pré helped Madelaine carry the burgers and fries out, plate after plate, and he set them round, either they had cheese or not, and if the person he set it in front of had the wrong one they would swap with a neighbor.

Du Pré's eldest daughter Jacqueline came in, bright silver beads of water on her capote. She threw the hood back and she laughed.

"Hey Papa," said Jacqueline, "you can maybe not be a waitress now, eh?"

She hung her capote near the woodstove. It began to steam. The stove was very hot.

"We are all right now," said Madelaine. "You are a crappy waitress. I don't give you no tips."

Du Pré nodded.

Old Booger Tom came in, moving very slowly, his right side stitchy. The old cowboy had broken every bone in his body one time or another and in very damp weather like this they all hurt.

Tom struggled out of his slicker and he hung it up and he made his way painfully to the bar and he slid up on a stool beside Du Pré.

Madelaine put a bottle of whiskey and a tall glass with ice in front of him and she went off to the kitchen to get slices of pie for the people who had finished their hamburgers.

"That damn hammerhead Bart," said Tom, "out working with the hands today pulling calves, got to hand it to him, though. He can be just as stupid as anyone who works for him."

Du Pré laughed.

Booger Tom had no doubt been up all night, and he was nearly eighty. Maybe more than eighty. These small wiry cowboys aged slowly.

"Dumb damn way to spend my life," said Booger Tom, "but I done it so I guess I ought not to bitch."

"You are through though?" said Du Pré.

"Pret' much," said Booger Tom, "few more'll drop but it ain't like it was. The hands can go back to their chores now. Calves come all in a mob."

The door opened and a man came in, a huge man Du Pré had never seen before. He was gray-haired and had a full beard, and his face was pitted from old acne scars and weathered rough and brown. He had on a stained parka that had seen hard use, and high laced boots made of leather and nylon, with very thick soles of white rubber. A round fur hat on his head, dripping rain.

The big man stripped off his parka and he took it outside and he shook it and he came in and hung it up with the mass of coats drying by the woodstove, and he took the mop from the bucket and cleaned up the mess he had made. He wrung the mop out and he left it standing beside the bucket.

His shoulders were huge, masses of muscle, and his hands were thick and he walked like a bear, rocking a little side to side.

He looked once around the bar and his eyes settled on Du Pré and he grinned and his face lit up like the sun. He laughed merrily and he walked over.

"Mr. Du Pré," he said, holding out his right hand, "I'm Burdette. The good Bart bade me come see you."

Du Pré looked at the giant paw. He shook hands.

42

Burdette sat on the next stool. The heavy wood frame squeaked.

Madelaine looked at the giant, half smiling.

"A Scotch, straight up, large, three fingers," said Burdette, "and I would like to buy whatever Mr. Du Pré and the Reverend Booger Tom may be having. My generosity is complete. Put it all on Bart's tab."

Booger Tom nudged Du Pré.

"Not only is he bigger than Bart," said Booger Tom, "I think he's crazier."

"I am an archaeologist," said Burdette, "and we have some business."

"See?" said Booger Tom.

"You look like someone Bart would know," said Madelaine.

"We were at school together," said Burdette. "I went on. Bart, well, his career took a different path."

"Where is this school?" said Madelaine.

"Yale," said Burdette.

"Bart went to this Yale?" said Du Pré.

"Indeed he did," said Burdette, "for a while. Actually, not very long. Actually, there was some quarrel with the dean. Bart, who is . . . high-strung . . . pitched a file cabinet through the office window."

"Oh," said Du Pré.

"There is more, yes?" said Madelaine.

"Oh, yes," said Burdette, "Bart followed that amazing performance by . . ."

"He throw the dean through the window, too," said Madelaine.

"Alas, yes," said Burdette.

"How you know that?" said Du Pré to Madelaine.

"You boys," said Madelaine, "all act the same."

✤ CHAPTER 8 ✤

Du Pré dribbled loops of yellow electrical cord on the muddy ground. It was a hundred yards from the outlet on the light pole to the seed bin and it took three of the thick yellow cords to reach it.

Burdette plugged a helium lamp into the socket and switched it on.

The slab of yellow compressed earth and the ochred bones leaped out of darkness, high relief.

Booger Tom spat in the mud.

Burdette knelt and he crossed himself and prayed silently for a few minutes.

Then he got up and stepped through the low wide door and knelt again by the burial.

Du Pré carried the helium lamp in and he set it to one side. He stood behind Burdette so that he wouldn't be in the light.

Burdette pulled on thin latex gloves and he took a worn cordura packet from his parka and he opened it. He took out some plastic bags, small ones that closed with a pressure seal. He handed Du Pré a notebook and pen, there were peel-off labels in sheets inside.

"If you wouldn't mind," said Burdette, "just writing a number on one when I ask you to, to go along with the tape I'll make." He had a tiny pocket tape recorder sitting on the concrete floor by the yellow slab.

Burdette scraped and picked with the dental tools he took from the nylon packet and he spoke briefly, using words Du Pré had never heard, and then he would ask Du Pré to write a number followed by another after a dash and he would take the label and stick it on the plastic bag.

It didn't take very long.

Burdette stood up slowly, like his right leg hurt him, and he thanked Du Pré for his help and he took the notebook and he put it back in his pocket and he folded up the tools and he stood back.

"Good place for this," he said. "I was thinking on spraying it with plastic, but I guess not."

The huge man stepped out, ducking his head, and Du Pré followed with the lamp. They swung the two corrugated steel doors shut and forced the latch down, sealing the rubber gaskets.

"Marvelous," said Burdette, "marvelous. This burial is three thousand miles south of any other I have ever seen. Wonderful. Wonderful."

And he laughed joyfully.

"Who are these people?" said Du Pré.

"They have a lot of names," said Burdette. "Usually that of some professor wishing immortality of the academic sort. I call them the Navigators."

Du Pré nodded. He took the ivory amulet from his pocket.

"Ah, yes," said Burdette. "Could I see that? I'll return it to you, of course."

Du Pré handed it to him.

"They put a sinew thread through here," said Burdette, "and then they tied it off so that it was long enough to fully extend the arm and hold the amulet like this and sight on a star on the horizon. If, say, they wished to cross the Atlantic Ocean from

45

Ireland to America, they could go across and come back and make landfall within forty miles of their destination. Pretty good for a chunk of bone and a thread."

"Benetsee calls them the Horned Star People," said Du Pré.

"The old man," said Burdette. "How very much I would like to meet him."

Du Pré looked hard at Burdette.

"Only," said Burdette, "if Mr. Benetsee would care to meet me. He is very old and quite wise. I don't intend to steal from him."

Du Pré nodded. Anthropologists and archaeologists were hated by Indians, for excellent reasons. Usually, they gave the Indians dead and living the respect entomologists have for their bugs. People but not quite human. Specimens.

"Well," said Burdette, "I believe that Bart will be back shortly. I came as quickly as I could."

"All the same to you," said Booger Tom, "I'm tired and old and cranky and I need a drink and I'm going to get one. And that fool Bart turned in the drive down there just now."

Du Pré and Booger Tom and Burdette walked back to the main house. It was getting dark and much colder. It would freeze tonight and already the mud was stiffening.

They took their boots off in the mud room and hung their coats on pegs and went on into the kitchen. Bart wasn't there yet. Booger Tom led the way to the living room and the small bar and he went behind it and he poured himself a drink and one for Du Pré and a Scotch for Burdette.

The front door opened and Bart came in. He was in his stocking feet and he carried several snowballs.

"Burdette," said Bart, pegging one at him.

The snowball knocked over a lamp near the window.

Burdette put down his Scotch and he charged, his feet slipping on the polished wood floor. Bart fired off a couple more snowballs before Burdette slammed into him and the two of them fell out the front door.

Booger Tom had nimbly followed and he shut the door and locked it.

"I ask little," said Booger Tom. "A nice drink. Quiet. Kids these days."

Bart and Burdette were roaring and battling outside.

Booger Tom found some Black Forest ham in the little refrigerator and some pickled onions and crackers. He put them on the counter.

Du Pré rolled up four thick slices and he chewed.

"Pret' good," he said.

Ow. Thump. Uhhhhh. Thud. Oooooomph.

"We could," said Booger Tom, "just shoot them."

Du Pré nodded.

Laughter.

Feet on the steps and the porch planking.

Someone tried the door.

Then they pounded on it.

"We'll be good!" yelled Bart.

"You let 'em in," said Booger Tom, "I'll not take the responsibility."

Du Pré went to the door and he opened it and they came in, all muddy and laughing.

That Bart he is sad most of the time, Du Pré thought, but when he is happy he is happy some.

"We were at Yale together!" said Bart. "Where I lasted two weeks."

"Eleven days," said Burdette. "I'm a scientist. I count things."

"Well," said Bart, "nearly two weeks. How did you find the bones?"

"Marvelous," said Burdette. "So far south. People are amazing. I often wonder just how long ago man came to the Americas. I am sure it was long before the few old sites we know of. The seas were three hundred feet lower, sometimes more. They could have come down the coasts, and they probably did, and the seas rose and all the traces are obliterated."

Bart found some bottled sparkling water and he twisted off the cap and he drank deeply.

"We violated about forty laws," Burdette said, "but that is an enormously valuable piece of evidence."

"So screw 'em," said Bart.

Burdette nodded.

"I was in Alaska when you called," said Burdette, "looking, oddly enough, at a similar site. Same people. Been digging on it for three years. Same people, the red ocher, the ivory amulets. Horned Star People. I like that. Du Pré said Benetsee calls them that."

"Ah," said Bart, "Benetsee."

"That old bastard," said Du Pré. "You be careful there, he is a joker you know."

Burdette grinned.

"Most holy people are," he said. "Not a bit stuffy. Knew one in Siberia who tattooed a Brahmin lady there on an expedition. She ran off with him, has not been heard of since."

Bart raised an eyebrow.

"Well," said Burdette, "as I thought on it, she could only look forward to returning to Boston and marrying some Back Bay asshole. Maybe the shaman didn't need to tattoo her, all I know."

Du Pré roared. So did everyone else.

"I have the samples," said Burdette, "I'll send them on, get us the dates, other useful information."

"Can you stay?" said Bart.

Burdette nodded.

"I assume there's a clean place I might disassemble that slab in," he said. "I don't need a whole lot. If I take it back to a top-flight lab the whole damn world will know. I can get enough out of it in sterile shape anyway."

"What you got to have sterile, that thing?" said Du Pré.

"Human hair," said Burdette, "lasts forever. If it isn't contaminated by the DNA of anyone handling it, we can get a good read. I can manage."

Du Pré finished his drink.

The telephone rang, Bart went to it and he lifted it up and said hello. He listened.

He held it out to Du Pré.

Du Pré sighed and he took it.

"Gabriel," said Benny Klein.

"Yah."

"We have a body, clear the hell over west. Almost in the next county."

Du Pré waited.

"It's . . . you'd better come look."

Du Pré tapped his fingers on the bartop.

"OK," he said.

"I'm over at that old abandoned school, sits out in that coulee past the Thorson place."

Du Pré though for a moment.

"Is it a hunter got lost?" said Du Pré.

"I don't think so," said Benny Klein.

✦ CHAPTER 9 ✦

Rancher saw him flying over checking for winter kills," said Benny. He was looking off away from the body ninety degrees. "Saw a couple coyotes moving off and when he checked what they were eatin' on he saw the legs and boots stickin' out of the snow."

A couple of deputies from the next county west were standing back by their four-wheel rig, the blue light revolving slowly.

"We don't rightly know what county it is in," said Benny. "This country never was surveyed carefully."

Du Pré knelt by the legs. The coyotes had torn the cloth of the trousers and eaten both thighs to the bones. The dark green cloth of the corpse's trousers was shredded. The torn parts fluttered in the little wind.

Heavy shoe packs, the rubber-bottomed leather-topped boots that had thick felt inserts. Standard cold-weather footwear in Montana.

"This is Dr. Burdette," said Du Pré to Benny. "He wanted to come. He is an archaeologist, looks at dead people. . . ."

"Not this recently dead," said Burdette.

Benny handed Du Pré a broom.

"You know how I am about this stuff, Gabriel," said Benny. His face was white and he was swallowing a lot. He'd vomit in a moment or two.

"We got a bad accident!" yelled one of the deputies standing by the four-wheeler. They got in and swung round on the rutted track and they drove off toward the county road.

Du Pré swung the broom back and forth, brushing the clotted snow away from the torso and head of the body. Ice had shelled over the coat and cap and head. But the coyotes hadn't been at the face, unless they'd chewed on it before the snow.

No, Du Pré thought, them coyotes find this pret' short time ago. They find him long time, he just be bones. Him. Them boots too big for a woman. Funny pants he got.

Du Pré knelt and he put the beam of his little flashlight on the chewed legs. The man was wearing wool trousers under waxed cotton pants. The trousers and overpants were both tucked into the high boots.

That is not someone who knows this country, Du Pré thought, this is someone buys expensive stuff, thinks it will work but don't know how to use it.

"Sign of the dude," said Burdette, "tuck the pants in."

Du Pré reached down and he grabbed the shoulder of the corpse and he pulled. There was a cracking sound and the frozen body moved and Du Pré turned it over.

The man had fallen on some thick high grass, so he hadn't frozen to the earth.

An ambulance wallowed up the track, a light van with four-wheel drive but not enough weight to keep from sliding whenever it hit a grade of more than a few degrees.

The wind from the north was cold and smelled of ice.

"Where do your medical examinations take place?" said Burdette.

"Funeral home," said Du Pré, "doctor from Cooper does it. If there is more to be done we send him to Helena, state lab. What the fuck is this dude doing twenty-five miles from anything, this broken country anyway?"

"Dying," said Burdette. "He was dying."

51

The ambulance came close and stopped and a couple of the volunteer firemen from Cooper who had taken EMT courses got out and they opened the back of the ambulance and pulled out a stretcher with a black body bag unfolded on it. They carried the stretcher through the snow and mud to the body and set it down.

"Ready to go, Benny?" hollered one.

"Ask Du Pré," said Benny Klein, the sheriff, hunched over with his hands on his knees, puking.

"Yah," said Du Pré, "I look round here, mark it maybe, I come to the funeral home later."

"A dudesicle," said one of the men. "Silly bastard, what the fuck is he doing out here? Look at them tucked-in pants."

They rolled the corpse and the snow onto the stretcher and folded the body bag over it and they carried the corpse to the ambulance and slid it in and they got in and went off.

Du Pré looked carefully at the place where the body had lain. Not anything but grass stems and grainy corn snow. Nothing glinting, no paper.

Burdette had a very powerful small flashlight out and he was spiraling out from the place Du Pré was looking at, hunched over, and moving quickly. For such a big man he was light on his feet, coiled and intent.

Du Pré stood up. His back ached. He was tired. He reached in his jacket pocket and pulled out a flask and he sipped some whiskey, hot going down, it felt good.

Du Pré rolled a cigarette and he lit it and sucked in the smoke. He rubbed his eyes.

The wind was picking up. More damn snow.

"Yo!" said Burdette. "Du Pré, do come here!"

Burdette was standing at the lip of a gully. He was pointing the beam of his flashlight down.

Du Pré walked slowly over and he looked.

A snowmobile. On its side.

Probably went off where we are standing, Du Pré thought, going pret' good, hit that cutbank, bounce back.

Guy lies there awhile, it is snowing, he wakes up, hurt pretty bad, gets up this far and dies.

Burdette slid down the hill and he went to the snowmobile and he reached out and casually turned it upright. There was a box behind the seat, a plastic trunk with the top hanging crazily from one hinge.

Burdette looked in it. He pulled out a dark green backpack, a small one, it had something heavy in it.

He looked round the snowmobile for a moment and then he struggled back up the side of the gully. He reached over the top and grabbed a thick sagebrush and pulled himself up rolling and he stood up in one smooth motion.

Good shape, Du Pré thought, maybe I don't fight with him.

"I'd come back in daylight," said Burdette. "For one thing, I just hate being out on these High Plains with the wind from the north smelling of snow. I'm funny like that."

Du Pré nodded.

They trudged back to Du Pré's old cruiser, and they got in and Du Pré gunned it and swung the back end around and they bounced over the stony track out to the county road. The road was broken and frost-heaved and Du Pré went down it fast, sometimes the cruiser sailed for twenty feet when they went over the top of a hill.

Burdette took the flask Du Pré offered him and he drank a long time.

"Leave me some there," said Du Pré. His head ached.

Burdette reached under the seat and he pulled out a full bottle of whiskey and he refilled the flask.

"Way you drive," he said, "I oughta drink all this, too."

Du Pré laughed.

"I am sorry," he said. "You look in that bag?" He turned on to the two-lane blacktop and he speeded up. This road was good.

Burdette fiddled with the nylon zipper on the backpack and he got it to open and he pushed the cloth sides away.

Du Pré glanced over. A rock.

Ordinary chunk of the landscape.

"It's a rock," said Burdette. He turned it over in his lap.

"Rock on this side, too," said Burdette, "and this and this . . . oh, my my my my my."

Du Pré had a drink and he waited. The snowplow gauges on the sides of the road were flashing past.

"Very interesting," said Burdette.

Du Pré waited.

"Fascinating," said Burdette.

"You are an ass pain like that Bart," said Du Pré.

"Yeah," said Burdette. "Comes of being a bright fat kid and wanting all the attention, except in the matter of being a fat kid. Well, it seems to be a tooth."

"The whole thing?" said Du Pré.

"No," said Burdette, "it's in a matrix of yellow clay and sand breccia. Typical fossil strata of this region. When things died they had to die on a beach or near a river mouth. Inland, something would eat them, in the sea, something would eat them, but the scavengers didn't go in much for beachcombing."

"What kind of tooth?" said Du Pré.

"Dinosaur," said Burdette. "Very big dinosaur. Ate meat, look at the serrations on this sucker. Mouth like my mother-in-law."

Du Pré laughed.

"Ex-mother-in-law," said Burdette. "Never did like me, that woman. Why, she correctly divined my lousy character and

54

general piggishness the very first time she laid eyes on me. Swelled up like a puff adder and spent the twelve years I was married to her lovely daughter hissing."

They are like that, thought Du Pré.

My dead wife's mother, she liked me, Madelaine's mother she liked me, too. Maybe they just don't hiss.

"I am an archaeologist," said Burdette, "so I am a bit out of my field, but I want to hazard a guess that this is from that motion picture star Tyránnosaurus Rex."

"Oh," said Du Pré.

"That's interesting," said Burdette.

"OK," said Du Pré.

"A thought," said Burdette, "perhaps not a good one, but I am distracted by your terrible driving."

Du Pré cranked it up another ten miles an hour.

"There are only four complete Tyrannosaurus Rex skeletons in the whole wide world, and a few years ago there was a big goddamned flap over one that was thought to be on private property."

Du Pré topped a hill and they flew. The lights of Cooper shone on the horizon.

"The skeleton was very valuable. An offer was made for it, some seven million dollars."

Du Pré slowed down a little.

"A Japanese company wanted it, to build a theme park around," said Burdette. "But that isn't what is so interesting."

Du Pré slowed a little more.

"This yellow clay, compressed, yellow ochre, it looks familiar."

"Them bones were buried in it," said Du Pré.

"Yes," said Burdette, "I believe that they were at that."

✤ CHAPTER 10 ✤

There it is," said the young doctor. He stuck a probe in a bullet hole high up on the man's back. The faint stench of rotting human was rising as the body warmed. "That's it. This guy's for Helena. We are not equipped to do a useful ME report on a homicide."

"Didn't kill him though," said Du Pré.

"This one didn't," said the doctor. "But, then, you found him. It shattered his scapula and tore up muscles and maybe a rib on the way out. Bleed pretty bad, but it would take him awhile to die."

"How long he was out there?" said Du Pré.

"Not long," said the doctor. "This time of year, under the snow and all, no more than a month. Probably not that long. He was warmly wrapped so his body heat would have held well, hastened decomposition. Folks aren't especially good keepers. The coyotes would have been done with him in a day or two anyway. But, who knows? Let the geniuses in Helena tell you. I'm just a country doctor. You know, the clap, childbirth if it isn't complicated, freeze off skin cancers, slap a cast on a clean break. I ship the interesting stuff out. This guy is interesting. Well, I guess I will pronounce his ass officially dead. It's seven forty two ack emma."

The two volunteer firemen zipped up the body bag and they put it on a gurney and they took it out of the back room of the little funeral parlor.

56

"Cheap Hollywood movie," said Du Pré, "fighting over some kind of dinosaur skeleton, chasing each other on snowmobiles."

"Not," said the young doctor, "my problem."

"That's evidence," said Benny Klein, breathing a little easier now that the body was gone. He was looking at the little green knapsack that had the big rock in it with the tooth.

"Dinosaurs ain't my thing anyway," said Burdette, "big fat silly bastards. Never liked 'em."

Du Pré yawned. They hadn't slept yet.

"Maybe it tell us where it come from," said Du Pré.

"Later," said Benny. "Guy's dead, I'm dead. Let's get some sleep."

"Maybe I take it down, that, Bozeman," said Du Pré, "ask them."

"Leave me a receipt if you do," said Benny. "Way things are going the FBI, the CIA, and all the rest of those bastards will be here later today, all screaming for that there dinosaur tooth."

"I could use a ride out to Bart's," said Burdette.

Madelaine would be tearing around her house cleaning like she did around now every morning. Her kids were old enough to fend for themselves and lately she had been moving furniture.

"I go there, too," said Du Pré. "Bart has a room for me."

They went out and got in the cruiser and Du Pré drove off up on the road to the bench and Bart's ranch which stretched from the bench well into the foothills of the Wolf Mountains.

A warm wind from the west was melting the snow. The Black Wind, the chinook. There was a thick black line on the western horizon. The gullies and coulees and creeks would be raging with water by the next morning.

Burdette had a pull on the whiskey and he lit a small mean

cigar. He rolled the window down. Big fat flakes were walloping down from the black clouds above.

"You know," said Burdette, "I have a feeling about all this. That it is going to be a very fascinating story. Very fascinating. Sixty million years' worth of it, you think on it."

"Benny will run a check on that snowmobile," said Du Pré.

"He's a nice guy," said Burdette. "Anyone got the guts to puke they see a mess like that I have to admire."

Burdette's accent was pure Montana, an almost southern drawl.

"You are from here?" said Du Pré.

"Yup," said Burdette. "Family homesteaded near Rapelje. That was a long time ago, but we're still around. Some of my folks still have a couple ranches, east of the Crazy Mountains there. Good country."

"How you become an anthropologist?" said Du Pré.

"Archaeologist," said Burdette. "I prefer my people long dead. Oh, as a kid I found arrow points and scrapers. Once a cutbank fell away on the little creek by our house. There had been camps beside it thousands of years ago, there were black bands from old fires, buffalo and beaver bones, goose bones, all layered like a cake. Then a guy came from Bozeman to look and he explained what I was seeing. He was there all summer, I followed him like a little duckling. Ain't that how it is with us guys. Look at a man doing something interesting and you think, well, I will do that when I grow up."

Bart was talking on the telephone when they came in. He waved and turned away.

Du Pré went to the room he used and he took a shower and fell into bed and went to sleep. He slept very hard but not that long and when he woke it was just about noon and some shafts of sun were stabbing down from breaks in the boiling black clouds.

He got dressed and pulled on some fresh dry boots and he went out to the kitchen and made himself something to eat.

The telephone rang.

"You are awake," said Madelaine.

"Yah," said Du Pré, "I am that."

"Sneak away don't move no furniture," said Madelaine. And she laughed.

"You are at the bar?" said Du Pré.

"Uh-huh," said Madelaine, "Benny tell me all about it. He is ver' tired but he came in to check some things for Susan, she is about crazy in those casts."

Susan cursed in the background.

"Bastard dump her here so he can go get some sleep," said Madelaine.

"I am taking that rock down to Bozeman," said Du Pré, "one that got the tooth in it."

"You come by here," said Madelaine. "Me, I want to see it. Them people at that museum they probably steal it, like they did that buffalo that them Oleson brothers give them."

Du Pré remembered. The Olesons had discovered an Ice Age longhorn buffalo skeleton, the hair all orange on the floor of a cave it had fallen into ten or fifteen thousand years ago. They took it to the museum in Bozeman and the museum claimed to have lost it. The skeleton was fourteen feet long and some of the bones weighed a hundred pounds each.

"No," said Du Pré, "it is evidence, murder investigation."

"OK," said Madelaine, "I still like to see it."

"I come by, have something, then I go," said Du Pré.

GOD DAMN Susan Klein roared in the background. Some glass broke.

"She is short-tempered," said Madelaine. "I tell her calm down or I shut her in the beer cooler."

"What happened?" said Du Pré.

"Booger Tom tease her," said Madelaine. "She throw a bottle at him. Miss."

Du Pré looked down. There was a cup of coffee there suddenly. He turned and saw Burdette padding away in sock feet.

"You come, she shoot somebody," said Madelaine. "Give them that first aid, maybe."

She hung up.

Du Pré picked up the coffee and went to the kitchen where Burdette was frying a mess of bacon. He cracked some eggs into hot fat and he pulled some pastries out of the oven, expensive ones Bart had flown in frozen.

"There is a man you should see," said Burdette. He had the green knapsack with the rock and tooth in it open on the counter. He was looking at the mortar. The pestle lay on the cutting board beside it, yellow powder on the blunt.

Du Pré stuck a finger in the mortar and he looked at the bright yellow powder that stuck to it.

"He's older than coal," said Burdette. "Aaron Morgenstern. He lives in the old Baxter Hotel, an apartment there. You should ask him about this yellow pigment."

"OK," said Du Pré.

"He was the man who explained the cutbank to me, more'n forty years ago," said Burdette. "He's a funny old bird. Ninety-one now. But he has all his damn marbles."

"Me," said Du Pré, "I am a little more than half that and I don't got all my marbles."

"I'm going to take a close look at the burial, the Horned Star People," said Burdette.

Du Pré nodded.

"Walrus ivory," said Du Pré. "Long damn way from any damn walrus, eastern Montana."

"Back when these people came through here," said Burdette, "the glaciers were melting and there were lakes and rivers everywhere. Rivers here every few miles larger than the Missouri today. The ice was a mile, or two, high. They probably came in their big skin boats."

Du Pré laughed.

"Voyageurs," he said.

"Men are voyageurs," said Burdette.

"Long time gone."

"They were Caucasian," said Burdette.

Du Pré shrugged.

"Some folks are not going to like that," said Burdette.

"Yah," said Du Pré, "me, I don't like finding, guy, dead in the brush, there."

They ate breakfast.

Burdette filled a small plastic bag with the ground yellow powder.

"Show this to Morgenstern," said Burdette.

"You maybe call him," said Du Pré.

Burdette nodded.

Du Pré closed the green knapsack and he went out to his old cruiser.

❖ CHAPTER 11 ❖

I t's all right, Bill," said the professor in the white lab coat.
"OK," said the security guard, "I just have to stop all folks
with backpacks."

"This way if you would," said the professor. He was young
and very intent-looking, wire-rimmed glasses. Some kind of
perfume.

Du Pré followed the man to a room surrounded on three
sides by plate glass windows. There were big plaster-covered
hunks of rock on pedestals. Some students were meticulously
scraping at the specimens with dental tools.

The professor pointed to a dark green marble table next to
a big stainless steel sink.

"A murder investigation," said the professor. "That's a new
one. Do you have a badge?"

Du Pré fished out his brand inspector's badge.

"OK," said the professor, "somebody kill somebody's cow
with this tooth?"

"I am a deputy," said Du Pré. "Badge is in my other pants."

"Other . . . pants . . ." said the professor. He opened the
backpack and he lifted out the tooth in its matrix of variegated
rock.

"T. Rex," said the professor. "Big bastard, too. We have a
smaller one here. I don't suppose you know where this came
from?"

"Next to the body," said Du Pré.

"Right," said the professor, "Well, it is in commingled Madison limestone with mudstones and . . . probably formed at a river mouth where it met the old ocean."

Du Pré nodded. The sea had once reached from the Gulf of Mexico to the Arctic Ocean. Sixty million years ago. Sharks a hundred feet long in it. These dinosaurs stomping along the beaches. Guy live then, he better be fast, alert.

"When the investigation is completed," said the professor, eyeing the tooth.

"We call you," said Du Pré, "after we call Oprah."

Du Pré zipped up the backpack and he hefted it and he walked out of the fishbowl room and toward the front door. The professor followed him for a little ways and then he threw up his hands and he went back.

Du Pré nodded to the guard as he passed. The man just stared at him.

Du Pré went to his old cruiser, all covered in mud. The rest of the lot was filled with the silly four-wheel station wagons the yuppies liked to get stuck in.

He put the knapsack on the seat and he got in and started the engine and he backed away from the curb and he went out the long drive and down to the center of town.

The yellow-brown Baxter Hotel was the tallest building in Bozeman.

Du Pré parked a couple blocks away. He walked back up the street and he went inside and he looked through the directory. Aaron Morgenstern. Eighth floor.

He rode the elevator up and it opened on a stuffy hallway with a thick red and black carpet in it, the place smelled of must and old sweat and tobacco.

Du Pré stopped in front of the door with the right number. There was an old brass gargoyle knocker beneath a peephole.

Du Pré banged on it.

He waited.

He banged again.

JUST A GODDAMN MINUTE YOU HEATHEN! someone roared inside.

The door jumped open. An old bent man stood there, still big and heavy, with a tall shock of white hair and thick bushy white eyebrows big as thumbs. Watery blue old eyes behind thick spectacles.

"Are you," said Morgenstern, in a rasping voice that was just a loud and grating whisper, "are you the goddamned Red River Breed with the damn dinosaur tooth that fool Burdette called me about?"

"Yah," said Du Pré.

"I thought so," said the professor. "Come in, God damn it."

Du Pré stepped in and he looked around amazed. The walls were full of light boxes filled with stone tools. A full-sized buffalo bull pawed the earth on a plinth. The buffalo had a saddle on it and several spears with aged eagle feathers hung on them leaned against the buffalo's horns.

A room beyond held a giant carved desk piled high with papers.

"Bring the damn thing over here," said Morgenstern, pointing to a small clear space on the desk top. Du Pré set down the backpack.

The old man waited for Du Pré to open it up.

Du Pré did and the old man bent over close and he looked at the rock and the tooth, mumbling umumumum-humhumhumumumumumyesyesyesyesyes.

"Hmph," he said.

Du Pré wandered over to a display case filled with war clubs and shields and knives. Some were very old, obsidian, a blade sunk into an elk rib, etched black on the bone. Bound with black sinew varnished with hoof glue. Arrows. The ones with the little points were for buffalo, a horn-strengthened bow could shoot the arrow clear through the animal if it did not strike a heavy bone.

A pemmican case, covered with stars and crosses. Métis.

"Hah," said Morgenstern. "Tell me, do you take a drink or not?"

"Yah," said Du Pré.

The old man shuffled over to a sideboard that held crystal decanters and he sloshed some brown liquid in a couple of glasses. He gave one to Du Pré.

Brandy. Du Pré smelled the grapes, the rough edge of resin.

"Greek brandy," said the professor, "aged long and well."

They drank. The brandy was very smooth.

"You take this to the museum?" said the old man.

Du Pré nodded.

"Wonder they didn't rip your arm off," said Morgenstern. "Bunch of goddamned thieves."

"I tell them it is evidence," said Du Pré.

"Hah," said the professor. He looked at Du Pré for a long time with his canny old eyes. He held out his hand.

"The powdered rock," he said.

Du Pré fished out the little plastic envelope full of yellow powder. The old man took it and he held it up to the light.

Um um um um um umumumumyesyesyesyesyes um.

Ah.

Ho.

Du Pré laughed.

"I got a friend, old bastard, you should meet him, I take you both some bad wine, good tobacco."

"Benetsee," said the professor.

"Yah," said Du Pré.

"Marvelous old thief," said the professor. "Haven't seen the old bastard in forty years. Last time I did, he stole my watch. Seth Thomas, too."

Du Pré roared.

"Pawned it," said Morgenstern. "I got it back. I still don't know how he did it. It was locked in my trunk."

Du Pré roared.

"I see you know him," said the professor. He walked away with the plastic bag. Du Pré heard water running in the kitchen. The professor came back, mixing the powder in a small white porcelain cup. He smeared some on Du Pré's cheek.

"Needs grease," said the old man, "But it's a goddamned good color."

The old man bent his head toward another room, one that faced south and had a lot of light. They went in. The room was not terribly big, and it was filled with mahogany map cases, stacks of them, some of the drawers six feet wide.

The old man bent over and he squinted at the labels on a set of wide drawers.

He pulled one open and he shut it and he pulled open another. There were two huge books in each one, leather bound, a full three feet long and two and a half wide.

"Lift that up if you would," said the old man. "Damn thing weighs a ton."

Du Pré lifted it. It weighed at least seventy-five pounds. The professor beckoned to Du Pré and he followed the old man to the dining table. He set the book down where Morgenstern pointed.

"Give my regards to Burdette," said the old man. "He's improved with age. When he was at school here I think I bailed him out of jail every damn Saturday night for four years."

Du Pré laughed.

"What he do?"

"Got drunk and picked fights," said the old man, "like any good cowboy. Damn kid, though, you know, take him in the field and he could spot a stone tool at half a mile, or, better yet, just where people would have camped a hundred or five hundred or a thousand or ten thousand years ago. Uncanny eye. Never could stand being a professor, though. Lasted about halfway through the first faculty meeting he ever went to. He quit before he killed them all."

"OK," said Du Pré, "that is all then."

The old man nodded. "Tell Burdette I'll know more in a few days," he said.

Du Pré closed up the backpack and he left.

The street was busy with people. It was afternoon. If he drove fast he could be home by midnight maybe.

He got chased by a highway patrolman halfway to Billings, but Du Pré switched on his light bar and the cop shut off his.

He slowed down to ninety when he turned north. The road wasn't as good and it was a little wet.

✦ CHAPTER 12 ✦

Yellow paint, huh?" said Madelaine. She was cleaning the top of the bar. It would close in an hour. There were a couple young cowboys still working on a pitcher of beer in the corner, but everyone else had gone home.

"Yah," said Du Pré, "I don't know so much about paint."

"You guys," said Madelaine, "you Salteur, you Métis, some of you paint up. Back then, my grandma tell me, you guys, you spend about four days painting yourselfs and then a week bragging and you go out to fight each guy, stand there, yell a lot, count up how many there are and you charge and they go home, and they charge and you go home. Bullshit, you guys."

Du Pré laughed. Indians fighting Indians was a pretty bloodless kind of war.

"It don't get wild," said Du Pré, "till them damn whites come, they are very serious about war."

"Paintmaking songs," said Madelaine. "I heard some once."

Du Pré nodded.

"That paint going to tell just where that damn dinosaur is," said Madelaine. "Everyplace a little different."

Du Pré nodded.

"That old professor say he know Benetsee," said Du Pré. "Benetsee steal his watch."

"Hah," said Madelaine. "More to that story I am sure."

"Maybe I see what Benetsee says," said Du Pré.

68

"You stuck between them two old liars," said Madelaine, "you go crazy. How many times you about shoot Benetsee?"

"Yah," said Du Pré.

"Guys," said Madelaine, looking over at the two young cowboys, "maybe I close up now if that is all right."

The young men stood up, draining the last beer they had. They got into their coats and they left.

Du Pré mopped the floor while Madelaine counted out the day's money and then they locked up and went to her house.

They sat in the kitchen both too tired to sleep. Du Pré sipped some whiskey and Madelaine had some pink wine.

Madelaine sighed.

"Miss my Lourdes," she said. Lourdes was in Chicago, Bart was paying her way through a good Catholic girls' school.

"We could have a bunch of kids," said Du Pré.

"Shit we have a bunch of kids," said Madelaine. "Your Jacqueline she give you twelve grandchildren and mine they have not started their damn litters yet and we are too damn old, Du Pré, go through that again. Shit all over *everything*."

Du Pré roared. Madelaine sat on his lap.

It was snowing very hard outside and the wind was picking up.

"Snow till June," said Madelaine.

"You be a grandmother pretty soon," said Du Pré.

"Rude thing that kid did," said Madelaine. "I am old woman now you go find some younger woman. I cut your damn balls off you do, but I suppose you try. You guys."

She put her head on his shoulder.

Du Pré worried the amulet out of his pants pocket and he held it in his palm.

Madelaine looked at it.

"Who are these people?" said Madelaine.

69

"Burdette say that the glaciers are melting, water everywhere, they come down the rivers that are gone now. Fly over the country, you can see where the old rivers ran," said Du Pré.

"How old?" said Madelaine.

"Ten, fifteen thousand years, don't know yet."

"Long time gone."

Someone tapped at the window and Madelaine jumped up, surprised.

The back porch door opened and Benetsee and Pelon came in. They were thickly covered in snow and they knocked it off and hung up their coats on the hooks and came in. They both wore high moccasins with quill work on them.

"Three in the damn morning," said Madelaine. "What you want you old drunk. Him, too?"

"Ah," said Benetsee, "I will think. Maybe I would like some good wine like you have, maybe something to eat, a smoke maybe. Pelon, too. He is trying to be good but it is not the medicine way, I tell him."

Du Pré got a couple big glasses and he filled them with bubbly cheap pink wine and set them down at the kitchen table. Madelaine was rummaging around in the refrigerator.

"Deer steak?" said Madelaine. "I got the other stuff. Du Pré?"

Du Pré put on his boots and he walked out to the meat shed and turned on the light and he skinned the carcass back a little and cut off four thick tender steaks. The deer had been hanging in the cold whole for weeks and the meat was so aged it could be cut with a fork.

He carried the meat in one hand and his knife in the other. Catfoot made that knife from a car spring, long time ago, elk antler handle. Held an edge good.

Madelaine fried the steaks very hot and she served up some bing cherry sauce and fry bread and corn with hot little flecks of peppers in it. They all ate a lot and then they sat back and

Pelon got up and he cleared the dirty plates and dishes and he washed them up and stacked them in the drainer that Du Pré had made from willow roots.

"Why you come the middle of the damn night?" said Madelaine.

"Du Pré," said Benetsee, "he goes to see my friend the old Aaron, old man, I want to know how my friend is."

How you know that, Du Pré thought, I have quit wondering a long time ago. You just do.

"He is a joker like you," said Du Pré.

"Paint," said Benetsee.

"Yellow paint, the rock around the dinosaur tooth," said Du Pré.

"Yah," said Benetsee.

"Paint?" said Pelon.

"Ceremonial paint," said Madelaine, "everybody they have their secret place they get paint, don't tell anyone. Crows are the worst, they don't even tell each other."

"Ah," said Pelon.

"Know where that paint come from," said Du Pré, "know where the dinosaur bones are. Them very valuable bones. Seven million dollars."

"Lot of money," said Pelon. He rolled a cigarette from Du Pré's tobacco.

"Where is this tooth," said Benetsee.

Du Pré sighed. He pulled on his boots and went out to his car and he got the backpack and he brought it in and set it on the kitchen table.

He unzipped it.

Benetsee looked at it.

"Oh, him," said Benetsee. "I know him where he is?"

Du Pré looked at him.

Benetsee held out his glass.

71

Du Pré filled it.

Benetsee drank.

"Him yellow in the rock near that butte," said Benetsee.

Du Pré waited. No damn use asking *what* butte.

Benetsee got up and he went out and put on his coat. Pelon followed. They stuck their knitted caps on their heads.

"You want a ride?" said Du Pré.

Benetsee shook his head.

"I am teaching him about snow," he said. He grinned. They went out and into the swirling flakes and they were gone.

"Hah," said Madelaine, "they are home already."

Benetsee came and went, on his own time and season.

"That is a real yellow got very little brown in it," said Madelaine. "I don't know paint in the ground that color, like in that rock."

Du Pré sighed. He was suddenly very tired.

They went to bed and couldn't sleep. They got back up.

"Something," said Madelaine, "is not right now. We should be sleeping."

"You got to work tomorrow?" said Du Pré.

"Yah," said Madelaine. "Go in at five, though. I can sleep late. My kids, they all run away." Two were in the service and the others were in school away from home.

The telephone rang and Du Pré winced.

No more goddamn bodies, this fucking snowstorm.

He picked it up.

"Du Pré?" said Bart. He sounded excited.

"Yah."

"Burdette found something," said Bart.

"That is very good," said Du Pré.

"You need to come out," said Bart.

Du Pré looked grimly at the snow splatting against the window.

"I don't got to come out."

"Oh," said Bart.

"I am ver' tired," said Du Pré. "You maybe find that Jimmy Hoffa I do not even care, you know."

"Burdette broke that mess of earth and bones apart," said Bart, "just cracked it right in half. And guess what?"

"There is that Jimmy Hoffa?"

"No," said Bart, "there is a vertebra from a Tyrannosaurus Rex, is what was in there."

Du Pré woke up.

"They were buried around it?" said Du Pré.

"Seems to be," said Bart.

"Ah," said Du Pré, "so I see you tomorrow maybe."

❖ CHAPTER 13 ❖

Good old Bob," said Burdette. "He was in no condition for me to recognize him right off. His slime glands ceased functioning when he died. When he was alive, you could see the iridescent trail."

"You knew him?" said Benny Klein. He had a wallet and the papers and cards in it spread out on his desk.

"Oh, yes," said Burdette. "He was one of them."

Du Pré looked at the driver's license. California. Berkeley. Robert Lewis Palmer. Address. Must wear glasses. Organ donor.

"You did not like him much," said Benny Klein.

"Fucking academic," said Burdette, "a real tenured mofo. Desperation is never pretty, but he was uglier than most."

Du Pré looked at Burdette.

"He just flat stole someone else's research and rushed it into print and took all the credit," said Burdette. "Destroyed the man's career while assuring his own prospered. He's about right. Ever since the university systems of this country began to shrink, the fights over the bucket have been getting more and more vicious."

"What is he doing driving a snowmobile, the High Plains?" said Du Pré. "He maybe find this dinosaur skeleton, not supposed to?"

Burdette shrugged.

"When we know," he said, "it will be a very interesting story."

"Snowmobile he was driving was stolen a couple years ago in Red Lodge," said Benny. "What it was doing between then and now I'd like to know, too. Bunch of things I'd like to know. But I got to take Susan down to the doctors and so I guess I'd better go. You boys have any good ideas while I am gone why don't you just assume I would like them. You pick up your badge, Du Pré?"

Du Pré nodded.

"That little bastard at the museum had everybody call me up to the governor, hollering that we'd better turn over the tooth to him for safekeeping."

"Governor?" said Du Pré.

"Yah," said Benny Klein. "I tol' him I was a lifelong Democrat. He said he was glad to know there was at least one in eastern Montana. He'd see if the legislature could protect me or something. Nice guy."

"Hide the tooth, Benny," said Burdette. "They'll steal it."

"College professors?" said Benny. "My my."

"Anyway," said Benny, "our good Professor Palmer went off to a conference two weeks ago in San Diego. Never showed up till the guy spotted him from the plane. My budget's so low a snake could see over it, and there's no way we can afford to backtrack him."

"Benetsee knows where that dinosaur is," said Du Pré. "Maybe that old professor I go and see in Bozeman does, too."

"All yours," said Benny. "I went out and sweated with Benetsee once and I will never forget it. Won't talk about it, either. I got to take Susan to Billings. Arrest anyone you like. 'Bye."

He went out of the office, leaving the wallet and contents on his desk. The green backpack with the dinosaur tooth sat on a filing cabinet.

"We need to hide that," said Burdette.

Du Pré nodded.

"I know a good place," said Du Pré.

Burdette raised an eyebrow.

"Beer cooler, the bar, Toussaint," said Du Pré. "We just put it in the old oak cold case there. No one opens it, got cleaning supplies in it, stuff like that."

They drove to Toussaint and parked in front of the bar and went on in. Buster Dunn's wife Barbara was behind the bar. She was sewing big silver buttons on a combed wool coat. She made them at home and sold them for big bucks at the ski resorts.

Barbara looked up. She put the soft rich black coat into a big clear plastic bag and she took it to the storage closet and set it up high.

"I shouldn't work on them here, anyway," she said when she came back, "the grease from the kitchen gets into the fabric. Smells. I never could do one thing at a time, though."

Du Pré went back to the beer cooler and he stuck the backpack and the tooth in the back of the old oak case, behind a couple of cases of bar polish. He shut the spring door. The case was more than a century old, lined with sheets of zinc riveted to wooden frames.

Du Pré went back out and he slid up on a stool. Barbara lit a cigarette and she waited.

"I hope Susan's doing well," she said.

"Yah," said Du Pré. "Before she kill us all."

"She sure don't like confinement," said Barbara. "You gents want anything?"

"Whiskey, water," said Du Pré.

"Scotch, water," said Burdette. "I think we might go and see Bart."

Du Pré nodded.

Bart was off moving thousands of cubic yards of gravels to

make way for the trout ponds. Sitting at the controls of his giant dragline, Popsicle, and listening to country music.

"Since," said Burdette, "the trout ponds don't make a nickel's worth of sense, I expect our Japanese investors have other things in mind. Like the rest of our friend in the cooler."

Du Pré nodded.

They drank.

"Bart he will call if there is anything," said Du Pré. "Me, I think maybe we go and see Benetsee. People getting killed over this I maybe yell at that old bastard some."

"May I come?" said Burdette. He looked as eager as a young boy who might get to go fishing.

"Sure," said Du Pré. "He can fool the pair of us easy as he fool me."

I know that old man all my life and him, he lives, that other world there. Talks to the coyotes, maybe he sail with them Horned Star People long time ago. He was old my father was young. Always been there.

Some people here they think he is just a dirty old drunk Indian.

Hah.

"You know that Bart, college?" said Du Pré.

"Not very long," said Burdette. "He was tossed out quickly. But I always liked him. Miserable family. He'd go on a drunk and end up in my rooms at Yale, sober up, I wouldn't see him again for a while. Once when I was in a really bad place, broke, and a chance at going on to get my doctorate but not enough money to do it right, and how he found out I will never know. Anyway, he had a key to my place. I came home from drinking a bunch, trying to forget my troubles, and there was a blank envelope on my desk, with a whole lot of money in it. No signature, of course, but it couldn't have been anyone else.

I asked him about it and he said he didn't remember doing any such thing."

Du Pré laughed. Bart, sure enough.

"I would have thought he would have drunk himself to death long ago," said Burdette. "Glad he didn't. Nice guy. Lonely."

Du Pré got up and he shrugged into his old leather jacket and he rolled a smoke and he waited for Burdette to come back from the john. They went out and got in Du Pré's old cruiser.

They drove toward Benetsee's. When they got to the top of a little hill Burdette motioned for Du Pré to stop. He got out and so did Du Pré.

The day was clear and the sun made the deep snow on the peaks of the Wolfs white as hot flames. The High Plains rolled below them, off to the west, the horizon a good fifty miles away. To the south the horizon was the last line of hills before the Missouri.

"You know about the glaciation?" said Burdette.

Du Pré shrugged.

"There were glaciers spilling down out of the Wolfs," said Burdette, "and some on the plains. There was a lake that reached halfway to the Arctic Ocean. It rose and fell. When I think of the Horned Star People I think of them in big skin canoes, the men and women using big carved paddles, coming through the mist. It must have been misty with the ice a couple miles high and waterfalls spilling off them. They came down here, in their boats, why we will never know. Long time gone, as you say. There's the track of a glacier there, can you see it?"

Du Pré squinted. He saw it, a faint outline of a giant mass of ice scraping down from the mountains.

"Benetsee got something in this," said Du Pré, "I don't

know what but he got some medicine reason he don't tell us."

Burdette nodded.

"I have thought that by the time we are through we will know some things that we wish that we didn't," said Burdette.

"He is joking a lot usually," said Du Pré, "but not this time."

Du Pré rolled a cigarette.

He lit it.

"Damn big country," said Burdette. He shaded his eyes with his hand.

It is that, Du Pré thought. Them Le Doux Springs, they are there thousands of years, maybe Bart find more buried near them. Thousands of years. Hundreds of years my people come there, pick them plums, make the racks of alder smoke the meat, fall, get ready for the winter. Lots of years. Them Métis playing that fiddle, dancing on a buffalo hide pegged to the ground.

Du Pré got in the car and so did Burdette. They drove on to the torn-up drive that led back into the trees to Benetsee's cabin. Du Pré tried to miss the deeper holes.

There was no smoke coming from the chimney.

They got out and went to the door and knocked but the cabin was empty.

They walked around back. The sweat lodge was open, the fires long cold. Water ran from the roof of the cabin in silver scarves.

Something sat on the top of the sweat lodge.

Du Pré walked over.

A carving. Of a long canoe patched with many skins, a man with wings for arms standing in the prow and paddlers bent to their tasks behind him, faces hidden by ruffs of parkas.

"Jesus," said Burdette, "I dreamed about that boat."

Du Pré nodded. He carried the carving back to the car.

✤ CHAPTER 14 ✤

Popsicle popped. The huge dragline was idling and the cab
door swung open, the little winds from the mountains
kicking at it. The backhoe and dump truck were parked well
away and Bart's Rover was next to them.

Du Pré parked the cruiser.

He looked at Burdette and nodded.

They split up and began to run. Burdette for the Rover, Du
Pré for the dragline. Water was bubbling up right in front of
the huge bucket set on the ground, the cable slack.

Du Pré ducked under the boom lines and he went around
the steel track on the far side. Bart was sitting on the ground,
blood streaming from his face.

Du Pré yelled at Burdette. He knelt by Bart, who had his face
in his hands. Ropy blood hung from his fingers.

"Bart," said Du Pré, "I am here."

He went away from the dragline enough to see Burdette
and he waved him toward the cruiser. Burdette nodded and he
ran back to the car.

Du Pré put a hand on Bart's shoulder. The big man rolled
and he struggled to get to his feet and he slumped back down.

Burdette drove up in the cruiser and he and Du Pré lifted
Bart, who was shaking a little, and they put him in the backseat. Du Pré dug some blankets out of the cruiser and he put
them around Bart.

"You take him . . . Masson it is closest. Right up the road

80

north. Twenty miles, maybe thirty. I will look around." Du Pré dug in the pocket of Bart's jacket and found the keys to the Rover.

Burdette got in the cruiser, backed and turned, and gunned it.

Du Pré yelled. A long roaring scream of rage.

He stood a moment and then he clambered up into the cab of the dragline and he shut it off. The huge diesel popped a moment and hung. Du Pré dropped back to the ground and he began to walk round the dragline.

Ground torn up by boots, here is where they fought. Bart he knock one down there, another behind him probably had a sap or a club. Drag Bart here, kick him some, kick him in the face.

Du Pré picked up the tooth white in the mud.

Somebody pay for that, a lot.

Backtrack, come from over there, Bart he cannot see them behind him, the dragline, they wait there, one . . . walk out there and wave and Bart trusts him and he gets down and then they jump him. He fights pret' good but they kick the shit out of him.

Got a broken jaw. They pay plenty for that, too.

Du Pré followed the tracks back to where the car was parked. He knelt down. There was a splotch of new oil on the ground. He looked at the tire tracks, couple on the front almost bald.

Old car.

Res? Indians done this?

Son of a bitch.

Bart was there a while, we come in on the road, turn on the highway.

Couple big trucks pass, couple pickups, no cars.

Thirty minutes from that turn to here.

If they are headed south.

Five minutes if they are headed north, over the first hill we do not see them going. Nothing up there, though, except maybe the west.

That goddamned dinosaur is west of here.

Du Pré got in the Rover and he drove off and when he got to the two-lane highway he floored it heading south. The big four-wheel wagon was more car than truck. Wouldn't go as fast as the old police cruiser and the power steering felt like mush.

Du Pré shot past the road east to Toussaint and Cooper and he saw the long black ribbon heading south over the plains, brown and dry, cut by water and wind. Antelope flashed white rumps and sped away.

An eagle sat on a dead cottonwood by a spring, bald, quiet, waiting.

Du Pré looked at the gas gauge. Quarter tank.

Crossroads bar with a pump maybe twenty miles, maybe more ahead.

I drive this a hundred and ten, my cruiser, this pig is eighty-five and not much more. The tires whirred on the road.

The beer sign was on in the roadhouse. Du Pré parked in front of the gas pump and he went inside. A young woman with a small baby was sitting on a high stool behind the bar. She looked up at Du Pré and then the baby began to bawl.

It took her a minute to shush the child.

Du Pré laid a twenty on the counter.

"Anyone in here last couple hours, buy gas?" he said.

"Yeah," she said, looking at him.

"Any Indians?"

"One," she said. "Bought a couple quarts of oil, too."

Du Pré went out and he ran twenty dollars into the tank and he got in and floored the accelerator.

Big country and dry.

The Missouri is down here not far. Big lake from the dam, got to go east or west there.

They will go east or west.

The Rover was topheavy and when Du Pré came to a curve he had to slow or the SUV would roll over.

Should have sent Bart in this damn pig, Du Pré thought.

He crested a high hill and he looked down a long stretch of road.

A car was heading south on it, several miles away. The sun glinted on the rear window and the car dropped out of sight.

Du Pré shoved his foot down. The Rover shot downhill, helped by the grade. The springs quivered when the SUV bottomed out and began to climb. Du Pré took the middle of the road. The steering gibbered in his hands.

Just before he got to the top of the hill a pickup came over and Du Pré twisted the wheel hard and shot past. The pickup was doing a good eighty and the driver's mouth dropped open. Du Pré dropped off the far side of the crest and his stomach heaved. There was a T-intersection down at the bottom.

He couldn't see the car.

Du Pré cursed. He slowed and stopped at the blinking red light and he jumped out and he ran out into the lane and he looked hard at the pavement.

Few little oil drops there, to the right.

Maybe the car, maybe not.

He got back in the Rover and he roared off to the west.

The road wound tight between slabs of old seabed lifted up, back and forth away from the tilts that would shed rubble on the road.

Du Pré came round a tight curve and he saw an old brown

car up ahead of him, blue smoke spewing from the exhaust. The vinyl top was piebald with rust. The right rear tire wobbled.

Du Pré roared up behind them.

Left my damn gun in the cruiser, Du Pré thought, it is just as well.

The car kept on. Du Pré was right up on the rear bumper.

Suddenly the car lurched to the right and went off on a gravel lot near a huge pile of road sand.

Du Pré braked and followed.

The car sat there.

Du Pré waited.

The door opened and an old white man, dressed in worn khakis, got out. He shuffled as he walked toward Du Pré, his mouth working. He was waving his fist.

"Shit," said Du Pré.

Du Pré wheeled out of the lot and left the old man cursing. He drove back to the T-intersection and he stopped and he rolled a smoke and he lit it.

He turned north.

Follow the wrong track don't matter you catch them.

Some hunter I am.

It didn't take nearly as long to come to the roadhouse this time as it had on the way down.

Du Pré stopped and he went in and bought a bottle of whiskey and some potato chips. He took a go-cup full of ice.

He drove north toward Masson, sipping whiskey and eating the salty snacks.

The Wolf Mountains rose black green gray blue and white on the east. No clouds and the sun bright on the snow.

Lots of snow up there.

Du Pré stopped by the turnout that led to Le Doux Springs

for a moment. He got out and looked at the muddy track. No one had gone in since Du Pré had left.

He drove on.

A fence was down where some drunk had driven through it, missing a shallow curve. The pickup the drunk had been in was on its side in a hayfield.

I find them three bastards I am breaking their damn heads, Du Pré thought, this silly stuff, why the hell they beat up poor Bart?

Masson was just a handful of trailers and small houses, a machine shop and a country feed and hardware store with a bar and restaurant attached. Du Pré went in and asked where the clinic was.

His old cruiser was outside a double-wide trailer. The clinic sign had blown down in the constant wind.

Du Pré opened the door and he went in.

There was a little office with papers on the desk and a computer terminal. File cabinet with one drawer open.

Burdette came down the narrow hall, turning sideways so his shoulders didn't brush the walls.

"He's OK," said Burdette. "Cut up some. Got hit in the mouth and he's taking some stitches there, couple places on his head."

Du Pré dug the tooth out of his shirt pocket.

"Well," said Du Pré, "they do this to him, too."

Burdette grinned.

"Not him," said Burdette. "His smile is intact."

Du Pré roared.

That Bart.

♣ CHAPTER 15 ♣

Hoo," said Madelaine, looking at Bart, "you face looks like a mother's heart, there. Whose husband you piss off?"

Bart shrugged. His face was bandaged and stitched and bruised and scraped. One eye was swelled shut, blooming purple.

He scribbled something on a pad and he shoved it over to Madelaine.

She looked at it.

"Ah," she sighed, "they kick you in the head for sure. Them Indians kick the shit out of you, a sacred site?"

Bart scribbled again.

"T. Rex," said Madelaine. "I see a really dumb movie about them T. Rex. Made about a billion dollars. There is this whole world out there Bart which they are very welcome to."

"So they don't know where it is either," said Burdette.

Bart shook his head.

His lips were swollen so grotesquely that he looked like he had two fat slabs of liver under his nose.

His nose was swollen, too.

"Oh, yes," said Du Pré, "this is yours." He put the tooth on the bartop.

Bart looked at it. He raised a clenched fist and flexed his bicep.

"I chase down some poor old guy in an old car," said Du .

86

Pré. "Scare him about half to death I bet. It was not the guys did this to you."

Bart shook his head. He scribbled on the pad.

THEY DON'T KNOW THE HALF OF IT.

The telephone behind the bar rang and Madelaine picked it up and she listened for a moment and then she said something and she waited and she said something again. She put the phone back down.

A man at the far end of the bar raised a glass and Madelaine went down and refilled his drink and she came back.

"Them Japanese wondering where you are, their ponds are not getting dug," said Madelaine. "That was Booger Tom. He told them you are here."

Du Pré snorted.

"So they are coming over, very upset about something."

"Talk to Booger Tom I bet they are upset," said Burdette. "Christ knows what that old bastard told them."

Bart's eyes were twinkling behind the bruised flesh.

"Take a couple hours for the Japanese to get here," said Du Pré.

Madelaine shook her head.

"They fly up," said Madelaine, "fly over Le Doux Springs, don't like what they see, fly on here. Got no airstrip over there anyway, they are in Cooper. Got no ponds put them big trout in."

Du Pré laughed.

Bart dabbed at his face with a bag that held crushed ice.

Du Pré went over to the jukebox and he put in some quarters and punched up some Cajun music. Good fiddle.

He went out to the cruiser and got his fiddle and he came back in and he tuned and played along with the recording. Stepping icy little notes in behind the breaks. Good practice.

He had played with three songs when two Japanese dressed in ski parkas and a young blond man in a revolting pink windbreaker came in. They looked around the bar a moment, letting their eyes adjust to the dim light, and they walked over to where Bart was sitting.

Bart turned around and they stepped back.

The two Japanese and the American talked for a few moments in rapid Japanese.

Du Pré cased his fiddle and he wandered over.

"Ah," said the American, "what happened to Mr. Fascelli?"

Bart was hiding his face behind the ice pack.

"Some people they beat him up," said Du Pré. "He is not talking. What you want?"

"The digging is behind schedule," said the blond American, "and no one told us that the springs had found new outlets. They have a very tight schedule and they were upset."

"Bart he is hurt," said Du Pré. "I will go down there and drag in the morning, you know. Some Indians beat him up, they said something about a sacred site."

"Shit," said the American. "Look, I'm the architect. We don't need a fight with the Native Americans. What the hell were they upset about?"

Du Pré shrugged.

"The spring will be late," said Du Pré, "you can't pour your concrete for maybe another month anyway."

"Shit," said the architect.

"Nothing can be done about the weather," said one of the Japanese, in flawless English.

Du Pré looked at him.

The two Japanese and the American moved off to the corner by the jukebox and they talked together rapidly. Then the Japanese left. The American came over to Du Pré and Bart.

"No problem," the blond man said, "but is it possible to have the ponds ready to pour by the fifteenth of May?"

Du Pré nodded, not really knowing.

"Well," said the architect, "I'll come by tomorrow and we can talk."

He went out.

Du Pré turned back to Bart.

Burdette was sitting hunched over, his face hidden by his hand. He was looking in the mirror in the barback. He got up and he went to the window by the front door and he looked out for a moment, then he went outside.

THANKS. I HURT.

Bart pulled the pad back.

Du Pré nodded.

Burdette came back in. His face was troubled. He went to his drink and he drained it and he shoved it over the bar. Madelaine filled it again and she took some money from the pile on the bar and she made change and put the silver and bills in front of Burdette.

The big man came over to Du Pré, and he stood so his face hung between Du Pré and Bart.

"That guy," said Burdette, "isn't an architect. He's an archaeologist. Hoffmann. I've met him a bunch of times."

Du Pré nodded.

"I doubt they know a thing about the Horned Star People," said Burdette, "but Hoffman's here for another reason."

Bart nodded. Du Pré rolled a smoke and he lit it and he squinted when the smoke hit his eyes. He sipped bourbon.

"Perhaps," said Burdette, "I should stay out of sight till he's gone."

Du Pré nodded.

Burdette went out and he drove off.

Bart scribbled on the pad.

I DON'T LIKE THIS.

Du Pré nodded.

Bart scribbled again.

PONDS MY ASS.

Du Pré laughed.

"I bet you ten dollars," said Du Pré, "we go back, your equipment is wrecked. They put sugar in it, something."

Bart nodded.

He scribbled.

WE QUIT. SEE HOW LONG IT TAKES FOR THEM TO GET SOMEONE ELSE.

Du Pré nodded.

Scribble.

TAKE ME HOME. CAN'T SEE WELL.

Bart got up and put on his coat and he was weaving a little, dizzy from the pounding he had taken. He went out the door.

"I be right back," said Du Pré. "We are going to Bart's."

"He maybe sleep," said Madelaine. "That poor face of his, it hurts."

Du Pré went out. Bart was sitting in the old cruiser.

Du Pré drove out of town and he turned right and went up the long rising road that lifted to the benchlands and he turned left at the crossroads and went west toward Bart's.

Bart sat slumped forward, his hands lightly touching his swollen face. Once when Du Pré hit a pothole and the car jerked Bart wheezed in pain.

Bart started frantically rolling the window down and Du Pré came to a dead stop and Bart vomited into the mud for a while. He was sweating and shaky when he stopped.

Du Pré got out and filled a paper sack with wet heavy snow and he brought it back and Bart sat for a while with his face in the sack, pressed against the cold melting ice.

When he straightened up and swung his legs back in the car

Du Pré drove on and he parked the car as close to Bart's house as he could when they got to the ranch.

He helped Bart inside. Bart went into the room with the huge bath with the water jets coming out of the tiles of the side every couple of feet. He turned on the pump that churned the hot water.

Du Pré waited until Bart was in the tub before he went back out to his car.

Some magpies were gathered near a fencerow, feasting on a deer that had gotten tangled in the wire in the blizzard and died. The birds quarreled and some flapped up a few feet and then they settled and pecked at the carrion.

The car Burdette was driving was over by the shed where the bones of the Horned Star People had been moved. The sliding metal doors were shut and Du Pré looked a long time at the building and then he shrugged and went to his car.

Booger Tom came out of his cabin and he waved at Du Pré. The old man picked up a piece of wood and he started to make kindling of it on the chopping block, a round of ponderosa that had taken the thumps of an ax thousands of times without splitting.

Chunk. Chunk. Chunk.

Du Pré got in his car and drove off. When he got to the road he sat for a moment and then he turned toward Benetsee's.

✤ CHAPTER 16 ✤

Pelon poured hot water from the kettle on top of the wood-stove into a cup. He handed it to Du Pré.

Tea. Chaparral. Oily. Dark.

Du Pré breathed the scent.

"He maybe be out a little while," said Pelon. "He poured three times, you know, some time back."

Du Pré went to the little window at the back of the cabin and he rubbed a clear place in the moisture that was clouding it.

The sweat lodge was shut. Not a wisp of steam coming out of the door flaps, so it would not be too long before the old man came out and went to the creek to jump in.

Some damn day he do that and his heart stop, Du Pré thought. If he got one. Maybe he just got an obsidian pump in there. He was old when my father was a boy, I think.

Du Pré looked at Pelon. When he had first come to the country his face was fat and smooth, full of water and cities. Now lines were etched deep in the skin round his eyes and two clefts reached up between his cheeks and his nose. His hands were worn and callused and his nails black and broken.

Used to have fat hands. Computers.

Du Pré picked up the jug of screwtop wine he had brought and he cracked the top away from the plastic ring and he poured a big glass for Pelon.

Du Pré rolled a thick cigarette and he lit it and he handed it over.

Pelon took a deep drag and then he drained the wine at one long deep swallow.

Medicine people. Drunks. Like me, Du Pré thought.

He sipped some whiskey from his flask.

Pelon belched. Du Pré poured him more wine.

"I come here listen to more of his damn riddles," said Du Pré.

"Yah, them," said Pelon. "Sometimes he gets me so mad I could kill him. I don't do it, of course, but his riddles, they make me mad, too."

Old man knows things. Mind like smoke in the sun. Shimmers. Can't see what it is.

Nobody is lying to me that much yet but I still don't like it.

"He come out," said Pelon. He hadn't looked.

Du Pré rolled another cigarette and he got up and filled another big jar with wine and he went out the front door and down the sagging steps and through the mud around to the back of the house.

Benetsee was standing by the creek. Steam came off his brown old body. He jumped in and disappeared.

Du Pré waited.

Damn old man he die there sometime.

Shit.

Du Pré set the wine and the smoke down on a stump that was dry in one place and he walked quickly over to the creek.

The water shimmered over gold sand and gravels speckled with dark round stones. The water weeds waved sinuously. A couple little trout darted out of cover to feed and then shot back inside the weeds.

Du Pré cursed and he walked downstream. He went around

a thick stand of red alder and he looked at the creek which was shallow and much faster now. A white patch across the creek changed from snow to a jackrabbit pumping long hind legs as it headed for the sagebrush beyond the pasture.

Du Pré looked up at the sky for patience.

Goddamn old man always does this to me.

He walked back up the creek and he turned and went toward the house.

Benetsee, fully clothed, was sitting on the stump. The wine was gone from the jar and the cigarette was half smoked.

"Hah," said Du Pré, "you have a good sweat there? Eh?"

"Uh," said Benetsee, "yes, very good, thank you. Good wine, nice smoke. You should do something about your temper, you know, it is not good for your stomach."

"You," said Du Pré, "are not good for my stomach."

Benetsee grinned.

"We go in," said the old man. "It is cold out, damp, not good for us. There is more wine in there, too."

Du Pré followed him. The old man skittered over the ground like a crab, mostly moving sideways.

Pelon stood up when they came in. He had another half jar of wine in his hand and his face was flushed.

Benetsee sat down in the chair and he waited while Du Pré rolled a smoke for him and filled his glass.

"Horned Star People," said Du Pré, "they come here a long time ago, start something. Someone is dead, so it is not a funny story anymore old man. I don't like jokes played on me got dead people in them."

Benetsee sat with his eyes closed. He smoked for a while.

"Thing about stories with dead people in them," said Du Pré, "is cops ask lots of questions so whatever it is I am not supposed to find out they probably will, you know."

Benetsee didn't move.

Pelon had gone outside.

An ax thudded into wood.

"Yes," said Benetsee.

Du Pré sighed and he sat down and he rolled himself a smoke and he lit it and inhaled. He took out his flask and had some whiskey.

"Me," said Du Pré, "I wonder about this dead guy. These Horned Star People, they bury their dead, Le Doux Springs, got a piece of this dinosaur in the middle of them. Them Japanese they want that dinosaur. Guy dead, he has a piece, that dinosaur. Very popular dinosaur, got such good friends they kill for him."

Benetsee didn't say anything.

Du Pré rolled him another cigarette.

"Ever' thing," said Du Pré, "you know some. You know about all of this old man."

Du Pré pulled out the walrus ivory amulet and he put it on the table.

Benetsee looked at it, a small smile on his face.

"Yah," said Benetsee, "not much good."

"So," said Du Pré.

"We maybe go and talk, them Crows," said Benetsee.

"Why I got to talk to Crows, I talk to you?" said Du Pré.

"I maybe go and talk to Crows," said Benetsee. "You talk, whoever you want."

Pelon came in carrying an armload of wood. He dumped it in the box by the woodstove and he opened the door and put in a couple of pieces. A little pine smoke puffed out. He closed the door. The draft made the fire roar, and then it got quiet again.

"I got to go, move Bart's dragline, other stuff," said Du Pré.

Benetsee drank his wine.

"I got to go and talk to Crows."

Du Pré nodded and he had a little more whiskey.

He picked up the amulet and he put it down again.

"Seven million dollars, lot of money," said Du Pré.

"Yah," said Benetsee.

"So this is not about money."

Benetsee looked at Du Pré a long time.

"I don't know what it is about," said Benetsee, "but it is not about money. Them Crows maybe know."

Du Pré sighed and he looked across the room at the shelves full of food Madelaine had canned and given to Benetsee. Stew and chili, corn, beans, tomatoes, pumpkin, plums, peaches. Feed the whole world, wipe its tears. Madelaine.

I sit this chair, listen to this old man not tell me things, wants me to go and talk to Crows. I like them Crows just fine, we fight them Sioux together, them Blackfeet, we fight them.

He will not tell me why?

"OK," said Du Pré, "Maybe I go and move Bart's stuff then we go and talk, them Crow."

Benetsee sat saying nothing.

Pelon started playing a flute, a long carved one, cedar, the sort the Coast tribes made and traded inland. A long slow song, looping and lonely and full of some great sorrow.

Du Pré had never heard it before.

He sighed and closed his eyes.

Benetsee began to sing.

Du Pré couldn't understand the words.

Du Pré nodded and he smelled saltwater and snow and pines in the fierce cold.

Black water so cold it rasped against the sides of the boat.

Du Pré heard a big drum.

Behind Benetsee's old voice keening there were others, high, sung in the throat, wavering like the calls of ghost birds.

Du Pré saw a long canoe on the black water, a man in the

bow with feathers on his arms and a beaked mask over his face. He stood up waving his arms and jerking his head like an eagle looking around and the paddlers behind him plunged the blades of their paddles, knives in the black water and it writhed like a stabbed snake wound forever round itself.

Du Pré heard clicking.

He opened his eyes.

Pelon was standing by the deep sink, banging a glass with a spoon.

Du Pré cursed and he stood up.

Benetsee was gone.

Du Pré hit the table with his fist.

No use in looking outside, the old man was gone.

❧ CHAPTER 17 ❧

You can't do this!" screamed Hoffmann. "We have a contract!"

"Bart is hurt," said Du Pré. "His jaw is broken. You sit up there, this thing, and it shakes. Plenty other contractors."

Hoffmann threw up his hands. The two Japanese were standing off by their rental car. They were paying no attention to Hoffmann and Du Pré.

Booger Tom spat. He wandered off toward the backhoe.

Du Pré clambered up in the cab of the dragline. He switched on the heater coils in the huge diesel engine and he waited until the ready light came on and then he pressed the starter and the engine mumbled and then it caught and roared and a cloud of black smoke shot out of the stack. Du Pré set the throttle and left it to warm at a high idle and he got out and checked the hydraulic lines. The lock pins were out and he got back in the cab and retracted them and he lifted the bucket and then the boom and then he put it in reverse and swung it around and he began to crawl toward the lowboy trailer.

The machine clanked up on the ramps and Du Pré waited till it was three feet from the spot it would sit on and he cut the power and threw in the clutch and he inched the huge machine forward till he could see the painted line on the frame just above the steel treads. He shut off the dragline and he got down and began to thread the chains and clip them tight.

Booger Tom had the backhoe up on its trailer and boomed down and Du Pré stopped and he went over to guide the old man as he backed to the hitch.

Booger Tom got it on the first try and Du Pré dropped the pin home and then he threaded the safety chain around.

Booger Tom had forgotten to lower the bucket and Du Pré jumped up to the seat of the backhoe and he lowered it and he took all the pressure off the hydraulic lines. They slumped a little.

Du Pré drove the SUV they had come down in up on the ramps behind the dragline and he lifted them up with the box controls at the back of the trailer and he chained the ramps up and put the sleeves through the hinges. Then he boomed off the front and rear bumper of the SUV.

Booger Tom left first. While the dump truck and backhoe weren't very maneuverable, the dragline with its tractor-trailer was a monstrous lumbering thing and Tom would be twenty miles down the road before Du Pré got on it.

That Hoffmann he put on a show but not much of it, Du Pré thought.

Well, we got them Horned Star People bones out of here. They ever find out about that they shit about ten colors.

Du Pré crept slowly through the mud. When he would hit a deep puddle the terrible compression of weight would shoot mud fifty feet and more. Up. Off to the side. Depending.

The big tractor screamed along in compound low.

Du Pré got to the county road and he pulled out very wide and missed the fence on the far side by a few inches. He ground along in third gear now, at about ten miles an hour, and when he got to the paved state highway he had to wait while the cars and trucks passed. The road stretched visible for a couple miles on each side and when there was no traffic at all Du Pré crept out and swung left and south and then he was able to step up the gears and lumber along at forty-five miles an hour.

He turned off to double-check all the chocks and chains at the first snowplow turnaround. All of them were taut but one. Du Pré reset the boomer and cranked it tight.

He stopped again at the roadhouse where the highway went east to Toussaint and Cooper and he went in rubbing his eyes. The day was blazing bright and the bar was very dim.

He got a bottle of whiskey and some soda and a glass and ice and potato chips and a pack of smokes. He'd left his pouch on the front seat of the SUV and the flanges of the ramps were so high he couldn't get the door open, without moving the SUV clear off the trailer.

"Popsicle, my ass," said Du Pré to the dragline. "Big Green Pig. Some hobby my friend he got."

Du Pré climbed up in the cab of the tractor and he mixed a drink and had it and then another one and he set it in the rack over the console and then he moved the big tractor-trailer out of the lot and crossed the north-south road and headed east. The highway was frost-heaved badly.

I am not legal to be driving this now, Du Pré thought, there is too much weight on this thing.

He pulled off by a historical marker and he let the SUV down and he got in and drove on. He threw the pack of tailor-mades out the window and he rolled himself a real smoke.

When he passed Booger Tom the old man sounded a long blast on the air horn.

It will freeze tonight I go and get the damn thing four A.M., Du Pré thought. Big fine for that, tear up these fine highways. Popsicle. Big Green Pig.

It was getting late in the light and the tops of the Wolfs blazed with alpenglow. A fingernail moon hovered near the highest peak.

Du Pré went past Cooper, and then he turned down toward Toussaint and he kept the lumbering SUV moving fast until he hit all the potholes right at the edge of town. They were very deep and would be deeper before they got filled.

Madelaine was behind the bar, sitting on a high stool. She had some beadwork she was getting ready for the summer powwows, little purses with coyotes and their young on them.

"You back pret' quick," said Madelaine, "drive that big rig fast, eh?"

"Leave it at the historical marker," said Du Pré. "Frost laws. I go and get it early in the morning."

Madelaine set down her beadwork and she put her reading glasses into their case and she wrapped it all up and put it in her big handbag.

She went to the kitchen and Du Pré heard a patty of meat sizzle on the grill and then bubbling when she plunged a mess of fries into hot fat. She came to the door and she motioned for Du Pré to make his own drink.

Du Pré went behind the bar and he got a glass and ice and some whiskey and he went back around and sat down and rolled himself a cigarette. He lit it and blew out the smoke and the door opened and the light cut in. He couldn't see who it was.

"Afternoon," said Burdette, as he slid up on a stool. He was smiling.

Du Pré nodded.

Madelaine came out with Du Pré's cheeseburger and she set it down and Du Pré listened to the fries whistle. Too hot to pick up yet.

Burdette ordered a brandy and Madelaine went to warm the snifter. She ran hot water on it and shook it out and she poured a slug of brandy in it from a squat bottle and put it in front of Burdette. She picked up his twenty and made change.

"The shit will now hit the fan," said Burdette. "Bart and I talked. We decided to announce that we found the burial of the Red Ochre People."

Du Pré sipped his drink and he waited.

"And then we did it. Called some television station that it turns out Bart owns."

You go crazy figuring out everything Bart owns, Du Pré thought.

Too much stuff.

"And they went bananas," said Burdette. "I expect the first wave of newspeople will be here in an hour or so."

He went outside and when he came back he carried a Plexiglas case, a cube a little more than a foot on a side, with a green cloth-covered base in it, and on it a skull and mandible, marked with the red ochre.

"Find one like this it could just be an aberration," said Burdette, "but there were seven in the burial, all long, so they pretty well have to be Caucasian. Twelve thousand years old. Read all about it in your supermarket tabloid."

Madelaine looked at the skull. She patted the case.

"There, there," she said.

Burdette smiled.

"Old person sleeping," she said. "Now there is light and a lot of people around."

The door opened and Bart limped in. His face was even more swollen now and some of the bruises had ugly yellow borders. But his lips had shrunk. He waved to Du Pré and Madelaine and Burdette.

Madelaine rattled her fingernails on the top of the bar.

"You sons of bitches," she said. "You announce this. Where you say you announce this from."

"Uh-oh," said Burdette.

"Uh-oh your fat ass," said Madelaine. "I know, them newspeople, they coming here, right? My Du Pré he get to shove that jerk what-his-name's head, the wall there."

Bart scribbled something on his pad.

He pushed it over to Madelaine.

"I call a couple people," said Madelaine. "They drink some, them newspeople. Big story, come to the Toussaint Bar, hear all about it. Susan Klein find out, this, you die maybe."

Du Pré sighed and he went out to his cruiser and he got a cordless drill out of the trunk and he came back and he drilled some holes through the sides of the Plexiglas and down into the scarred old wood of the bar. Then he put twelve heavy tempered screws through the holes.

He hit the Plexiglas case with the drill. It went thump.

"Very good," said Burdette. "I hadn't thought of that."

Du Pré shrugged and he put the drill away and he carried it back to his car.

Madelaine made herself a barbecue sandwich and one for Burdette and she had a couple of glasses of pink wine. The two women who spelled her at the bar showed up, faces flushed from the cold. They were laughing but then they came close and looked at the skull and they got quiet.

"What a story," said Burdette.

A light plane flew over.

Du Pré had a nice stiff drink.

They waited.

✦ CHAPTER 18 ✦

Burdette and Bart sat like two stone guardians on either side of the Plexiglas case.

The skull reposed. It glowed. Tricks of light and shadow gave it an eerie cast of life. The black eyeholes were deep with time.

The reporters milled and shouted questions.

Burdette read a short prepared statement. The skull was Caucasian and similar to skulls found in all lands surrounding the North Pole. It was fifteen thousand years old. It had been found within a hundred miles of where it now sat.

Photographers jostled each other and complained bitterly about the Plexiglas and they pleaded for someone to remove the skull from the case so they could photograph it without the glare the plastic added.

Madelaine and the other two women were shoving drinks over the bar.

Du Pré was standing down at the end where it opened to the barroom to keep the reporters and photographers from getting behind the bar.

"Hit one of them," said Madelaine quietly, when she was near.

Du Pré laughed.

"You don't love me," she said. She went back down the bar toward the hands holding money.

A television crew shoved their way in and a fight broke out between them and some journalists.

Du Pré picked up a softball bat sitting against the beer case and he walked to the punching reporters and he eyed a camera on the shoulder of one of the crew.

"This stop," said Du Pré to the wide-eyed man, "or I smash your camera there."

The cameraman screamed for a few moments and the fight quit.

Du Pré told them all to get out and not come back. He slapped the bat in his palm while he did. They left grumbling.

"Excuse me," said a breathless young woman with a pad and pencil in her hand, "were you there when this was found?"

Du Pré shook his head.

"Who was?" said the reporter.

Du Pré looked at the ceiling. He looked back at the reporter. He shrugged.

"You bastard," she hissed. She turned back toward Bart and Burdette.

"Did the earthquake turn this up?" said a voice behind him.

Du Pré shrugged.

"You're that fiddler, Du Pré," said the voice.

Du Pré turned. A fat disheveled man wearing thick glasses stood there, galoshes open, shirt misbuttoned, shrewd black eyes behind the smudged lenses.

"There aren't any digs around here anyway," he said, "it was the earthquake, right? Tipped something up?"

Du Pré shrugged.

The man slipped out the door.

Now they fly all the whole length of that tear in the earth, Du Pré thought, and the only place I know there is digging is

Le Doux Springs. Hope Bart and Burdette got it all out of there.

Smart guy.

Them Japanese are not going to be happy.

Du Pré heard singing outside, the words were Sioux. A drum.

Du Pré began to laugh. He went to the window and looked out.

A knot of Indians in ceremonial dress were standing out in the parking lot singing. The fat reporter was talking to one of them.

Du Pré squinted.

"Ah!" said Du Pré.

It was Benjamin Medicine Eagle.

That little prick Bucky Dassault he is here, got on the eagle feathers and the beaded clothes, Sioux give them out, child molesting.

Benjamin Medicine Eagle and his chums began to walk toward the bar.

When they got to the porch Du Pré opened the door and he stepped out and let it swing shut behind him.

"We got a court order here," said Bucky. "That skull belongs to us."

Du Pré looked at him. He looked at the five men with him.

Never see these Indians before, but some of them beat Bart up I bet, Du Pré thought, dressed Crow some.

"You got a court order," said Du Pré, "you go find that Sheriff Benny Klein."

Who is in Billings.

Bucky looked at Du Pré. He was scared to death. He swallowed and he swelled.

"We take that skull now," he said.

Du Pré roared with laughter. Three of the men with Bucky were young and they looked tough. They glared at Du Pré.

Them three, Du Pré thought, we talk a little later.

"Got a court order!" yelled Benjamin Medicine Eagle. "We take the bones of our people!"

Du Pré looked at him.

"Whose people these?" said Du Pré. "Them Sioux don't even get to South Dakota till seventeen seventy-six. Us Métis run their ass, the Great Lakes. Them Blackfeet, they are in Land of Little Sticks, before that. Fifteen thousand years them bones are here. White bones."

"We always been here!" yelled Benjamin Medicine Eagle.

"Yah!" yelled one of the young thugs behind him. The man was missing a front tooth.

"OK," said Du Pré, "I go and get Burdette, you talk to him. You can't get in there anyway, there is no room." He turned and went in the bar and he flipped the lock when the door shut.

Du Pré wound his way through the reporters, all in knots and mumbling.

Bart was holding ice to his broken face.

"Hey," said Du Pré, "you got that tooth I give you?"

Bart nodded. He fished it out of the watch pocket of his jeans.

He dropped it in Du Pré's hand.

"Guy you knock this out of, he is out front," said Du Pré.

Bart started to get up.

Burdette reached over and pushed him back.

"Keep the reporters off the skull," said Burdette. "You aren't healed up yet. Gabriel and I will stand in for you. Just this once."

Bart nodded.

Du Pré picked up the softball bat.

"Only," said Burdette, wagging a finger at him, "if you promise not to hit anyone in the head."

"Yah," said Du Pré.

They walked out from the bar. Burdette was pulling on a tight black pair of driving gloves. He smoothed the Velcro tabs down.

Damn guy is so big, ought to eat hay, Du Pré thought.

Burdette stopped by the door.

"Now," he said, "we don't want to kill anyone. Right?"

"Yah," said Du Pré, "not here anyway."

"Benjamin Medicine Eagle," said Burdette, "bitched up a Shoshonean site I was digging. Sneaked in and wrecked it. Two years' work."

"Me," said Du Pré, "I don't like him either."

"OK," said Burdette.

"I go," said Du Pré, "hang this tooth in front of the guy. Arrest him, beating up Bart."

Burdette nodded.

He motioned to the cameraman. The man hesitated and then he came over.

"Things," said Burdette, "are gonna get very Western out there in about ten seconds."

The man nodded.

"I'll follow," he said. He waved to a woman holding a boom mike and a tape recorder.

Du Pré opened the door and he walked out and he went to Benjamin Medicine Eagle. Burdette hung back a little.

"You!" screamed Medicine Eagle.

Du Pré motioned to the young thug with the missing tooth. The man pushed past Medicine Eagle.

Du Pré opened his hand. The tooth sat in his palm.

"This yours, asshole," said Du Pré. "You are under arrest, beating up my friend Bart." He tucked the tooth in his pocket.

"What?" said Medicine Eagle.

The young thug was still gaping when Du Pré swung the bat

and caught him in the knee. He screamed and went down and then Du Pré went after another one.

There was a loud wet thump behind Du Pré. The young thug turned to run and Du Pré cracked him across his forearm and the bone snapped loudly.

The other three started to run but a patrol car across the street switched on its light bar and spots and the two deputies got out with drawn guns. The three punks stopped, hands in the air.

It started to rain hard on their feathers.

Du Pré turned around.

Benjamin Medicine Eagle was flat on the ground on his face out cold.

The man Du Pré had hit in the knee was writhing on the ground and clutching his leg.

Du Pré took out some handcuffs but he couldn't find the key to open them. He grabbed the man by his hair and he started to drag him over to the patrol car.

Benny Klein's truck came screeching up and Benny jumped out.

"What the fuck are you doing?" he said.

"This guy beat up Bart, two of them over there, too," said Du Pré.

The deputies were stuffing the last of the three into the backseat of the patrol car.

"You prove that?" said Benny.

"Sure," said Du Pré, pulling out the man's front tooth.

❖ CHAPTER 19 ❖

Du Pré sipped his whiskey. He watched himself on the evening news bashing the one guy with the softball bat and then the huge bulk of Burdette flashed past and there was a terrible thump but no one could see Benjamin Medicine Eagle behind the big man. Then the rest broke and ran and the camera zoomed forward to focus on Medicine Eagle facedown in the mud with the rain on his feathers.

"Violence broke out at a press conference in Toussaint, Montana," said the reporter, gravely, to all America, "over who has the right to buried Indian artifacts and bones. . . ."

"Not that little cocksucker," said Burdette, "I may assure you."

There were still reporters in the bar, drinking and asking questions of anyone who came in.

Buster Dunn was flying the fat man with glasses—the one who'd asked about the earthquake—over the long jagged tear in the earth that ran along the border of the Wolf Mountains.

Du Pré looked at the screw holes in the old dark bar top.

"Maybe you better patch those, Susan Klein kick your ass," said Madelaine to Du Pré. "She like this old bar."

Du Pré nodded.

Me, I like this old bar, too, got my father's initials in it, bunch of places, got my grandfathers' both of them, think I found my great-grandfather's but maybe not he never learn to read and write. Pret' old bar, here, come all the way up the Missouri, steamboat, then it is hauled in a wagon here. Three buildings built up and fall down around it it is still here.

Like us Métis.

"You guys have trouble this," said Madelaine. "Why the hell you have that damn photographer come with you?"

"Resisting arrest," said Burdette.

"Oh, yes," said Madelaine, "that resisting arrest, there, I hear that damn Bucky Dassault resist arrest there. You hit him so hard he is still out cold I bet."

Burdette shook his head.

"No," said the big man, "he's well and talking to some lawyer about suing me and everybody."

"Yah," said Madelaine, "that is about right. Poor Bart's face."

"I have half a mind to lead these clowns on a long goose chase," said Burdette. He looked at the reporters nursing drinks and staring at him.

It had gotten very cold out and the temperature was dropping so fast that Du Pré could hear the water slowing as it ran off the roof. Ice was clotting the drains and gutters.

One of the reporters pulled a cell phone out of his pocket and he popped it open and listened and he shut it while he was getting up. He didn't say anything but all the others did, too, except one pair who must have been told to stick tight to Burdette.

Everybody rushed out and cars started and went off.

"I think," said Burdette, "that they found something."

He yawned.

"Yah," said Du Pré, "I bet they did."

Madelaine sounded her fingernails on the bar, rippling taps.

"They are gone," she said. "Maybe I close this place up."

"Oh," said Burdette, "have mercy."

"Yah, that," said Du Pré.

"Shit Jesus!" said Madelaine. The door to the bar had opened and she was staring goggle-eyed at someone.

Du Pré turned.

A man stood inside, wearing a long fur cloak and leggins of fur lashed crisscross with raw white hide. His boots were fur, too, and spiraled up his calves with the same babiche.

His face and hair were bright vermilion. Spikes of fat and ground red earth stuck up from his scalp. His eyepits were black and his eyes glittered in the carbon. He carried a long spear with a foreshaft of bone tipped with the white tooth of a shark. He carried a carved white bone atlatl in his left hand.

"You are still maybe serving dinner?" said the red man.

Pelon.

"Pelon, damn you," said Madelaine. "It is not fucking Halloween. You and that Benetsee you have a good time, there? Them reporters out there thinking maybe them old bones come to life? Jesus."

"Him I don't know," said Pelon. "We get dressed like this, he goes off, tells me to come to this place this time."

Du Pré and Burdette roared with laughter. Du Pré laughed so hard that he started to cough and he couldn't stop.

Pelon walked over, the rawhide ties on his clothes skreeking a little. He stank like raw salted hides.

Du Pré looked at the hides.

Dogs. Two golden retrievers, a Lab, and some curly brown coats he couldn't identify.

"You wearing somebody's pets," said Du Pré.

"Oh," said Pelon, "some dumb city bastards they come here let their dogs out and they pack up and kill some sheep so the man owns the sheep shoots them, nails the hides to boards, his fence. Benetsee and me we take them, save him trouble."

Du Pré nodded. City people were always bringing their

dogs, who they let run. Their dogs met other dogs and once they were a pack they went looking for things to kill.

"Nice spear," said Burdette.

"Benetsee him make that," said Pelon. "Has two, these shark's teeth in a little pouch."

Pelon handed the spear to Burdette, who looked at it carefully.

"Well," he said, "he's got the sinew ties right. The Horned Star People had an unusual way of lashing. It made the sinew tighten when any stress was put on it."

Du Pré looked. Over, back, under, up, back.

"Where is Benetsee?" said Du Pré.

Pelon shook his head.

"Oh, yes," he said. "He is where all them reporters are I bet."

"You stink," said Madelaine. "Them dog hides don't get cured too good, eh?"

She came round the bar with a spray can of disinfectant and she sprayed Pelon liberally. Burdette and Du Pré moved away from the fumes.

"Jesus," said Madelaine, looking at the long tan fur, "you got bugs in that fur, there."

"Benetsee say I wait here till they come back," said Pelon.

"Yah," said Madelaine. "You do that, but I take you outside and I give you a good shot of poison, them bugs. Beetles you got, I see. Maybe fleas."

"Fleas eat living creatures," said Burdette.

"Benetsee's goddamn fleas, probably eat anything they want," said Madelaine. "Medicine fleas you know."

Madelaine got another spray can out and she led Pelon outside. He went along meekly.

"Benetsee," said Du Pré, "he is picking on someone else, me, for one time, I guess."

Burdette nodded.

"I have known a few true medicine people," he said. "They aren't anything like the movies have them for sure. Rotten senses of humor."

Madelaine came in and she went back behind the bar and she put the can of bug spray away and she washed her hands.

"Him stay out there, them bugs die and drop off," said Madelaine.

Someone yelled outside, but the words were unintelligible.

The fat breathless shrewd reporter banged through the door, his glasses wildly askew.

"I got to rent a car!" he said. "I'll pay two hundred dollars for a ride."

Burdette and Du Pré looked at him blankly.

"Four hundred," said the man. "It's only a few miles, no more than five."

"What," said Du Pré, "you want to look at?"

"Dunn flew me over the earthquake fault," said the reporter. "We saw some guy . . . dressed like the guy outside, anyway . . . dancing around something. I called my assistant here."

"And the word spread like wildfire," said Burdette.

"It was strange," said the reporter, "it was like there was a fire around this spot but no smoke."

"You got this assistant," said Du Pré.

"Isn't answering his phone," said the reporter.

"OK," said Du Pré, "I take you."

The reporter waved some money at Du Pré.

Burdette got up, too.

"Who is that guy out there?" said the reporter.

"He is a drunk," said Du Pré. "Wanders around, kills dogs, dresses up in their skins. Gets like this we take him to a hospital."

The reporter nodded.

"Hey," he said, "I'm in a hurry."

Du Pré and Burdette shrugged into their jackets.

"Maybe you take that damn Pelon, his bugs," said Madelaine.

Du Pré shook his head.

"Ah," said Du Pré, "all this, I don't spoil that Benetsee's joke."

"Bugs," said Madelaine.

"Come on, guys," said the reporter.

✤ CHAPTER 20 ✤

"Can't you drive any faster?" said the fat reporter. He leaned over the seat.

"No," said Du Pré.

"Shit," said the fat reporter.

They could see the cars parked by the road up on the bench, but not the people who had been in them.

Du Pré drove lazily and the cruiser slopped a little on the frozen mud as they crawled up the grade to the top of the bench.

The reporters were crowded around a stone outcropping, the ordinary gray-yellow limestone of the old seabed.

A small man in furs, with a red-painted face and a red ruff of some spiky hair was dancing on top of the outcropping. A couple of four-wheel drive SUVs had pulled into the field and their lights shone on him.

"I bet they cut Bart's fence to do that," said Burdette.

"Yah," said Du Pré, "well, we will run them out and put it back up."

"Run them out?" said the reporter.

"It is private property," said Du Pré. "You don't even get to walk on it. Your fat ass, it stays out on the road."

"Bullshit!" said the reporter.

Du Pré fished his 9mm out from the glove box and he checked the chamber.

"You fat fuck," he said, "you will stay on the road or I shoot you in the leg."

The reporter slumped back in the seat.

"I known him a long time," said Burdette, "and I am sure he will be happy to shoot you in the leg. If not, I will."

Du Pré parked behind the clot of rental cars and he got out and so did Burdette and they waited for the fat reporter to struggle through the doorway and get to his feet.

"Find a ride back, someone else," said Du Pré.

Some of the horses in the big pasture were running back and forth on the ridge to the right.

"Saw the hole in the fence," said Burdette.

Du Pré handed him a roll of mending wire and some snips.

"I get these assholes out of here," he said.

Burdette reached down and he got a cut end of wire and he made a loop in the end and then he started on the other.

The fat reporter was pacing back and forth by the cars.

Du Pré walked up to the knot of reporters. They were looking now and again at the red-painted furman on top of the rocks. Halfway down the rock face half a skull sat in a small hollow, and red streaks ran down the gray-yellow stone below.

Du Pré stepped into the headlight beams.

"You cut these fences," he said. "You get out of here now. I give you one minute."

"We're filming!" someone yelled.

Du Pré nodded. He took out the 9mm and he shot the right front tire of the SUV nearest him, and the left front tire, and then he stopped.

"You will go now," he said.

The reporters ran for the road, and they stumbled over the low wire that Burdette had patched together.

117

Du Pré wandered over past the headlight beams. A man was opening the door of the SUV.

Du Pré pointed the gun at the radiator.

"That silly car of yours stays here," he said. "Bart maybe sue you or something."

Hiyihyyyyyyiiiiihiyihihiyiyiyihiyi, Benetsee sang.

Du Pré wandered up to the rock face and he looked up at the half skull.

Plastic mask for a kid, cut in half, stuck in there.

Red paint, kind you mix with water.

"Old man," said Du Pré, "what are you doing, this."

Benetsee stopped hopping around and singing.

"They want to find something," Benetsee said, "so I help them."

The old man disappeared behind the lip of the rock. Then he came around the left side, little stabbing steps as he came down the steep hill. The bone foreshaft fell off his spear. He stopped and picked it up and shoved it back on the haft.

"I don't let them horses out," he said.

Du Pré nodded.

"We got two fine cars here," said Benetsee. He looked in the one that didn't have holes in the tires. "Keys in it, too."

The old man took his spear apart and he put it in the SUV and then he got in and turned the key. The engine caught. Du Pré reached in and pointed to the shift on the console.

"You know how to drive?" said Du Pré.

Benetsee shook his head.

"It is automatic," said Du Pré. "It is in park, that is P, drive is D, reverse is R . . . there, them lights."

"Don't need reverse," said Benetsee.

Du Pré shut the door laughing.

Benetsee raced the engine and shifted and the SUV lurched and turned and made off up a steep trail. Then the old man started to go almost straight across and the SUV looked like it would roll. But it didn't and it ground over the top and was gone.

Somebody down on the road was screaming.

Du Pré reached in the SUV with the dead tires and he pulled the keys out and he threw them off in the dark. He punched the lights off.

Burdette was waiting, the last strand of barbed wire in his hand.

Du Pré stepped over the two lower strands and he helped Burdette pull it tight and tie it off.

"Bastards!" someone yelled.

Burdette and Du Pré walked back down to the cruiser. They got in and Du Pré turned the old car on and drove off to a turnaround where he could change direction. Other cars were following him now.

When they passed a green sedan, the fat reporter was hanging out the window waving his fist and screaming bad words.

"Press relations have soured," said Burdette.

They got to the top of a little rise before the road ran down the steep grade to the plains.

Benetsee was standing beside the road.

Du Pré stopped and the old man got in. He reeked of rotting skins and cheap wine.

"Jesus," said Burdette, "I forget how aromatic life was back in the Old Stone Age."

"Got a smoke," said Benetsee, "got some wine?"

"That Madelaine she spray you with gasoline, set you on fire," said Du Pré, "you come in, her bar, smell like that."

"Nah," said Benetsee, "Madelaine respect old people."

"Respect the Church, too," said Du Pré, "she still kick Father Van Den Heuvel's ass he piss her off. She kick God's ass."

Du Pré rolled Benetsee a smoke. He stopped the car and he

went to the trunk and opened it and he fished out a jug of cheap fizzy wine and he cracked the top and carried it back to Benetsee.

"Got a glass?" said Benetsee.

"Drink it out of your damn shoe," said Du Pré, "Now what you do with that car you take?"

"Give it away," said Benetsee. "Don't go fast enough."

He drank wine from the jug. Gurgle Gurgle Gurgle Ah.

"Where did you learn to weave the sinews on the spear?" said Burdette.

"My father," said Benetsee. "He learn it from his."

Burdette had some of the cheap wine.

"Christ," he said, "I haven't tasted anything that vile since graduate school. One is very poor in graduate school."

Du Pré drove on slowly.

A few of the cars the reporters had shot past, slewing on the slick frozen mud.

The Toussaint Bar was still open, so Madelaine hadn't made good her threat. They went in and saw Pelon over in a corner dancing while a TV cameraman filmed him.

"*Star Search!*" yelled Pelon when Du Pré and Burdette and Benetsee came in. "They want me that *Star Search!*"

Madelaine was taking money and mixing drinks and pulling beers and tossing bags of chips and pretzels on the bar.

Bart sat at one end of the counter with Booger Tom.

Madelaine looked at Benetsee.

"You got them bugs in that fur, too?" she said.

Benetsee grinned.

"Du Pré!" said Madelaine. "You take that old bastard out there, you spray him down with this." She slid the can of insecticide over the bar.

Du Pré and Benetsee wandered out to the front porch.

Benetsee held his arms out straight from his shoulders.

"Ver' funny," said Du Pré.

pssst pssst pssst psst psssssst.

"Horned Star People think so," said Benetsee.

Du Pré nodded.

psssst pssst psst psst psst.

A few small beetles fell out of the dog fur onto the boards.

"What is this about, old man?" said Du Pré.

"Fools," said Benetsee.

"Horned Star People," said Du Pré, "long time gone. Longer to that dinosaur, that Tyrannosaurus."

"Yah," said Benetsee.

They went inside.

✦ CHAPTER 21 ✦

Y ou sure you want it this way?" said Benny Klein, "I mean, these guys beat the shit out of you, Bart."

"They don't know dick," said Bart. "That fucking Benjamin Medicine Eagle put them up to it, I guess. And he's so dumb I would expect all he did is bitch about the white man messing up a sacred site and off they went and they found me."

"Awful nice of you," said Benny, "the county being so broke and all."

Bart grinned through his swollen face.

"Benetsee came in, took one look at them and said, 'not them Crow,' " said Du Pré. "What Crow we want there, anyway?"

"It works out," said Bart. "Believe me it works out."

Benny opened the door of the cell and the three young Indian thugs filed out sullen and bewildered.

"You got anyone you can call?" said Benny. "I want you the fuck out of my county right now."

"We got our car, Medicine Eagle's," said one.

"Good," said Benny. "You go and get your car, Medicine Eagle's, and get down the road."

Benny dropped a plastic dishpan that held their wallets and belts and loose change and car keys.

"What about that dead guy, the archaeologist?" said Du Pré.

"Our friends here were all in the joint when the good Mr. Palmer found himself dead in the middle of nowhere, riding a stolen snowmobile," said Benny, "and damned if I am not grateful to our Mr. Palmer for being so very dead in another county."

Du Pré snorted. The newspeople were over there in force, long after the body had been found. The T. Rex tooth was still in the old cooler at the Toussaint Bar.

The young thugs went out the front door. The last one slammed it.

"Not them Crow," said Benny, "our good Benetsee. Not them Crow."

"Only thing he ever says to me I understand is wine, tobacco, pour me wine, roll me a smoke," said Du Pré. "I never, me, understand anything else he ever say."

"Is it just me," said Benny, "or is this seven-million-dollar dinosaur skeleton at the bottom of all this?"

"Stands to reason," whispered Bart.

"Benetsee tell me he don't know where it is, them Crow do," said Du Pré.

"Well," said Benny, "do you know which Crows Benetsee is talking of?"

Du Pré shook his head.

The telephone rang and Benny picked it up. He listened for a moment, making faces. He put his hand over the mouthpiece.

"Those two SUVs on your place?" said Benny. "You going to be nice and give them back now?"

Bart laughed and then his face hurt and he stopped.

"Booger Tom hauled them out by the county road," said Bart. "I don't guess they are too bad broken up."

Benny mumbled into the mouthpiece.

"It is illegal to brandish and threaten with weapons trespassers," he said, "and I want you boys to quit that there brandishing."

"I just shoot them tires," said Du Pré.

"I don't want to talk about it," said Benny. "I want to go and get a cheeseburger and a drink and go home and hay my horses."

They left the jail and drove to the Toussaint Bar. Madelaine was behind the bar and Susan Klein was sitting in a wheelchair, grading wool. The table in front of her was piled high with skeins.

Madelaine went off to make cheeseburgers without asking who wanted them. Benny leaned over and he kissed Susan.

"I'm getting pretty good on this thing," said Susan, whipping out from behind the table, wheels weaving through the chairs.

"She gets out next week," said Benny.

"Yeah," said Susan, "all the way to crutches and casts."

"That old man been by here?" said Du Pré to Madelaine.

"Yah," said Madelaine. "Hour maybe, he come in, have some wine, some tobacco, some beef, corn. Not wearing them damn dog skins this time. Stink, terrible, they stink."

Du Pré nodded.

He went to the old cooler in the back and he dug the green backpack out and he brought out the stained sack and he set it on the bartop and he unzipped it and pulled out the chunk of bright yellow and brown and gray rock with the huge tooth gleaming in it. He set it on the bartop.

"Tooth like that I don't want to see the rest of him," said Madelaine.

Du Pré nodded.

Madelaine went back to the kitchen and she got the cheeseburgers piled on plates and she brought them out. She left them on the bar for Du Pré and Bart and Benny to pick up.

Benny took a huge bite of his cheeseburger and he chewed it and he looked at the dinosaur tooth.

"That's evidence," he said, "which come to think on, I did not know where exactly it was."

"I am going to take this, Bozeman," said Du Pré. "Maybe they know where this rock comes from."

Bart was chewing delicately. His face hurt.

Du Pré finished his cheeseburger and he kissed Madelaine and he took the green backpack with the tooth and he went out to his old cruiser and he put the backpack in the trunk. The wind was raw off the Wolf Mountains and there was a thick black band of cloud to the west.

He drove out toward Benetsee's but the old man was gone and Pelon was gone, too.

He drove to his old place, where his daughter Jacqueline and her Raymond lived now, with their twelve children. The youngest ones were racing around the yard getting all muddy and happy.

Du Pré knocked on the door and Jacqueline came and she smiled when she saw her father.

"Papa!" she said. "You have eaten? You are hungry?"

"I have eaten," said Du Pré. "I needed to get something of Catfoot's I think is maybe in the attic, up there, I can't remember."

"Lots of stuff up there," said Jacqueline. "Pretty scary."

A baby began to bawl in the back bedroom. Jacqueline smiled at Du Pré and she went off to tend it.

Du Pré pulled the ladder down from the door in the ceiling of the hallway and he took a flashlight from the kitchen and he went up. The attic was very dusty and hadn't had anyone in it in years. A couple old steamer trunks sat against the rafters and a long rack of clothes that the moths had eaten big holes in. Cardboard boxes. A couple of metal trunks that Catfoot had welded up to carry things in the back of his old monster of a truck, a cobbled-together four-wheel drive that sat on big tractor tires. He had used it prospecting for gold and other minerals. Long since sold for scrap, when Catfoot died the truck died too and no one could get it to run again.

Du Pré opened both of the trunks and he found the leather case he was looking for and he shut the trunks back up and he went back down the ladder and he put it up and slid the panel over the hole.

Jacqueline was standing in the kitchen, a baby on her shoulder.

"You, Madelaine come for dinner soon?" said Jacqueline.

"Yah," said Du Pré.

"Maria she tells me she will come home this summer for sure," said Jacqueline. Du Pré's youngest daughter was out east in school, working very hard. Economics.

Little Métis girl studying that economics, thought Du Pré, we been poor always she should know that.

"You find what you need?" said Jacqueline.

"Yah," said Du Pré.

He kissed his daughter and he went out to the car and he drove off toward Cooper. He stopped in front of the hardware and feed store and he went in and bought a couple six-packs of batteries and he went back out and replaced the batteries in the instrument. He drove out of town to a snowplow turnaround and got out and he went to the back of the cruiser and he picked up the green pack and carried it away from the cruiser.

Du Pré rolled a very thick cigarette and he smoked it slowly and he had some whiskey from the bottle under the seat.

Catfoot, Catfoot, Du Pré thought, my papa, there is not much he did not do if it was outside, then, my papa.

Dig for that gold, the bed of the old Red River.

Run them horses, the cattle, train them good shepherd dogs.

Du Pré looked at the tooth in its matrix of varicolored rock.

He pulled the instrument out of the case and he switched it on and pressed the check button and he watched the needle and then he let it sit and click and he remembered the background reading.

He waved the Geiger counter's probe at the rock.

Pokpokpokpokpokpokpkpkpkpkpk.

He moved the probe closer.

The Geiger counter whirred and popped.

Du Pré went to his truck and he got out a geologist's pick and he chipped off a piece of the bright yellow rock and then smashed it on a flat piece of rock in the muddy part of the turnaround.

He put the probe of the Geiger counter next to the crushed yellow ore and the machine's needle went off the right side, bouncing against the stop.

Du Pré nodded.

He cased the counter back up and he put the rock in the backpack and he drove off to Bart's. Burdette's rig was parked over at the metal building. There was no one in the house.

Du Pré put the backpack and tooth in the bottom of the freezer, under fifty pounds of steaks cut and wrapped.

Du Pré had a whiskey.

He tapped the lump of rock in his shirt pocket.

Bright yellow.

Make good paint.

See what that old professor Morgenstern has to say maybe.

Oh, yes.

❧ CHAPTER 22 ❧

Du Pré's feet felt uncomfortable walking on the thick old pile of the carpets down the long hall to Morgenstern's apartment. He had called from a booth at a gas station on the east side of town.

"I wondered how long it would take you," said Professor Morgenstern, "and I frankly thought longer."

Du Pré lifted up the old brass knocker and he let it drop once and the door swung slowly open. The old man stood there, looking through his thick spectacles, his old eyes washed out and shrewd.

He looked at Du Pré for a long time. Then he motioned with his huge old liver-spotted hand for Du Pré to come in.

"How is my friend Benetsee?" said Morgenstern.

"He is good," said Du Pré, "always the riddles that he talks, though. Crows but not them Crows."

"Long dead Crows," said Morgenstern.

"We got a guy dead up there now," said Du Pré.

"Palmer," said Morgenstern. "Never met him. Read some of his papers. Wouldn't trust the man an inch."

"He come here?" said Du Pré.

Morgenstern shook his head.

"No," the old man said. "Just you and Burdette. Burdette a long time ago now."

"Burdette looking for paint?" said Du Pré.

Morgenstern grinned.

"He's not as clever as you are," said the old man. "He just wanted to say hello and look at my collections of stone implements."

Du Pré nodded.

"What do you know about paint, Mr. Du Pré?" said Professor Morgenstern.

Du Pré shrugged. He took the piece of rock from his shirt pocket.

Morgenstern reached out his shaking old hand and he took the yellow stone and looked at it carefully. He motioned for Du Pré to follow him and he went to the big room with all the map cases and Indian artifacts arranged and carded and numbered.

Morgenstern put the piece of rock against the flat of a little anvil mounted on his worktable and he tapped off a few chips. He put the chips in a mortar, a big white porcelain one, and he ground them with a big pestle with a wooden cap handle.

He dribbled a few drops of baby oil into the mortar and he stirred the powdered rock and oil with a small flat stick.

Morgenstern grunted softly while he worked.

He stuck his finger in the paint and he smeared some on his cheek.

Bright, very bright, yellow.

He took a small sheet of white paper from a drawer and he made a few smears on it. Thick, thin, the ends tapering to scrapes like the fingerpaints of children.

"Great-uncle Arthur," said Morgenstern, "I expect you don't know him. Arthur Waters. Came from some money in the East, father bought into the railroads early on. Arthur had plenty of money. The Waters side of the family is mad. Absolutely barking. Came to Montana in eighteen sixty-six. As a small child, he wanted to be an Indian. Got his sister to pierce his ears so he could wear what he thought were Indian earrings. Ran about the estate on Long Island in a loincloth and moccasins. Made the moccasins. Somehow he made it through Harvard, but, then or now, if you have enough money you can get through Harvard. They are practiced at it there."

Du Pré rolled a smoke and he lit it. The rooms stank of old cigars.

"When Arthur came, of course, the Sioux were killing every white man they could get hold of. The Blackfeet were about gone of smallpox and measles. But the Crow, the fortunate Crow, they were friends to the whites, seeing as they were stuck between the Sioux and the Blackfeet. Uncle Arthur joined the Crows. Took an Indian wife. Ate buffalo. Time to time he'd find a telegraph office and find out how his railroad stocks were doing. The Crows tolerated him. Supposedly savage peoples have always regarded the insane as God's Own."

Du Pré looked for an ash tray. He found one under a pile of newspapers.

"Paint," said Morgenstern, "Arthur became obsessed with the paints of the Crows. Very special some of these paints. A family might know where a deposit of paint pigment was and they would use it in trade. So much for the communal spirit. Greedy as anyone, those Crows."

Du Pré felt tired. He went to a high stool and he sat.

Professor Morgenstern had an audience and he would lecture.

The old man walked to a mirror and he looked at the stripe of yellow paint on his face.

"Good paint," he said. "Durable. Good battle paint."

"Arthur cataloged paint," said Morgenstern. "He collected it and he bribed the owners to tell him exactly where they got it and he put it all in books. These books in this case. There are ten of them."

Professor Morgenstern pulled out the top drawer of the map

case. He lifted out an enormous leather volume, a full two feet by three, and he clutched it to his old chest as he shuffled to the workbench. He opened the big book.

Du Pré went over and he looked.

Smears of red-brown, with notes. What mineral, and where exactly the pigment occurred.

Professor Morgenstern flipped the pages. Reds and browns, a few black streaks at the back.

The next volume held blues and greens. Malachite and azurite, copper compounds.

An entire volume of vegetable dyes now gone with few exceptions to a pinkish-gray, pale smears on the page.

"Yellows were rare and common, too," said Morgenstern. "The variations were very subtle. Lots of samples in this book. See if we can match yours."

Yellow smear after yellow smear. They all looked pretty much the same and further they were dulled by the years.

Du Pré took the Geiger counter out of his bag and he passed it over a page of samples. The machine clicked when he got to the bottom. Faster, faster.

Du Pré nodded to Morgenstern. The old man turned the page.

The counter rattled faster at the bottom of the page.

Du Pré nodded.

Morgenstern turned ten or so pages.

The whirring speeded up.

A few more.

They got to the last page. Same rattling, but nothing approaching the fever of the piece of stone Du Pré had brought.

"Sometimes they mixed several pigments," said Morgenstern.

Du Pré nodded. He sucked his teeth.

Morgenstern looked at Du Pré.

"Very odd," the old man said.

Du Pré waited.

"I don't know how to explain this," said Morgenstern.

Du Pré frowned.

"There's a page missing," said Morgenstern. "The very last one."

He pointed at the spine of the book.

Du Pré squinted.

Someone had cut the last page very neatly away, close into the spine of the book.

"Christ," said Du Pré.

"I am not all that familiar with these," said Morgenstern. "For all I know it could have been stolen about nineteen twenty. I have looked at them carefully, but not that carefully and as you can see . . . wait a minute. There is an index. If I can find it."

The old man went to an old-fashioned rolltop desk and he rummaged through the drawers, taking out a couple ledgers, small ones, and a metal box.

He found a maroon leather book, fat and crinkled with age and wet.

He grunted and turned the pages.

His breath whistled in his nostrils.

Du Pré looked at the sun coming through the streaked windows.

"Two pages," said Morgenstern. "I wonder who could have taken them?"

"Anything about where the paint it comes from in there?" said Du Pré.

"No," said Morgenstern. "This is just a brief summary, bright yellows, mineral."

Du Pré nodded.

"I am going to find that dinosaur," said Du Pré.

"I expect so," said Morgenstern.

"What you do with seven million dollars," said Du Pré.

"Beg pardon?" said Morgenstern.

"Them pages are gone," said Du Pré. "You know where. Maybe I do too."

"That's insulting!" said Morgenstern. He looked as though he was going to cry.

"Uranium," said Du Pré. "My papa Catfoot he look for that uranium. Right after the war, off in that Big Dry country don't got nothing in it. He tell me long time ago, lots of uranium there, shaped like the quarter moon, belly up against them buttes."

"Oh," said Morgenstern.

"Horns of the moon go around each side," said Du Pré.

"I wouldn't know," said Morgenstern.

"Benetsee knows," said Du Pré.

Morgenstern looked out of his dirty window.

"I expect he does," he said.

✤ CHAPTER 23 ✤

Du Pré parked in front of the Museum of the Rockies. He looked around the lot at all the yuppie vehicles, SUVs and Volvos and a BMW or two. His old cruiser was out of place.

A campus security officer in a four-wheel-drive sedan drove past, staring at Du Pré.

Du Pré rolled a cigarette and he lit it and got out and walked slowly up to the main entrance. Two young women walked past him and they glared at his smoke.

Maybe I give them my car, Du Pré thought, got more Montana dirt on it than in this whole place I bet. Probably they know about the Métis, here, pronounce it Met-iss-ay.

He stubbed his smoke out and he went through the big doors and up to the counter and he paid his five dollars' admission. There was a half-scale tepee in the foyer, made of chrome-tanned cowhides with the brands on the flanks. The poles were stacked wrong.

"Where them dinosaurs?" said Du Pré to the young woman behind the counter.

She pointed toward a hallway.

"Unh, good," said Du Pré.

He went down the hall and turned right and walked through a display of fossils, bones, the skull of a three-horned beast, and he stopped at a window looking into a big room. Several people in white lab coats were standing by a lot of rocks up on stout tables, mostly covered with plaster. A couple

134

of young people were scraping at the rocks with dental tools.

The older people were talking and gesturing and sometimes pointing to the plaster-covered rocks.

There was a big card mounted on a stand in front of another window.

"Tyrannosaurus Rex, specimen found in west central Montana," said the card. There were drawings below of the big lizard dying, arcing as it went through rigor mortis, dotted lines of debris piling up on it, and then a rendering of the fossils weathering out of the formation they had rested in for tens of millions of years.

The room was entirely surrounded by windows. Du Pré walked around slowly, past a couple of doors. He stopped and looked back in. He put his arm up on a square glass case. There was a photograph in it. Du Pré glanced at the photo and then he bent over to look more closely.

THIS SPECIMEN WAS STOLEN FROM THE MUSEUM. REWARD FOR RETURN.

Du Pré nodded.

That specimen, it is in Bart's freezer, under a bunch of beef, Du Pré thought.

A tall dark-haired man inside the room looked at Du Pré a moment and then he came to one of the doors and out and he walked over to Du Pré smiling.

"May I help you?" he said.

"Yah," said Du Pré. "Me, I wondered about these T. Rexes, I did not know how big they are, what they look like in the stone."

"OK," said the dark-haired man, shrewdly, smiling a little. "I'm Lou Giannini. Professor. Don't hold it against me. Happy to answer any and all questions."

A woman inside the room tapped on the window and motioned for Giannini to come in. He shook his head and made a chopping motion with his right hand. She shrugged and walked away.

"I just show up," said Du Pré, "so if you are busy I maybe come back another time."

"Not at all," said Giannini. "For one thing, guy like you is the kind of guy shows up here time to time and says I have this great whacking beast weathering out of the butte on my south forty and what is it? Nope, I'd a lot rather talk to you than those folks in there. One thing, they talk all the time anyway. The chattering classes, someone called us. Ouch, but right."

Du Pré nodded.

"It's pret' big, huh?" he said.

"Forty feet," said Giannini, "a full-grown one. Maybe even bigger, how the hell we know how big a T. Rex gets? There are only four complete skeletons in all the world, all we know we got four runts."

Du Pré laughed.

"We just got this one a couple years ago," said Giannini, "after a big fight about who owned it. Guy thought it was on his ranch, but it turned out to be fifty feet onto leased public land, so after all the ruction we ended up with it. Guy had it all sold to a Japanese company, too, they wanted to build a theme park around it."

Du Pré nodded.

"I could take you in there but there isn't much to see," said the professor. "All cased in plaster, so we don't bust it when we move it."

"Somebody already steal a piece of it," said Du Pré, pointing to the empty case with the photo in it.

"No," said Giannini, "that was from another place, another whole skeleton, I imagine. The tooth and part of the jaw were well-preserved and the damage was due only to strata subsiding as the bones fossilized. No, the tooth, there, is one of the enduring mysteries of this place."

Du Pré looked at him.

"This museum was begun on a few dollars in contributions from people in town here, forty years ago," said Giannini. "They had a few things in a couple of Quonset huts on the campus, and for the first ten years or so they hadn't any money or even a permanent staff. The old county families gave stuff as the old generation died off. It was never cataloged as it came in and it was pretty much stuffed in some old chicken sheds. Lots of things badly damaged by rats and water. Terrible. Anyway, when finally there was enough money to do something and they pulled this stuff out in the late Sixties, the T. Rex tooth was in a wooden box along with a lot of other mineral samples but there was no record of who had given it or when."

Du Pré nodded.

"It wasn't especially valuable because it was completely singular," said Gianinni. "We don't know where exactly it came from. The matrix was odd, in that it had a lot of carbon and uranium oxide in it—pretty radioactive—but then there is so much uranium in Montana in small deposits."

Du Pré nodded. Yah, my papa he looks for them small deposits, all he find, too, them small deposits, not big enough to mine.

"We've looked, of course," said Giannini, "but so much has happened in the last thirty million years in Montana that it is all jumbled up."

Du Pré nodded.

"You find these dinosaurs," he said, "what rock are they in."

"Fossil beaches," said Giannini. "If the dinosaur died on

land something would eat it, and if it died in the seas, something would eat it. Had to die on the beach, scavengers didn't go there so much. In Montana, it is yellow-brown sand, and mud. Here, see that chunk of rock there?"

He pointed to a slab of rock sticking up out of plaster. Brown and dark ochre yellow.

Just like the rock on that damn tooth, only it don't got that yellow uranium on it, in it, thought Du Pré.

"How this get stolen?" said Du Pré. He looked at the photo of the tooth that sat in Bart's freezer.

"Whoever did it," said Giannini, "knew about museum procedures. They came for it at shift change when the alarm system was down, and they just lifted the case off—it has a couple screws at the bottom of the glass—and held up the case with one hand and lifted the tooth out with the other. Had to be a strong person, the tooth weighs a hundred pounds with the matrix and the case far more than that. Put it in something, a box or a bag, and walked calmly out. We reamed out the security staff, thinking one of them might have stolen it, but, no dice. All clean."

"You got maybe a book I could buy on this?" said Du Pré.

"Got one I'll give you," said Giannini. "I just published a popular guide to fossil hunting. Not terribly technical, but pretty thorough. Come on, I'll get a copy for you."

He led the way down to his office.

I ask him about them other mineral samples, that box with the tooth, he will get suspicious, Du Pré thought, maybe they don't mean anything anyway.

Giannini took a slender paperback off a shelf absolutely stacked with them and he handed it to Du Pré.

"I thank you," said Du Pré.

"Where are you from, if I might ask?" said Giannini, putting his hand on his chin.

"South of the Wolf Mountains," said Du Pré. "Little place called Toussaint."

Giannini nodded.

"Never been there but I know where it is," he said. "Funny country. You know, the other stuff in the box with the tooth was odd, it came from all over, and it was all rocks that the Indians ground and used for paint. Had stuff in there from Idaho and Alberta and Wyoming and Yellowstone Park and even some from eastern Oregon. Couldn't figure that either, unless the yellow uranium was what they were after and the tooth didn't interest them at all."

Du Pré shrugged.

That old fucker Morgenstern is maybe knowing a lot more than I am hearing, him, Du Pré thought.

"If you find anything," said Giannini, "We'd appreciate knowing about it. If it is a T. Rex, we can find a donor to buy it from you if it is on your land."

Du Pré nodded.

He went out to his old cruiser. The security detail was parked and staring at the old battered cop car.

Du Pré drove out of the lot.

The security detail didn't move.

✦ CHAPTER 24 ✦

Never had one before," said the sheriff. He was sitting at his cluttered desk sipping stale burnt coffee. The office smelled of wet wool and tobacco and disinfectant and burnt coffee. "They say that if'n you don't solve a murder in forty-eight hours you ain't gonna. We've had three in the county the last ten years, all wives havin' had it with their husbands beatin' them up when they's drunk. Never had a murdered guy just a-layin' out there."

Du Pré nodded. There was an oil electric heater in the corner of the office. The rest of the county building was boarded up and closed off. Another county dead and gone.

"None of my business," said Du Pré, "you know, we just wondered."

"Make it your business," said the sheriff. "God knows we can't make anything of it. Some fancy professor shot and dead a couple of weeks or so out in the Wind Buttes, there. I lived here all my life and I only flew over 'em. That's some desperate country there. Not even the cattle will go into it. Won't even go there to get cover from a storm. I don't know anyone ever went out there."

"He wasn't there, though," said Du Pré.

"Where we done found him, he must have come in from the other side," said the sheriff. "It's twenty miles maybe across that, not bad goin' if there was snow on the ground. Out of the wind pretty much, the buttes you know, they are all slap-jawed round there."

"OK," said Du Pré. "The state cops they maybe look?"

"Glanced at it," said the sheriff. "They pret' much don't take on cases ain't nothing in it for 'em. I talked to the guy's wife. They's divorced. Told her he was dead up here. Know what she said?"

Du Pré rolled a cigarette, nodding.

"She said that was good, made her day. She hated the son of a bitch." The sheriff rolled himself a smoke, too. "Said that was just fine with her and if I didn't mind say it again, she liked to hear it."

Du Pré laughed.

"She like hearing that he is dead, eh?" he said.

"That she did. Now, we shipped his dead ass out and the ME in Helena looked him over. Had two twenty-two slugs in his chest, went in didn't come out. Bled enough to get weak and he died out there in the snow. Slugs were hollow-points and they hit bone, wasn't enough left to make out the gun they come from if we ever even find it."

Du Pré nodded.

"I maybe look, the stuff he had with him?" Du Pré stubbed his smoke out on an ashtray mounded with butts.

The sheriff went over to a file cabinet and he fished out a plastic bag. Wallet, change, a pocket comb, pens, a small note-book. Little plastic case for emergency matches.

"Clothes he had on is with his dead ass in Helena," said the sheriff. "We don't got a cooler for 'em any more."

Du Pré walked over to some large-scale contour maps pinned to the wall. He stared at the Wind Buttes. Over a thousand square miles of nothing. No water there. Soil taken by the wind.

A good two-lane highway on the west side, though, and a crossroads bar with motel. Grocery store. The bar would be the local post office, employment agency, walk-in mental health clinic, fire station, just about everything for fifty miles in any direction.

"That's where the car he rented was," said the sheriff. "Rented an SUV in Spokane. Rented a room at the motel, only customer they had. Ate two meals there, it was snowing like hell, went outside when some car or other pulled up. Nobody went to look. Next morning it's still snowing and he's solid gone. Now, nobody was asking for the health and whereabouts of Professor Palmer. He was on sabbatical—them professors get a year off with pay every twice in a while, them tax-supported bastards, wish I got a couple years off with pay—and like I said his ex-wife damn near shouted hooray. I called her finally."

"What is this?" said Du Pré, pointing at a cluster of squares on the map.

"Old ranch," said the sheriff. "You know the story, it's nineteen ten and them Norskys come to homestead and they try to ranch where they got no water or grass or nothing. Them people starved out in the Twenties, Svensons or something like that. Then about nineteen thirty maybe they just walked away. Left everything. Left a couple old Model T's in the barn, I got one of them I was a kid, it started after a little work, put on new tires and drove the sumbitch away. Good startin' old car. Left the clothes in the closets and pans on the stove. Just snapped and gone. But they did know how to build them cabins and barns. Never rotted down, got them funny corner joints them Norskys made, you know what I'm talking of?"

"Yah," said Du Pré. The corner joints were cut so every surface angled down.

"Them buildings is still standing," said the sheriff. "Folks go out there to camp sometimes, I guess, the spring there has bitter water but if you take in your drinking water you can use the spring to wash up and such. Drink it it'll give you the shits right now."

"You don't mind I maybe look around out there some?" said Du Pré.

"Be my guest, don't get lost," said the sheriff. "We got no money in this county for searches. You come from the country. I have to go and fish you out of there you're gonna get a bill for the full amount it costs."

Du Pré nodded.

"That country's so poor you couldn't raise hell on it," said the sheriff. "I suppose them flatlanders will want to call it a wilderness, have another place to get lost in. I was talkin' to some sheriffs over to the western part of the state. They's all tired of fishing them little bastards out of trouble. Tell you that."

Du Pré nodded.

"One thing though," said the sheriff. "Maybe you can find out who the hell the Walker is out there."

Du Pré was cleaning his fingernails with his penknife.

"Walker," said Du Pré.

"Folks fly over it now and again," said the Sheriff, "sometimes they see tracks, sometimes they see a man walking through that country. Not often, and when they go back for another look, he ain't there. I seen him myself. Don't run or nothin', but time you turn the plane around and go back he ain't there."

Du Pré nodded.

"Spooky," said the Sheriff. "My mama used to sing an old ballad, 'The Walker in the Snow,' you ever hear it?"

143

Du Pré nodded. The Haunted Hunter, the Walker in the Snow. Old trapper's nightmare, freezing to death before he can get back to camp, his ghost forever walking through the cold toward the fire, warmth, life. Never makes it.

Du Pré thought about the half dozen times he had come close enough to dying of hypothermia. Too cold. Only thing in the country, only really dangerous animal was a cold wind.

Lots of voyageur songs about the Beast, the cold wind sucks your blood and makes you crazy, sink to you knees, die there.

"When you see this Walker?" said Du Pré.

"Any time," said the sheriff. "He don't got a horse. On foot. Just him. Ain't a prospector, though maybe. Crazy. Maybe he's a ghost."

"Yah," said Du Pré. "We got them ghosts, sure."

Du Pré took the wallet out of the plastic bag and he looked through it. No money. Driver's license, credit cards, slips of paper with phone numbers on them, receipt for a rental car, a Jeep Cherokee, Spokane.

Picture ID, University of California at Irvine.

Pale bearded man, big-framed glasses. Aviator glasses.

Big pale vain bearded man.

Last time I see him his face it is burgundy, deep purple. Lucky guy the coyotes don't come yet, eat his face, the rest of him.

Nothing in that country, a coyote can eat even. That is why he is not so chewed.

"So what you do with this?" said Du Pré. He waved the bag of stuff Palmer had had in his pockets.

"Stays in the file," said the sheriff. "Unsolved homicide. I got better things to do than run down whoever killed some fucking flatlander. I done checked at the roadhouse, he didn't make

144

any calls and didn't get any calls. Not a one. Used his cell phone I hear, call his school twice, the state boys were going to look into it. What was he a professor of anyway?"

"Archaeology," said Du Pré.

"Yeah," said the sheriff, "now I remember."

"Nobody saw the car that came to the motel?" said Du Pré.

The sheriff shook his head.

"It was snowing, one of them hard spring snows. I checked with the guys that ran the plows and they didn't see anyone out on the road but a couple grocery trucks come through every week and one or two other cars. Lots of snow, the cars was covered and nothing more than some headlights in the snow and they was gone."

Du Pré looked at the map.

"Where you see the Walker?" said Du Pré.

The sheriff walked over to the map. He sucked on a toothpick and he stared at the ink contours.

"Trail's through here," he said, pointing. "Old Indian trail. What the hell they'd want with that country I don't know either."

The sheriff pointed, touched the map with a forefinger. He ran his finger up through the cuts between the buttes.

"Goes like that," he said. "No damn water ain't poison on it though."

Du Pré nodded.

"You going back there?" said the sheriff.

Du Pré shrugged.

"If you do," said the sheriff, "you keep to the higher ground. Flash floods. Sounds crazy, but it can rain over here like hell and be sunny over here. And then you got a wall of water thirty feet high coming down this wash here."

The sheriff pointed.

"All at once," he said, "it can just come on you."

Du Pré nodded.

"Yah," he said, "I seen some of them before."

✤ CHAPTER 25 ✤

I guess we're like everybody else," said Benny Klein. He was sipping a drink. The remains of his slab of prime rib lay congealing in grease on the platter. The single daffodil in a small vase on the table was drooped and brown at the edges.

Du Pré nodded.

"Nobody give a shit this Palmer is killed," he said. "Sheriff there tell me that the guy's ex-wife laughed when she heard the news. You know, when somebody educated got a job like that gets killed there is usually a big fuss."

Poor people get killed not so much fuss.

"You know," said Benny, "mean as it sounds I am just as glad it's out of my jurisdiction."

"That Burdette say Palmer is a real bastard," said Du Pré. "I still maybe like to know what this real bastard is doing dead with a stolen snowmobile and a dinosaur tooth stolen from that Museum of the Rockies. I like to know what them Japanese maybe have to say about this."

Benny nodded.

"It ain't right, for sure," he said.

Maybe that Palmer he needed killing, Du Pré thought, me, I have met some people needed killing in my life, there. They are dead now, yes.

Susan Klein came over to the table, moving damn fast on her crutches. She set them against the pony wall that screened the hall to the bathrooms and she pulled a chair out and she sat.

Du Pré would have gotten up and pulled it out for her but it only made her mad to be coddled.

"That dinosaur tooth was stolen from the museum?" said Benny.

Du Pré nodded.

"I expect we ought to let them know we have it," said Benny, after sucking his teeth a minute.

"They got lots them dinosaur teeth," said Du Pré. "This one got too many friends around here get mean about it. I want to find out who is doing this, why."

"Suit yourself," said Benny.

"Du Pré," said Susan Klein, "always suits himself."

Madelaine came over from behind the bar and she picked up the platter and the empty glasses. She went off toward the kitchen.

"Them Japanese are after a T. Rex fossil," said Du Pré. "They don't got any other reason, be at Le Doux Springs. Trout ponds, my ass, they build those down near the mountains, maybe even the park there, have a golf course, lodge, maybe skiing off season. No damn reason for them to be at Le Doux Springs."

Benny nodded.

"Well," he said, "maybe you should go and chase them down and just see what they got to say."

"They are maybe waving around seven million dollars, that will get someone killed, you bet," said Du Pré.

"Lotta money," said Benny Klein.

"I go over there tomorrow," said Du Pré.

"Well," said Benny, "take somebody. I don't want you gettin' the shit beat out of you like poor Bart."

The door opened and Pelon came in, and he stood for a while in the dark, eyes blinking behind his thick glasses. Then he shuffled over to the bar and he sat up on a stool. Madelaine came out of the kitchen and she saw him and she smiled and crowed.

"Ah, Pelon!" she said. "You don't got them dogskins, all them bugs! You are looking much better now, yes!"

Pelon laughed. Du Pré looked at him a moment and then he walked over.

Pelon's skin was burned, windburned and roughened. His hands had many splits on the skin and dirt worked into the creases deep. He had scrubbed himself but he couldn't get all of it out.

Benetsee's apprentice, Du Pré thought, they got something to do with this, too, my old friend, my new one here.

"Eh, Pelon," said Du Pré, "you are well, I maybe buy you a drink. I maybe want to talk, Benetsee."

"Gone," said Pelon. "He been gone, time now."

Du Pré nodded. The old man drifted in and out, north, south, east, west, traveled on foot.

Maybe he change to a raven, fly some.

He change to a coyote, run some.

Me, I don't believe medicine people do that. Don't want to.

"Maybe I come and sweat," said Du Pré.

I do that before, some time, Benetsee he talk in the sweat lodge out of Pelon's mouth.

What is this?

"You come here for me," said Du Pré. It was not a question.

Pelon nodded. He drank the wine that Madelaine had brought. He looked down at the floor.

Du Pré rolled him a cigarette and one for himself. He lit them both and handed Pelon's to him.

"Me," said Pelon, "I don't understand his riddles any better than you do, Du Pré. I am not doing well and he shows up, in a city, brings me here, more than a thousand miles. We walk and walk but we don't walk all that much. We got on a train, freight train. It stops for us, middle of nowhere, we got on. Train it is carrying cars. Benetsee he opens the hood, one of the cars, keys are taped to the battery. We get in, ride in the car, smoking, looking out at the sagebrush, the little towns. Don't stop much. Train it stops again, middle of nowhere. There is a coyote sitting looking at us. It is night. Next morning we see them Wolf Mountains. We walk some, we come to his place. I don't eat, all that time, feel fine. We sweat. I hear things. Hear my people, people who are gone, they talk to me. People gone so long that I am not born before they are gone they talk to me, too."

Du Pré nodded.

"We sweat maybe," said Pelon.

Madelaine brought two gallon jugs of wine in a cardboard box, and there were packages of cooked meat and crackers and cans of sardines in the box, too.

"This, Benetsee," said Madelaine. "You, too."

Pelon nodded.

"I go sweat, him," said Du Pré.

"Uh," said Madelaine, "good, yes, Du Pré you do that." She drummed her fingernails on the bartop. "That old man piss me off," she said.

Pelon laughed.

"I am his friend and he don't talk to me," said Madelaine. "Don't talk to no one."

Pelon shrugged.

They finished their smokes and Du Pré carried the box out to the cruiser and he put it in the trunk and got in and so did Pelon.

"I got one thing, do, before," said Du Pré.

Pelon nodded.

Du Pré drove out to Bart's and pulled up by the metal building where Burdette was working on the Horned Star People's bones. Burdette's SUV was there. There were lights on in the building.

Du Pré fished the Geiger counter out of the trunk of the cruiser and he went in. The door was unlocked. The building was cold and there was a sharp chemical smell.

Burdette was hunched over a work table in the back, a bank of very bright fluorescent lights hung low over it. He glanced at Du Pré and he waved some small metal instrument at him.

Du Pré made his way past boxes and bins of parts to Burdette.

The jackstrawed bones of the Horned Star People were set on the table in five sections. Burdette was digging at the yellow earth that the people had been buried in. Yellow and then the red ochre, bright, almost vermilion.

Burdette glanced at the Geiger counter.

He nodded.

"It's uranium ore," said Burdette. "I sent a sample out east and the printout from the lab is over there somewhere."

The vertebra of the T. Rex was sitting in the center of the table, upright like a plug. White and red and yellow and tan minerals gleamed through the soft yellow ore.

"Pretty pure," said Burdette. "Damn near yellowcake already. Refined ore."

"I am going to sweat, Pelon," said Du Pré. "Then I maybe go talk to them Japanese."

Burdette put down the pick and he wiped his hands on a white cloth. Yellow smears came off his hands.

"The rest of the beast is west of here someplace," said Burdette. "That tooth is part of it and so is this chunk of spinal column."

"Tooth was stolen, Museum of the Rockies," said Du Pré.

"Pretty dumb," said Burdette, "that's a very famous tooth,

there. Lots of photos and analysis done on it. I can't imagine what the hell Palmer was doing with it."

"Waving it under the noses, them Japanese," said Du Pré.

Burdette nodded.

"Seven mil is a lot of money," he said.

"Yah," said Du Pré, "he don't steal it though."

Burdette looked at Du Pré.

"Me," said Du Pré, "I got friends I don't want to know too much about. You got friends like that, Burdette?"

"Many," Burdette said.

"Bart he is my friend," said Du Pré.

"Mine, too," said Burdette.

"I sweat, Pelon," said Du Pré.

Burdette nodded.

"Then we talk some, eh?" said Du Pré.

Burdette nodded, and he bent back to the bones.

✦ CHAPTER 26 ✦

Du Pré wallowed up the muddy path to Benetsee's.
I keep meaning bring Bart's backhoe, fix this road, then
it gets dry again and I forget, only been meaning to do this,
five, ten years.

Du Pré cranked the wheel and the old cruiser lurched off
into some fairly tall grass, brown from the winter. Du Pré shut
off the engine and he looked over at Pelon, who was looking
straight ahead.

Pelon got out slowly and he looked for a long time at the old
cabin with the antlers and long porch where wood was stacked
in the winter.

The front door was open a little.

"Somebody been here," said Pelon.

Du Pré got out and he pulled his 9mm from under the seat.

"Don't need that," said Pelon, "they are gone now. They
were looking for something."

Du Pré walked toward the porch, his eyes flicking over the
ground.

Boots. One pair got a star in the sole, hiking boots.

Two men. Maybe one of them is six feet, not heavy, the
other shorter and heavier. Walk like city people, feet out like
damn ducks.

Du Pré put the gun barrel against the door and he pushed
it open.

Papers strewn everywhere.

153

Magazines. Torn-apart magazines.

Ashes from the stove out on the bricks underneath it.

Cupboards open. Bottom ones have doors anyway. I made them long time ago for Benetsee.

Pelon looked along the shelves on the back wall.

"Hooboy," he said, "they steal that medicine bag, they be sorry."

Du Pré looked at Pelon.

"Coyote stuff," said Pelon.

Benetsee he talks, them coyote all the time. God's Dogs. Know all of God's jokes, them coyotes. I bet they are sorry.

"Took that ivory thing, too," said Pelon. "Horned Star People thing they navigated with."

Du Pré nodded.

"Took all them paints, too," said Pelon. He pointed to a rack that had held the tips of buffalo horns made into little bottles, stoppers of soft willow.

Du Pré gathered up the pages torn from the magazines and he stuffed them in the stove and lit them with his cigarette lighter. The fire caught and roared quickly. Good draft.

They wandered out back. The ragged old sweat lodge stood open and cold, a sleeping bag that served as the door flung up on top of the mound of canvas and old quilts and plastic.

Du Pré walked to the creek and he looked into the deep long slender pool that they jumped into after a sweat.

Something black and a foot long down there.

Not a stick. Funny shape for a rock.

Du Pré sighed. He took off his clothes and he dove down into the icy water and he grabbed the black thing. Stone. He gasped when his head came out of the water and then he scrambled up on the bank and he danced in the pain of the cold. His feet and hands stung like needles were stuck in him.

"Brbbbbblllllllbbbbb," said Du Pré. He looked at the thing in his hand. Close-grained black stone all carved. Long canoe, high ends, the carver had drawn lines and filled them with vermilion. Paddlers and a man wearing bird wings with a beaked head in the prow. Very worn, very old. Very very old.

Horned Star People carving, Du Pré thought, where is that Benetsee?

He leave it down there for me, the old bastard, so I get this nice cold bath. I bitch at him he say my Madelaine like me better I don't stink so much. Hah. Old bastard.

Pelon was splitting wood into thin pieces, two and three feet long.

Du Pré shrugged into his clothes and he went to the growing pile of split wood and he took armfuls over to the pit where the stones were heated. He made a crisscross stack and began to put the rocks for the firepit up high on the ricked wood, so they would be where the flames were hottest and heat rapidly.

I pick these stones for Benetsee long time, Du Pré thought, he knows he wants damn stones from Yellowstone Park and some from where the glacier push down from Canada, there, north bank of the Missouri. Some from out east, they weather out of pale clay. Got to have just the right stones, heat up but never break.

Pelon came with the last armload of wood split very fine and he put the thin pieces in the pile, threading them through.

He took a can of lighter fluid from his shirt pocket and he squirted a lot down low and then Du Pré lit a match and tossed it in.

In ten minutes the fire was roaring hot, white flames licking at the stones. In ten more minutes the ricks of wood began to slowly sink, laying the stones down gently on thick beds of glowing red-yellow coals.

Pelon went over by the creek and he sang for a few minutes, the high prayers, smoke and eagles, long time gone.

The stones were white with ash and heat.

Du Pré took the metal-handled shovel and a rake and he loaded the broad scoop with the hot rocks and he carried them to the pit in the sweat lodge and piled them carefully on the finer gravels in the bottom of the pit.

Pelon was naked, he had smeared some charcoal on his face. He went into the lodge and Du Pré put the flap down. He stripped and crawled in to the hot wet dark. The stones glowed dull red in the pit.

Pelon was singing, high constant ululations. He would sing and pray. Du Pré didn't know many of the words, they were not Cree and not Sioux.

That Pelon he belongs to a tribe I don't know.

I can hear the prayers though.

Louder than I pray to the Virgin, them saints.

Pelon cast more water on the stones and the heat leaped out in the steam. Du Pré's lungs were full of moisture and he coughed up gobs of phlegm. Cure your smoking, this.

Pelon sang.

Heat.

Wet.

Dark, only the faint red glow of the stones piled in one corner of the little sweat lodge.

Du Pré relaxed. His muscles lost their tension and he slumped down and leaned back on his elbows.

The Walker in the Snow.

Them Horned Star People, Red Ochre People, long time gone.

They got clear up to here. Find that dinosaur skeleton.

I bet they make paint from the uranium.

Paint from the ochre.

Long time gone.

Du Pré felt sleepy. The lodge was very hot and he had eaten well recently and had some whiskey. He could taste the whiskey on his breath.

Pelon ululated for a long time.

He began to pray again.

Cree words this time. Grandfathers, grandmothers, help us now.

Du Pré listened.

Pelon stopped. He cast more water on the stones.

Sssssssssssssssssssssssssssssssssss.

Du Pré had his eyes shut.

He saw a dark red plain with green lakes and mountains of white ice on each side. Dark red rivers ran between the lakes. Mists rose. It rained, dark red rain.

Mammoths screamed by the water, trunks upraised.

The water steamed mist. The land was green with thick high grass and trees stippled the plains. Huge flowers.

Du Pré rose up above the land, like a hawk rising. The lakes went far off over the horizon.

Waterfalls thundered off the mountains of ice.

Rain. Cold, cleansmelling rain.

Du Pré saw the huge canoe down below. Thirty paddlers and one man wearing the wings of a bird and a beaked mask standing in the front.

Du Pré dropped like a hawk stooping.

He was on the shore. The canoe was passing.

The bird-man in the prow held something out from his neck, between his thumb and forefinger, looking down his arm toward the sun low and red above the mountains of ice.

Ha hoo ha hoo ha hoo hahoo.

The paddlers changed, digging their paddles in on the beat.

Du Pré followed the canoe, like a seagull does a ship.

The canoe came to the end of the ice. There was a circular valley full of worn buttes, a big one. The lakes filled the land between them.

The paddlers headed for a smallish flat-topped butte, red and yellow and brown in the strange misty light.

The pulled round it and then headed for shore.

There were people painted red dancing on the shore.

Du Pré floated on to the land and he walked through the red-painted dancers.

Something white gleamed in the rock. A tooth, a huge skull half out of the stone, giant bones with ends protruding.

The bird-man walked to the bones and he fell down and screamed.

Mammoths screamed.

The mists rose.

The dead were piled in front of the dinosaur, bound up with ropes and coated with bright red ochre.

Du Pré began to cough and choke.

He struggled through the doorway and he stood up and staggered to the creek and he fell in.

The cold didn't bother him.

He sank in the water.

When he rose up and shook the water from his eyes he saw a coyote standing on the bank a few feet from him.

Du Pré looked at the coyote.

The coyote turned and trotted off through the alders.

✦ CHAPTER 27 ✦

"What you thinkin', there, Du Pré?" said Madelaine. She looked down the bar at one of the Oleson brothers who had started on his twice-yearly drunk. He could be counted upon to end in jail spring and fall. Madelaine had already taken his truck keys away from him.

"You don't got another key, there, you?" she said to the old man. "I am not letting you get drunk, my bar, you got keys. No drunk driving."

Oleson had sucked his false teeth for a moment and pulled out his wallet and fished another ignition key out of it.

"I don't trust that old fool," said Madelaine to Du Pré. "You maybe go out there, take off that distributor cap, huh?"

Du Pré nodded.

"He start playing that damn hardänger fiddle I go fix his truck," said Du Pré. "I go to Bart's drink, too."

Du Pré was not an admirer of Norwegian music, especially when the player was a deaf old arthritic drunk who played once a year and never practiced.

"He clear the place out sure enough," said Madelaine.

"Nother!" said Oleson. He was drinking shots and beers.

Du Pré sighed and he went out the back door and around to Oleson's truck and he opened the hood and he pulled the wires off the distributor and reset them. No way it would run now.

He went back around and in and made like he had been back in the kitchen helping Madelaine.

There was no one else in the bar.

"Nother!" said Oleson. He had taken out his false teeth and set them beside his shot glass. Madelaine took him another drink and she picked up the false teeth with a thick paper napkin and she went back and put them up on a shelf.

"He got the camper on the truck?" said Madelaine.

Du Pré nodded. Good thing, otherwise Madelaine would take the old man home so he didn't get wet and catch cold.

Did that two years ago, he puke all over the bathroom, shit all over everything, pass out facedown in the bathtub.

"So what you thinking?" said Madelaine.

Du Pré shrugged.

"Du Pré," said Madelaine, "you are up to something I know. Don't you shoot nobody, please."

"I think maybe I take that Bart we go look them Le Doux Springs," said Du Pré.

Madelaine nodded.

"You maybe go out into them buttes, too?" she said.

"Yah," said Du Pré.

"You think you maybe want to find that dinosaur?" said Madelaine.

Du Pré shrugged.

"Guy's dead, that dinosaur," he said.

"Tooth is stolen from that museum, Bozeman?" said Madelaine.

Du Pré nodded.

"You are worried, Du Pré," she said. "Me, I bet you think that Burdette kill that guy. Maybe you think Bart knows something, too."

Du Pré laughed.

I don't get to tell her nothin', he thought, she tell me before I know what it is that I am thinking.

"Bart would not do that," said Madelaine.

Du Pré nodded.

Maybe Bart would not do that. Me, I do a bunch of things I once think I never do. Maybe we all do that, get older.

"Talk to Bart," said Madelaine. "He is your friend, you know, maybe he help you, this."

Du Pré nodded.

"You don't trust Bart," said Madelaine. "You really hurt him he get drunk maybe."

"Yah," said Du Pré.

"Du Pré," said Madelaine, "you like this story, them Horned Star People come up Red River in their boats, through the mist, the lakes long gone where there is desert now, long time gone, long time gone. You got to find out that story. Maybe you don't got to tell all of it but you got to find it out, yes?"

Du Pré laughed.

"You don't got to do nothing," said Madelaine. "You are not a deputy when you hand that badge back. You give it to me now, I hand it back."

She opened her hand palm up. Du Pré laughed. He took the badge off his belt and gave it to her.

"Go find that Bart," she said.

The door banged open and Bart came in. His face was mottled yellow and purple and green, but the swelling was way down and he was smiling.

"You," said Madelaine, "him, you and him go find that dinosaur."

"When I find things," said Bart, "my face looks like this." He pointed at the damage the young Indian thugs had done.

"So find that Benjamin Medicine Eagle, make him look like that," said Madelaine.

161

"It's a thought," said Bart.

"Go talk, them Japanese," said Madelaine. "They call for you here this morning."

"Huh?" said Du Pré.

"Just go to Le Doux Springs talk to them," said Madelaine. "They say they really need you, dig them ponds."

Du Pré nodded.

Bart looked at him.

"Oh, really?" said Bart.

"Nother!" said old man Oleson. Madelaine poured him a tall stiff one and waved his money away. She filled his beer glass.

"Du Pré look like this he is seeing them dreams," said Madelaine. "You go, sweat, you got good dreams, means you do something, you know. It is not that television, you know."

Du Pré nodded.

"Dreams," said Bart.

"Yah," said Du Pré.

"OK," said Bart. "Le Doux Springs it is."

"There is something here that I do not understand," said Du Pré.

"Yeah?" said Bart.

Du Pré shook his head.

"We maybe go see that Burdette first," said Du Pré.

Bart nodded.

"OK," he said.

"Du Pré," said Madelaine, "you wait, you know everything first, eh?"

Du Pré nodded.

Du Pré and Bart went out to Du Pré's old cruiser and they got in and Du Pré wheeled it around and he headed out of town and then up the bench road to Bart's ranch. Thick black rain clouds were stacked against the Wolf Mountains.

Du Pré shot up the wide gravel road that led to Bart's house and outbuildings. Burdette's SUV was parked near the metal building and lights shone out the windows.

The door was locked. Bart thumped on it a couple of times. They waited.

Footsteps inside.

The door swung open quickly.

"Afternoon," said Burdette. He was holding something in his right hand behind his leg.

Du Pré looked at him.

Burdette tucked the automatic in his waistband. Big one.

"Scholarship can be hazardous," said Burdette. "I am about to drive to the nearest FedEx box to send samples off."

He turned and walked back toward the workbench with the ochred bones and the dinosaur vertebra. When he got to it he crossed himself before bending over something on the table right in front of him.

Bart followed Burdette and Du Pré shut the door and came after.

"What news, gentlemen?" said Burdette.

"I think maybe you shoot that Palmer," said Du Pré.

Burdette shook his head.

"Not me," he said.

"OK," said Du Pré, "you steal that damn dinosaur tooth, them pages from Morgenstern's books, got the paints in them."

Burdette kept staring at the small piece of bone in front of him.

"Burdette," said Bart, "I won't stomach murder."

Burdette nodded.

"I did not shoot the good Dr. Palmer," said Burdette. "I did swipe the tooth and the pages, yes, but . . . look, there's a lot to this you don't know and I can't tell you."

"Like that seven million dollars them Japanese pay for the T. Rex?" said Du Pré.

Burdette straightened up and he turned to Du Pré.

"Not me," said Burdette. "Palmer wanted the damn money. It's why he's dead."

Du Pré waited. Bart coughed.

"I wish," said Burdette, "that I could tell you. But I cannot. I can only tell you that the answers are . . . you can find them. But be very, very careful in the looking, gentlemen."

"Don't be arch," said Bart.

"I gave my word," said Burdette, "and I keep my word, Bart."

Du Pré nodded.

"Benetsee he been by here?" said Du Pré.

Burdette nodded.

"Yes," he said, "some time ago. He wanted to pray over these bones."

Du Pré nodded.

"How old are they?" he said.

"Seventeen thousand years," said Burdette. "Caucasian, like the burials in Arctic Russia, on Ellesmere Island, on Bear Island, but we've never found anything to equal these."

"Who did Benetsee pray to?" said Bart.

"I don't know," said Burdette. "It was in a language I have never heard. Not Siouan, Athapascan, Cree, Uto-Aztec. Songs. Benetsee sang songs. The hair stood up on my neck."

"But you did not kill him?" said Du Pré.

Burdette shook his head.

✤ CHAPTER 28 ✤

Du Pré looked at Le Doux Springs. They had dug in now and the gravels had fallen away and they were cones of shimmering water stuck down in the gravelly moraine. A new creek burbled out of the lower one and then cut across the grass to the old creekbed.

More water now than before, Du Pré thought, that earthquake block something underground.

Three Japanese in expensive English waxed cotton coats and overpants and sou'westers were standing near Bart. They were listening intently.

"You aren't going to get the T. Rex anyway," said Bart. "We don't know where it is, exactly, but that's all government land out there where it has to be."

"Trout ponds?" said one of the Japanese.

"Oh, bullshit your damn trout ponds," said Bart. "And if you thought I could be paid off to excavate a hot T. Rex for you you've been eating rotten sushi."

"We had that offer," said one of the Japanese.

"Palmer?" said Bart.

"We don't know who from," said the other. "We don't know anything about Palmer, we don't know who killed him, we would tell the police if we did."

"Right," said Bart, "now you tried to buy that other one the guy thought was on his owned land, down there by Hardin, and it wasn't. It is not going to happen, gentlemen. And if you've been spreading money around and that is getting people killed well then shame on you."

"No money," said one of the Japanese.

"My offer for this place stands," said Bart.

The three Japanese walked away ten steps and then began to chatter rapidly.

Du Pré knelt down and he looked down in the clear cold water. Out in the center it was twenty feet to the bottom now. The surface roiled a little. Millions of gallons of melted snow rising up.

Du Pré looked out across the High Plains to the West. He stared and he stared.

"What do you see?" said Bart.

"Uh," said Du Pré, "them Horned Star People they camp here, come by boat, so maybe the water is this high, I am trying to figure how it goes west. Lakes in the sky. Rivers in the sky. Sweat lodge, I see them big skin boats, come up here, Hudson's Bay. The Red River."

"Missouri's only about ten thousand years old, right?" said Bart.

Du Pré nodded. The north bank of the Missouri was as far south as the tall ice came, pushing up berms of rock and gravel and earth in front. Ice a mile, two miles high. The Wolf Mountains had rivers of ice running out of them.

Water everywhere. Grass. Huge animals all gone now, mammoths, them big ground sloths twenty-five feet long, buffalo with horns eight feet tip to tip, horns like longhorned cattle.

"I have the exact elevation," said Bart, "from the survey."

Du Pré nodded.

The Japanese came back.

"OK," they said, "it's yours."

Bart looked at them for a moment.

He pulled out his cell phone and he dialed and he spoke for a few minutes, turned away from them and Du Pré.

"Gabriel," said Bart, "I think I'd best go with these gents to Billings and get this title transferred. Foote will be here in six hours with the paperwork and the check."

Du Pré nodded.

Rivers of ice.

Giant mammoths and mastodons.

Damn noisy place, ice booming and breaking, hairy elephants all bellowing.

Bart went to Du Pré's cruiser and he took out a small bag and he went off with the Japanese.

Du Pré waited until they had dropped out of sight off the moraine, where the road curled back and forth, and then he went around the springs to the great tear in the earth that the quake had ripped.

Rain and wind were softening the sharp edges.

Du Pré walked along until he came to an old streambed stuck in the gravels. It had been covered over time out of mind by soil and sand blowing in the wind. Du Pré stood up on a boulder and he looked at the layered soil on each side of the old streambed.

Little black line there. Old fires. A bone.

Du Pré tugged. A goose's thighbone came out of the wall of the cut.

Brown worn thing there. Dark brown, soft surface.

Old buffalo bone.

Du Pré stared and stared and he saw a pale green rock, just barely visible.

Du Pré took off his folding belt tool and he opened a long screwdriver and pried gently.

Pale green flint, chert, whatever. A scraper.

Long time people camp by these springs.

Long time gone.

Waters reach out west there.

The land was pale and windcut, wide bands of chalky-white clay compressed to rock, buttes weathered away. Land used to be all the way up to the top, them buttes, Du Pré thought. Water don't take all that, I bet wind take most of it.

He went to his cruiser and he opened the trunk and took out some maps all rolled up like wallpaper. He sat in the front seat staring at the maps for a long time.

Caw.

A big raven flew past low, headed west.

Storm come, he will be in a nice thick spruce, Du Pré thought.

A wet black band sat on the western horizon.

Du Pré rolled the maps up and he put them in the backseat and he reached under and got a bottle of whiskey and he cracked the label and unscrewed the cap and he drank. He rolled a smoke. He looked off at the rain clouds.

Damn wet tonight.

He started the cruiser and he drove slowly down to the north-south highway and he turned right and drove up to the roadhouse five miles away. He got out and went in and had a big steak and potato and salad and a few drinks. He bought some candy bars and some jerky, the smoked pressed kind that tasted terrible but his good jerky was home hanging dry in the meat safe and he didn't want to drive all the way back there.

He went west on the country roads, winding among the buttes, and he came down to the little town about nine in the evening.

The sheriff's car was out in front of the boarded-up county courthouse. Du Pré got out and he went in, chewing some minted gum.

There was no one in the office. Du Pré waited awhile and then the front door of the courthouse opened and the sheriff came in carrying a six-pack of beer and a Styrofoam box.

"Have a beer?" said the sheriff. "The hamburger and fries is mine."

Du Pré shook his head.

"I maybe go look around," he said, "I maybe rent a horse, saddle from someone."

The sheriff nodded.

"Gonna get wet out there," he said.

"I got a slicker," said Du Pré.

"Well," said the sheriff, "I got a horse or two and a saddle, I expect you could use. And my place is the last one before the badlands there. Don't have to pay me."

Du Pré nodded.

"Still after that dead professor and his murderer?" said the sheriff. "I don't give a shit personally my own self."

"Yah," said Du Pré.

"This is about something I don't know nothing about," said the sheriff, "and frankly I don't care to. It's early of a Friday night and the domestic violence should commence in about an hour. I got enough of that. Some asshole from California wants to come here get shot what has that got to do with me?"

Du Pré laughed.

He opened one of the beers.

"County's dyin'," said the sheriff. "I lived here all my life and I hate to see it. Ranchers going under, this never was that much for stock and it's nothing at all for crops. Still, folks hung on here four, five generations, till them damn environmentalists showed up."

Du Pré sipped his beer.

"Ain't had outside jobs in the county since the uranium mines right after the war."

Du Pré nodded.

"Everybody was going to get rich," said the sheriff, "but then they found a lot more uranium in one place up in Canada and they didn't need to pecker around here, these little deposits."

Du Pré rolled himself a smoke.

"But there's one thing I would sort of like to know," said the sheriff.

Du Pré sucked smoke into his lungs.

"I maybe find him out, you," said Du Pré.

"Neighbor was up flying over there," said the sheriff, "the Walker was out there, going along a ridge, but then he ducked down and he was gone just like that. Always just like that."

Du Pré nodded.

"I'll call my wife," said the sheriff, "tell her you're coming for the horse and saddle. That way she won't shoot you."

Du Pré nodded.

❖ CHAPTER 29 ❖

The sheriff's wife leaned on the stall boards and she spat brown on the straw. She was heavy-boned and tall and tough. She wore old faded blue overalls and rubber irrigation boots. She laughed very easily.

Du Pré smoothed the saddle blanket and he tossed the rig over and reached under and got the cinches and ran them through the buckles. The horse took a deep breath and held it. Du Pré walked a little forward and he grabbed the horse's nose and blew hard in his nostrils and the horse sneezed and his belly shrank and Du Pré tightened the cinches in a hurry.

The horse looked at Du Pré with bored eyes and he switched his tail one slow time.

"Ol' Dan there is a smartass," said the sheriff's wife, "but he's a good old horse, right gentleman."

Du Pré nodded.

"Yah," he said, "he is a nice horse, there. Got a good sense of humor."

It was raining like hell outside the barn and the metal roof rattled with the big drops.

"There's folks out there you know," said the sheriff's wife, "ever' once in a while I see some tracks or somebody'll be flyin' over and they will see some feller lopin' along but they always duck down right away. Gyppo miners maybe. There's agates out there, them mossy kind, and some jasper got pretty colors. God knows what else. A few wild horses and burros.

Not much. You know out there is where that damn fool Hornaday from the Smithsonian found them last fourteen wild buffalo and shot 'em all and spent the rest of his sorry life wonderin' why he'd done it."

Du Pré looked over at her.

"Last of the big herds," said the sheriff's wife. "Used to be millions and then the hunters come and starved in the Indians. Killed everything."

"You see any of them people?" said Du Pré. "I do not know exactly what I am looking for but that guy was dead, there you know, I wonder who killed him?"

"Somebody wants to shoot a goddamned Californian ain't got nothin' to do with me," said the sheriff's wife.

Du Pré nodded.

"It's murder, though," he said.

"Justifiable homicide," said the sheriff's wife. "Oughta be a bounty on the sons of bitches."

"That map," said Du Pré, "I go down this long draw out back and then left and past that old homestead, eh?"

"Sure do," said the sheriff's wife. "That old homestead was my grandparents' dream you know. They're buried there and so's my folks. They hung on. Seven of us kids and I'm the only one left in Montana. Tried to raise wheat and couldn't most years. Finally about half made it with cattle but then it got so expensive to fence things off they couldn't make it with them either. Or sheep. Last year when my pa had it he sort of give up and died, docs said it was cancer but I just think his heart was broke. He loved that country. It's harsh as a cold hell but it grows on you you know."

Du Pré set the headstall on the horse and he opened the gate and led the animal out. He set his own saddlebags behind the slicker roll and he tied them with the worn old latigos.

"Folks leaving here every month now just walkin' away,"

said the sheriff's wife. She took a tin of snuff from her pocket and opened it and she took out a big pinch and put it in her cheek. "County's dyin'. Some little bastards from out East came through left flyers sayin' this was gonna be part of some damn thing called the Buffalo Commons and us ranchers was bad people, bad for the en-vir-on-ment. Got some foundation would pay us about four cents on the dollar for what little land we got and what little water we got. Otherwise the flyers said we'd just be drove off. They was smart enough not to deliver 'em in person, some folks here would flat shoot them. Some families been here four, five generations you know. They got their people buried in little old ranch graveyards. They never have made a dime but they are mighty good at hangin' on."

"Yah," said Du Pré.

West it is changing but it always has changed. Ask my people. We come south every fall hunt buffalo, make winter meat, make pemmican. Kill all our buffalo, too. Kill us we fight them. We fight them English twice, lose both times.

Le Doux Springs. Damn Bart buy it, good, me, I hate it being some silly place for fat Japanese come, fly fish from a dock. Concrete pond. Shit.

"So I go left that butte behind your old place?" said Du Pré.

The sheriff's wife nodded.

"Right side has a shelf across the trail, maybe fifteen feet high, can't get a horse up it. Wild horses can make it but then they're small. Just a little patch of path sidestepped in the rock."

"You never see them miners up close?" said Du Pré.

"Nope," said the sheriff's wife. "They keep to themselves. I expect they come in off the highway over yonder. There's an abandoned mine in about five miles, silica sand it was, mined it during the war. Even had a rail spur but it's all torn up now. Anyway, the road was well-made and had culverts where there ever was any water runnin', so it has hung together. Once in a while the next county puts a road grader on it to fill the ruts, every other year or so. Hunters use it. They go back in there and camp, there's a big spring by the mine got good water. Lots of them springs out there are poison."

Du Pré nodded. You want to drink from a spring, you make damn sure there are plants and insects in it. If it hasn't got things living in it this is not a good sign.

Me, I am a kid, I drink from a sulphate spring I shit for a week, I don't do nothing else.

Catfoot he laugh and laugh at me, say, my son, maybe you listen your old papa once a while now. Ha.

Damn right I did after that.

"Long time ago there was a fossil expedition, I hear," said the sheriff's wife, "about eighteen ninety maybe. They went out there and then they didn't come back. Found the horses dead here and there but they never did find the four men. Not a trace. So their bones are still out there."

Du Pré nodded.

Country eat you up, swallow, you are gone. Lots of people up in the Wolf Mountains, lying on the bed of the Missouri, crawled off to die in the dry country and the coyotes eat them.

"Fossil hunters was from Yale," said the sheriff's wife. "They had a bunch of gold with them and they offered to pay for any fossils folks could find for them. So the gold is out there, too. My pa hunted for it all his life, looking for some rotting leather bag with money in it. That's about right come to think on it."

The rain was bashing down harder now.

"This'll let up, fifteen minutes," said the sheriff's wife. "Funny country rain like hell but it never lasts long."

Du Pré rolled a smoke.

"Keep that away from the straw," said the sheriff's wife. "Let's go outside we got a little roof over the door."

174

Du Pré nodded. He felt foolish. You didn't smoke in someone's barn or if you had any brains, your own.

They went out a sagging door and stood under a porch roof. There was no porch. Just plastic buckets and piles of junk.

The rain sluiced off the roof, cloaks of clean gossamer bending the light from the ranch house into sheets of flame.

"My husband keeps babbling about that damned Walker in the Snow," said the sheriff's wife. "I think he sees him when he's had too much of that damn shine the neighbors make. Piss-yellow stuff got oils on the top of it you pour it in a glass. I ain't never had the courage to try it myself."

"He say what him look like," said Du Pré.

"Moves fast," said the sheriff's wife, "ragged dirty dark old clothes and a cloth bound round his head and old moccasins got broken soles. I seen them tracks once in a while. Must have wet feet all the damn time. But them damn tracks are spooky, they just start someplace and then they end someplace. Lots of people have seen them goin' across new snow, just start and stop, like that guy stepped out of the air and then back up into it, you know, places like this all got their ghosts. There's a tale about a big Indian bust out of the res and got hunted down in there, shot in the spine and he crawled a couple miles 'fore they run him down and they finished him. Sometimes it sounds like him howling, the wind out there, sometimes there's marks in the ground like someone's been draggin' themselves along by the elbows, crawling on their bellies."

Du Pré nodded. Ghosts, sure enough. I got some ghosts fifteen thousand years old, white ghosts, red ochre on them, come sailing up Red River from that Hudson's Bay. Long time gone.

The skull that had sat in the Plexiglas case came to Du Pré's mind. Old eyepits stained red, shadowed, thinking something.

Long time gone.

"Rain's letting up," said the sheriff's wife, "You got a reason to go off in the night be careful don't fall down them gullies."

Du Pré listened to the rain. It did not sound like it was letting up at all.

"Five minutes it'll piss away to nothin'," said the sheriff's wife.

Du Pré finished his cigarette and the rain pissed away to nothing.

The sheriff's wife slid the door open and Du Pré led the horse out and he checked the cinches again and then he swung up.

"Good huntin' at night there," said the sheriff's wife. "I'll get the gate for you."

She walked ahead of him and she put her shoulder to the post and she opened the gate.

Du Pré rode slowly down the white trail. The clouds overhead were breaking up and there was enough starlight to see the brush and the land all pale and dead-looking.

Nice Montana woman, Du Pré thought, wonder why she was trying to get me killed?

✤ CHAPTER 30 ✤

Du Pré ran the horse at a canter up the trail that hugged the side of the butte. It went up straight from the dry pasture behind the old abandoned homestead to a wide ledge of rock that held the butte like a plinth. In some places the yellow stone fetched out fifty feet from the darker rock that sat on top of it. It was as level as a pool table and when the Rockies lifted the plains at their feet for some reason this formation hadn't tilted at all.

Du Pré rode for a few miles and then he saw a spot where the trail narrowed and he stopped and he got down and led the horse forward. There was a cleft in the rock thick with twisted little aromatic cedars and a wet place on the butte's wall where a spring seeped once in a while.

Du Pré wrapped the reins around a dead juniper and he went to the dark cleft and he looked down in the wash below. It was wide and white in the starlight with shadows where boulders sat or mother rock not yet broken away from the earth stuck up.

Du Pré looked out to the west. There was another black line of wet cloud there. Lightning flashed inside the dark billows, sudden yellow glows that died slowly in the eye.

Du Pré waited.

A mule deer ran flat out down the wash and then shot up the side of the low hills across the gully. The deer stopped and turned and looked right at Du Pré.

Wind at my back he smell me, Du Pré thought.

He looked at the hands glowing on his watch, the big expensive one that Bart had given him.

"Guy owns one of these things guy ought to own a yacht," said Du Pré to Bart when he'd first looked at the watch.

"Consider it done," said Bart. "I'll have one in your back pasture there in a week or two. How long you want it."

Du Pré shook his head and looked at the sky.

"I take the fucking watch, Bart," he had said, "I find some damn yacht in my pasture I saw it up, stuff it up your ass. Yes."

Bart grinned.

Two-thirty.

A sheet of lightning shot across the distant black clouds. Fire in black velvet.

Du Pré fished a bottle of whiskey out of his damp saddlebags and he had some and he rolled a smoke and lit it and he went to a flattish rock by the lip of the plinth of yellow stone and sat down.

A coyote flitted down the trail and then up the side of the hills beyond. The coyote sniffed the wind, nose held up, and then it bolted for cover.

Du Pré felt the vibration in his ass. The stone was shaking a little because the earth was shaking a little.

Three hours, rain to flood, Du Pré thought, good thing to know.

He looked to his right, up the long wide draw.

A wall appeared, twenty feet high, the color of the land. It was moving and moving very fast. It smashed into a horn of stone in the center of the gully and water shot up a hundred feet.

The flood wave rumbled. Du Pré glimpsed boulders time to time tumbling along.

The flood roared past. A few pieces of wood danced on the white foamy lip of the flood.

It filled the gully twenty feet deep and it slapped against the walls of the mother rock, and a couple slabs shuddered and slipped off.

The deer was still standing across the gully looking down now at the flood.

The water level fell rapidly, ten feet, five, three, one, and then the bottom of the gully began to poke through.

A desert bobcat soaked and disgusted limped along behind the flood. It found something and pounced.

Just hang to the left there in that gully keep going, Du Pré thought, there is no damn place get a horse up there anyway.

A small band of wild horses came down the gully, carefully picking their way, and then they found the trail the deer had bounded up and they scrambled and then neighed and pranced at the top.

Du Pré swung up on the horse and he rode on for three or four miles and then he looked to the west and saw the clouds moving in and slashed cuts in the black, lightning shimmering behind the rain.

He unrolled his slicker and he put it on. He wished he'd brought a cover for his hat. He jammed his hands in his pockets and found it and he stretched the clear plastic over his battered filthy Stetson.

He found a ledge that hung over a little and he stood in it holding the horse's reins. The ledge broke the force of the rain but rivulets writhed down snaking from the soaked rock above. The horse stood patiently even when the water cascaded down his face.

Du Pré rolled a cigarette and he smoked it under his hat.

The rain tapped to a halt and then a brisk wind started and Du Pré could feel it dry and cool. Moisture wicked off his slicker and in ten minutes it was dry and so was the horse. He rolled the slicker up and put it back in its ties.

The saddle was still damp where the oiled leather had taken on a little water.

Du Pré swung up and he rode on. The ledge narrowed and split and a gangplank of rock led down to the badlands between the buttes. All scoured by wind and sand. The rock was soft and carved into smooth eerie shapes above the lines where the more abrasive floods had cut into the formations. Some rocks were standing on tiny bases, balanced by the carving of wind and water. A black seam of coal appeared, five feet thick and stretching off into the dark.

This was all swamp once, Du Pré thought, trees everywhere, dinosaurs and big sharks behind me, hundred feet long with teeth the size of ax blades.

Things were tough out back then.

He glanced at his watch.

Two hours, little less.

Du Pré cantered on through the maze. Once he came on his tracks and he cursed and then he laughed.

Some greenhorn thing that.

Find my own tracks.

Don't think I tell anybody that.

Shit.

He went on, sighting up at the Dipper and the polestar and he faded to the right when he had no choice. Another huge butte loomed to the west. He got to it and he led the horse up on the ledge and he watched for half an hour and then the water sluiced across the floor of the maze, not very deep, a foot or two, and then he could hear it gathering and then roaring down through the gully.

Keep to the left that nice woman said.

Guy on the snowmobile he die of bullets, them.

Wonder how many she drown these good directions.

I like stories. I find out this story, too.

Professor Morgenstern he is missing two pages, them books.

Benetsee he is walking here, he is that Walker in the Snow.

Nobody else just light to earth, rise again, that old man. Old bastard he is playing his damn games with me again.

This world, other world, flits back and forth like a damn bat.

Speaks to me through Pelon's mouth.

Red River.

Du Pré thought of the big skin boats floating up the water that had stood here, miles of ice in the sky north and south. But them glaciers had not touched this. They came some places and not others.

Don't touch the Sweet Grass Hills.

Geology.

Catfoot he study damn geology want to find that gold. Uranium. So we can blow the whole world up.

Made better war paint, war was personal. You smell who you kill.

The water was gone and the little pools left were shrinking fast. Du Pré picked his way up the damp gravels and on toward the west. The huge butte reared up. There were cedars around it on a formation of stone that hadn't crumbled and water cascaded down in little veil falls from the top, breaking into mist in the wind.

Something snorted.

Bighorn sheep. Funny damn place for them.

Du Pré wandered on. The sky cleared and the stars shimmered in the black, lighting the pale dead country.

Lots of life here but it is hidden.

Badlands. Secret places.

The winds moaned in the torturous channels they had carved.

Music of the dead.

Du Pré fished the whiskey out of the saddlebag and he drank as he rode. He put it back and rolled a smoke and lit it and he felt warm and he unbuttoned his shirt at the collar. The breeze cooled the hot spot where his neck met his chest.

Rocks cascaded down from the side of the butte, great hollow thwocks. Spattering rattles dying to nothing.

The country was rising and the windcarved rocks were getting shorter.

Tongue of water reaching here.

Red River.

Long time gone.

About up here maybe.

Answers.

✤ CHAPTER 31 ✤

Dawn.

Rising light pale on the washed layered stone. Coyotes howled and yipped a hunting chorus and then they fell silent, running after prey. The wind rose coming down from the higher plains to the west. It smelled of rain and cedars.

Du Pré shivered. He unrolled the slicker and put it on to cut the cold wind. He shook the long tails down on either side of the horse and he snapped the loops around the high tops of his boots. He put his 9mm in the holster hanging from the saddlehorn.

One dead I know about. Maybe more. Why they end up dead? That damn Burdette he set Palmer up, for sure, somehow. Why?

The west was clear. The last clouds had scudded over fast, pushed by the high winds that screamed a little far off like the dead's lost voices. High overhead.

The wind began to moan in the soft sand-rubbed rocks. One note was deep as a woodwind with a tree for a reed.

A mad land, Du Pré thought, crazy land. Beautiful but it don't have much life on it.

He shivered.

The horse chuffled and danced. Du Pré clucked and the gelding went forward up the trail winding between the soft molded rocks, once mud at the mouth of a river flowing down from mountains worn away to nothing at all. Out past the sandbar, mud settling in the sea.

Du Pré looked up the watercourse and he thought of ice a mile high to the west with waterfalls cascading down and the water brown with dust.

The horse stopped. The trail had forked and Du Pré got down and he looked at the ground. Wild horses. Deer. Coyotes.

Du Pré swung up and he headed to the right, where the trail came close to the hulk of the butte. A long butte shaped like a narrow thin gourd.

The light glowed deathly pale but was gaining strength.

Some of the strata above Du Pré were pale, some dark. Fractures ran down angled to the tough competent yellow rock that the butte sat on. Scrubby cedars taken root in the fissures reached for the sun.

Du Pré came round a spur of green slaty stone and he stopped. An old mine head, timbers splayed and leaning, went into the rock a few feet up from the bottom of the gully.

Du Pré got down and he fished his big square camp light out of the saddlebags and he stepped up over the spoil and some timbers flat on the ground and he shone the light into the mine. A jumble of rock and wood blocked the shaft thirty feet back. The ceiling had collapsed.

Du Pré flicked the light back and forth, holding it near the ground.

Footprints in the dust. A man, small, he had sat on a wedge of rock for quite a while. Moved his feet back and forth.

Not very damn long ago either.

A black beetle struggled along the floor of the mine, up and over the dust ridges, across one of the footprints.

Du Pré walked in slowly, shining the light at his feet.

Beetle tracks across the footprints.

Not many. Not many at all. These prints are maybe one, maybe two days old.

Thin trickle of water ran off to the side. Du Pré could hear it gurgle.

Chittering. Bats on the ceiling, dozens of them.

Back already. Must be spring.

Get hot here in the day, down in the badlands, they catch the sun. Maybe it has them insects flying even sometimes in the winter.

Du Pré backed slowly out of the mine and he straightened up and he shut off his light and he turned round and looked over across the lumpy mudstone formations.

A mule deer, a big buck, stared back at him.

Du Pré nodded.

Plenty people know I am here.

He dug some jerky and candy bars out of his saddlebags and he ate them and washed the salty meat down with some water from his canteen.

The sun was touching the top of the butte high overhead and the light spilled down the striped rock face.

Du Pré looked east. Pink under a few high clouds, little puffs like cotton balls drifting away.

Du Pré rolled himself a smoke and he sipped a little whiskey for the chill.

A raven flapped down the coulee, wings barely moving, it disappeared behind a blob of rock worn nearly through at the base.

Du Pré went on. The horse was tired and moved slowly though steadily with the gravels giving way a little each time he put a hoof down. Then he stepped up a shelf and the ground was firm. The gelding picked up his pace.

The weird windcarved rocks passed by.

Du Pré looked across a meadow to a copse of willows hard against the rocks of the butte. Tall grass stood on either side of a tiny creek that wound out on the floor of the valley and then sank into some fissure in the rock.

Du Pré rode the gelding toward the hidden spring.

He got down and he stood listening for a moment.

Water chuckling.

Wind rubbing on the rock overhead.

Du Pré saw a path through the willows, a short one, the stand was barely twenty feet across. He bent over and went in.

The water came out clear, bubbling out of a grainy yellow-brown sandstone, a layer of rock that angled up as it went east.

Du Pré nodded. The entire butte must feed this spring. Water sinking slowly down and gathering in the porous yellow-brown rock and then rising up when it hit the impervious dark green stone below.

Du Pré looked above the spring and he jumped back.

A buffalo skull sat on a ledge. The skull was painted with stars and hooked crosses and stripes. Red ochre paint and bright yellow paint.

Uranium paint.

Du Pré went back out to the horse and he checked his 9mm. Round in the chamber. He put down the hammer. The gun had no safety. It was a combat pistol. He fished a couple more magazines out of his saddlebags.

He went to the little creek and he stepped over it and he went around the copse of willows on the far side.

A hitching post made of red cedars stood in the rocks. On a ledge above a wickiup, very old, and pictographs cut into the rock.

Du Pré scrambled up to the ledge and he went to the wickiup. Streaks of carbon from the century-old campfires still stained the overhanging rock. Figures of men and buffalo, geometric designs, suns or stars were incised in the soft stone.

Du Pré looked inside the wickiup. A firepit. Fresh ashes. Maybe a couple weeks old, maybe less.

A small pile of stones sat on another ledge to the left of the cedar trunks leaned against the rock face to form the wickiup.

Du Pré knelt. He lifted up scrapers, spear points, the tiny arrowheads for the buffalo arrows, letting the shaft into the chest. The shaft killed. Some of the scrapers and spear points were very old. Some of the arrowheads were very new. Made very recently, the knapping bright.

Du Pré slid down from the ledge and he walked out past the horse so he could see up the valley. There was some grass in bunches here and there and the spring gave good water all year, probably. He walked to the creek and he reached down and lifted up a handful of pebbles. Dark cherts mixed with softer rocks.

Du Pré smashed one of the chert pebbles with a rock on another and he looked at the fine-grained colloidal quartz.

Very good material for making stone tools.

The mine must have been for jasper.

He walked up beside the butte rising nearly straight up.

Dark nodules of chert stuck in sandstone, and at the base of the rock a litter of flakes and broken spear points. They hadn't washed away because the rock reared up and made a little basin. But there was enough water running through to wash soils away, so there the remains of the factory sat.

Men sat here with pads of leather on their palms flaking off tiny pieces of chert to leave a sharp edge stippled like a string of tiny clamshells. The edge would hold a long time. Harder than steel. Du Pré had dressed out deer with an obsidian blade bound to an elk rib. The serrated edge cut skin and flesh smoother than a sharp knife.

The paint on the buffalo is fresh. Some of these flakes are fresh.

Getting very close, Du Pré thought.

Horned Star People they paddle through here maybe, there would be a beach up there. Rise and fall maybe, the ice don't melt all at once the same way.

Du Pré walked back to the spring. He lifted himself up to the ledge where the painted buffalo skull sat and he looked hard at the dark rock.

There.

The Horned Star symbol, very faint. Wind and dust had worn it back to just a trace in the rock. Same symbol was on the ivory star sighters the Horned Star People wore.

Long time gone.

Nobody come here but maybe prospectors one time. Nothing but maybe some jasper, that is sold by the pound, you don't get rich on it.

Cows don't come up that draw, they don't like them rocks.

Wild horses would.

Du Pré went to his saddlebags and he fished out the whiskey and he had a stiff snort and he rolled a smoke and lit it.

Ver' close now.

A pebble landed at Du Pré's feet.

He looked back toward the spring.

A man stood in the willows. He was dressed all in stained buckskins, red leggins wrapped around his calves and over the tops of his moccasins. A red cloth wound around his head.

Face painted bright yellow with black stripes like a tiger's.

Sunglasses.

Gloves.

A very modern assault rifle.

The man moved forward. He waved his rifle at Du Pré's middle.

Du Pré lifted his 9mm out of his waistband with thumb and forefinger and he dropped it on the ground.

❧ CHAPTER 32 ❧

Du Pré walked up the trail. The painted man followed, leading Du Pré's horse. He carried the rifle lightly. There was no place for Du Pré to run to. Cowboy boots aren't much good for speed anyway.

Another painted man appeared on a ledge of rock, standing motionless. Assault rifle across his chest.

Du Pré looked for a moment and then he looked back down at the trail, so he wouldn't trip on the rocks.

The trail forked. Du Pré glanced back and the painted man made one economical gesture. To the right.

Du Pré took the fork. It went through a little gully and then up on hardpan. A few sagebrushes spackled the yellow-white earth, a few strands of grasses lay yellow on the baldness.

Tough country.

The sun was getting warm on Du Pré's back. He shrugged out of the slicker and he rolled it up and walked back to the horse and he tied it on. The painted man just looked at him.

The raven flew past again, wings pumping against the wind from the west. The bird cawed once and was gone.

A jackrabbit jumped out from under a sagebrush and it sped off, long hind legs pumping.

Du Pré rounded a slab of rock and another painted man stood there. Stone Age clothes, sunglasses, assault rifle. A flat black automatic pistol in a beaded holster on his belt. Elkhorn handled knife.

Du Pré stopped. The painted man pulled a kerchief from his pocket and he blindfolded Du Pré and then led him to the horse and helped him up.

Du Pré heard more horses. Hooves clattering on rocks as the mounts danced when the painted men swung up.

They moved off at a brisk pace.

Du Pré didn't try to see. He left the kerchief alone. It smelled of cedar and woodsmoke.

They rode for hours and Du Pré lost all sense of where he was. The sun would warm his back and then his front. It was rising and soon it was overhead and no help for directions.

Du Pré reached back and got the whiskey from his saddle-bags and he drank some and one of the painted men laughed.

They never spoke.

Finally they stopped. Du Pré felt a tap on his leg and he slid down, a little stiff from the ride and off-balance from the blindfold. He stumbled and the painted man caught him by the arm in a strong grip and held him till he could stand.

The man kept hold of his arm and he guided him along a path. Du Pré smelled damp stone and water, moss and the bitter scent of willows.

The painted man tugged at his arm and Du Pré sat down. A chair. The painted man fiddled with the blindfold and it fell away. Du Pré blinked.

He was in a huge cave that bellied out behind a narrow entrance.

A fire smoked. The blue tendrils lifted up, headed for a tiny slot of sky high overhead.

Du Pré rubbed his eyes. He took out his tobacco and rolled a cigarette and offered it to the painted man who stood behind him. The painted man took it. Du Pré rolled another for the other man and then one for himself. He lit his and passed his lighter back. A moment, and then a gloved hand appeared in front of his eyes with the silver Zippo. Du Pré put it in his pocket.

The cave was dark but not pitch. Du Pré's eyes were dilating and he could begin to see the walls. They were covered with paintings of buffalo and horses and men.

Modern paintings. Only had horses this country maybe 1700. Du Pré saw stripes of the yellow paint on a far wall. Something gleamed white, a short band of opalescent stones buried in the rock. A huge yellow-white rock stuck out straight, the end rounded like the joint of a leg bone.

Shit, thought Du Pré, it is that damn dinosaur, there in the rock.

A narrow black pool of water sat in front of the rock face. It was black and glassy on the surface.

"I look at that?" said Du Pré to the painted men. They nodded.

He got up and walked to the white stones stretched five feet along the rock.

Teeth. The damn dinosaur's teeth.

Leg bone. Some ribs sticking out there.

He was looking at the dinosaur down from the top. He looked over at a dark cleft and he started. The great skull sat there staring out of time tens of millions of years deep. Du Pré lit his lighter and the yellow flame cast the giant skull into planes and penetrations. The eyeholes were black as a moonless night.

Du Pré stared.

He heard some movements behind him.

The painted men were opening cans of food and putting the food in a big skillet that sat on the coals of the fire.

Corned beef hash. Beans.

Du Pré was starving. His mouth watered.

One of the painted men handed Du Pré an enameled metal

plate heaped with food. A heavy silver spoon with a blue plastic handle. Coffee steamed in a blackened blue pot set on a steel trestle over the coals.

Du Pré ate and ate. There was more in the skillet. He stuffed himself.

The painted man nearest to him handed over his saddlebags. Du Pré dug out the whiskey and he poured a good shot in his coffee. The metal cup burned his lips. He offered the bottle to the painted men and they shook their heads.

He dug out his camp light and showed it to the painted men. They nodded and gestured to the cave.

Look at anything you like.

Du Pré walked to the rock face that held the giant dinosaur. Thirty feet long, more, probably, forty.

Big son of a bitch.

Du Pré shone the light down in the black pool.

He gasped.

Reddened skulls all piled under the clear water. A jumble of bones beneath them. The water was cold and clear. The bones had a thin film of whitish lime on them the deeper they lay.

Du Pré shone the light on the rock face.

A big Horned Star was cut deep into the rock.

Jesus, Du Pré thought, I cross myself for this sure you bet. He mumbled prayers. Catholic. Cree. Even Sioux.

Them Horned Star People they make it all the damn way here from the Arctic Ocean, bury their dead, bring their dead here. Damn, something, that. Look at this.

The cave smelled of sweet grass long burned. Du Pré shone the light on the floor. Usually a lot of shit and rotting animals.

Du Pré walked back to the painted men.

"I got to take a leak," he said.

One got up and padded out of the cleft in the rock and Du Pré followed. The painted man led him a hundred yards away from the cave mouth and he pointed at a spot. There was a kettle cut in the rock and a pile of shit and leaves in it. Du Pré pissed a long time. Some dung beetles wallowed out of the pile when his stream hit.

He walked back toward the cave. The horses were all gone. The painted man swept away their tracks with a broom.

Du Pré heard a light plane's engines snarling far off. The painted man looked toward the sound and the west. The plane glinted silver, a small flash in the sun, and then it was gone.

Du Pré smelled the heavy sweet grass smoke. A big bundle smoldered on the campfire.

That sweetgrass it don't seed well, but you can cut the roots and carry them wrapped in wet moss and plant them. All them old Métis camps got sweetgrass thick around them, lots of other places. How you tell there was a camp there got used a lot.

Thousands of years some of them, places where the game always came.

Du Pré breathed in the sweet smoke.

He took his light and went back to the dinosaur sticking out of the rock wall. A chunk was missing, the vertebra that Burdette had found in the Horned Star People bones from Le Doux Springs. A tooth, the one that had been stolen from the museum.

Du Pré shone the beam on the rock below where the tooth had been.

AS 1888.

Morgenstern's ancestor maybe, Du Pré thought, the crazy man did all the books on Crow paint.

Yellow lines of uranium ore filled all the spread fissures in the mother rock, the yellow and brown fossil beach.

Coal around here somewhere.

Du Pré walked over under the cleft in the céiling of the

rock, a good fifty feet overhead. He shone his light up. Thick soot from tens of thousands of campfires coated the ceiling.

They come by here.

Du Pré shone his light on the back wall.

GD and a cross 1886.

Gabriel Dumont? The little general, that Louis Riel?

Du Pré laughed. Us Métis we are always there. Give maps to them Lewis and Clark, they never find the Columbia, don't got out maps.

Du Pré laughed again.

Red River.

✦ CHAPTER 33 ✦

It rained again that night. Du Pré stood outside watching the water build and gather on the great flat plain that lay between the buttes marching west. When it got to the choked gullies and coulees it roared and foamed and took off as a sudden wall.

The two painted men never spoke and one of them always had an eye on Du Pré, but they did not threaten him or seem terribly concerned that he might run or grab a gun. The assault rifles never were far away from the painted men, but never brandished.

Dinner was buffalo meat, fat back ribs roasted on the coals. Du Pré had had this a few times in his life when he visited cousins in Canada. They poached buffalo from a great northern herd cut off by the tundra and undiscovered until the 1950s.

Buffalo and fry bread with cherry sauce and canned apricots for dessert. Then one of the painted men offered Du Pré some vitamin pills.

But they would not speak.

They were waiting for someone. Du Pré was waiting for someone.

That old bastard Benetsee he come I chew his ass some good, Du Pré thought, play his damn medicine games with me. Old bastard.

The painted men had built the fire up. The Tyrannosaurus

teeth gleamed in the veined rock of the far back wall. The black pool lay beneath, full of red ochred bones.

One of the painted men clanked past carrying a white plastic trash bag. He went past Du Pré and he turned west and he was gone for twenty minutes and when he came back he was empty-handed.

Dump it down an old mine shaft.

How long they been here, watching? Du Pré wondered.

Crows. These are Crow people, Absarokas. Fight them Sioux with us Métis.

Du Pré rolled himself a smoke and he lit it and he looked up at the clouds passing over, bellied here and there like breasts. But no lightning in these and the rain had all been on the front edge of the storm.

Damn lake must have tongued up this far. Shit, it must be eighty miles from Le Doux Springs.

I got to fly over this one day.

"I am waiting here for who?" Du Pré said to the painted man. "That Benetsee? Someone else. I am not back there will be people come, look for me."

The painted man shrugged.

So there are some other people down the damn mine shaft with the rest of the garbage, Du Pré thought. Oh, yes. They been keeping this place a century? Nobody gets drunk or pissed off, blows the cover?

He went back inside. The painted men were sitting by the fire. They had pads of leather on their palms and the hard tines of deer antlers in their right hands and they were flaking chips from the edges of spear points. Very rapidly.

Du Pré had some more whiskey and he lit another smoke.

He looked at the fire and then he felt his neck hairs rise. Someone was looking at him from behind. He turned.

A man stood in the doorway. He was wearing old black

clothes and his face had no paint on it. Long white braids hung down on his chest. He carried a long wooden staff and he wore very expensive high brown leather boots with thick white rubber soles.

The old man stood there a moment.

"Du Pré!" he said. "You come, we talk." He walked outside. Du Pré got up and he followed.

"You got some friends," said the old man. "We maybe kill you you don't got those friends, they speak well of you."

Du Pré offered the old man tobacco. The old man nodded. Du Pré rolled him a cigarette.

"Used to be a lot of places like this," the old man said. "This is the last one, Du Pré, the last place the whites they don't know. We come here take care of it, make paint, pray sometimes. Tough country, eh? There are a few buffalo left in here, Du Pré, ones the whites never killed. Not very many."

"You know my friend Benetsee?" said Du Pré.

"Oh, yes," said the old man, "know him a long time."

"He come here?" said Du Pré.

The old man turned and looked at Du Pré his deep black eyes in his wrinkled brown face.

"What you think he does?" said the old man.

"He comes here," said Du Pré, "he tell me to talk to the Crows."

"Hah?" said the old man. "Don't do that much good Crows don't talk to you damn Cree."

"The professor, the archaeologist, that Palmer, you kill him?" said Du Pré.

"He came here, steal," said the old man.

"What he stole was stolen from the museum, Bozeman," said Du Pré. "So you shoot him?"

"He was coming here," said the old man.

"Maybe," said Du Pré, "but he is twenty miles from here, dead, with this snowmobile that is stolen, Red Lodge. And this tooth stolen from that museum."

The old man nodded.

"But you don't tell no one," he said.

Du Pré rolled himself a cigarette.

"Murdering people is not very good," he said. "You kill others here maybe?"

The old man looked off.

"Long time gone," he said, "couple prospectors maybe, seventy years ago."

"He steal those pages from that Morgenstern? Those paint pages?" said Du Pré.

The old man sighed. He nodded.

"Old man is sick," said the Crow. "That Palmer he come, give him some brandy got drugs in it, Morgenstern pass out and when he wake up he is in the hospital, someone call in say he is ver' sick. He is there a week maybe. That Palmer then he is here asking questions, old uranium mines, so this person offers him that tooth. Takes him out in that country and he has the tooth hidden, Palmer takes it, they are on snowmobiles. Pays some money. So this person shoots him, leaves him there, the tooth is stolen, the museum anyway."

"That tooth Morgenstern's great-uncle find it yes?"

The old Crow nodded.

"He was a strange man," he said, "tracked this place down. It was the only one we kept, only one so far away from anything the whites wanted that they wouldn't maybe find it. But he found it. Got one of the family dug paint here drunk and got directions, just showed up. He was friend to the Crow so they don't kill him, he promises he won't tell no one where this is. I don't know how that damn tooth ended up, museum.

Don't matter. Anyway, someone lets Palmer know about the uranium, the tooth, how much the Japanese are paying the Thunder Horse."

Du Pré nodded.

"Your friend say you don't tell," said the old Crow.

"Horned Star People," said Du Pré.

"We know about them long time," said the old Crow. "We don't know they are white, don't know how long time gone they are here. Plenty time on this land. Crows been here a long time we think but the Horned Star People maybe think we are not here long. Back long time we are Sioux anyway."

Du Pré nodded.

Even got a few Blackfeet-Sioux, Canada, languages are some different. Little tribe caught in the middle.

"I don't tell no one," said Du Pré.

The old Crow nodded.

"One of the young men, get your horse," he said. "You maybe be back home tomorrow, early in the day."

Du Pré waited a few minutes after the old man left and then one of the painted guardians came leading his mount. His saddlebags were tied on the back.

"Maybe," said the painted man, "someday we play some music together, Du Pré, me, I play that guitar some."

Du Pré nodded.

"Pret' holy place here," said the guardian. "We maybe keep it, you come you want to. There is someone watching always. You maybe be careful don't leave tracks, though."

"Yah," said Du Pré. "I come here I come at night. After one rain and before another."

"Yah," said the Guardian, "you don't maybe ride on the high paths, leave tracks that mud."

Du Pré nodded and he swung up. The night was clear and

cool and there was a new line of clouds far off. But they were forty miles west and moving slowly.

He chirred to the horse and the gelding took off back to home and a barn and feed. He clattered down the tongues of gravel laid by the floods from pan to pan and made very good time.

Du Pré let himself through the gate just after dawn. The sheriff's wife came out of the house, her rubber boots squelching on the mud. She opened the barn door and Du Pré led the gelding in and he offsaddled and he hung the saddle on the tree and hung the headstall on the tack board and the blanket he put out where the sun could dry it.

The sheriff's wife looked at Du Pré a long time.

Then she nodded.

"So you'll be back," she said.

"Yah," said Du Pré, "but I only come at night you know."

The sheriff's wife nodded.

"Won't need directions from me then, will you?" she said.

Du Pré laughed and he walked over to his cruiser and got in.

✤ CHAPTER 34 ✤

"That Bart and Booger Tom and that Burdette are over, Le Doux Springs," said Madelaine. She was slicing limes for the afternoon's cocktails. The big quartered plastic box was piled with lemons and onions and olives already. The onions and olives were pickled and lasted forever because very few people wanted them in their drinks.

Du Pré nodded.

"You are starving maybe," said Madelaine. "You want a cheeseburger, fries maybe, nice salad?"

"Sure," said Du Pré.

She bustled off to the kitchen. Meat sizzled on the grill and then there was a boiling sound and the fries plunged into the hot grease. Madelaine rushed out with a big salad and she shoved it under Du Pré's face and she rushed back to the kitchen.

Du Pré went round the bar and he got a tall glass and ice and some bourbon and water and he went back around and he sat and sipped his drink.

He looked at himself in the mirror. Dark with soot. His clothes smelled of the sweet grass and cedar burning in the cave.

Du Pré smiled.

Madelaine came back out with his rare cheeseburger and fries and she set them down. Du Pré wolfed the food. He finished his drink and Madelaine made him another.

The door opened and Susan Klein came in, walking with just a cane.

"Out!" she said. "I want my bar back!"

"I been fired I think," said Madelaine.

Du Pré grinned.

Susan hobbled around behind the bar.

"Really," she said, "I expect I can stand four or five hours is all. I still hurt like hell. But, take some time why don't you? Maybe you could come back early evening."

Madelaine nodded. She hugged Susan.

"The new mirror isn't as nice as the old one," said Susan. "Too bright. Take half a century to weather down nice and we'll all be dead."

Du Pré laughed.

"Maybe we go, them Le Doux Springs," said Madelaine, "see what that Bart and that Booger Tom are up to."

"Sure," said Du Pré.

They went out and got in the cruiser and Madelaine ran back and got a bottle of fizzy pink wine for herself and a pint of bourbon and a package of Bull Durham for Du Pré. Cups and ice.

Du Pré made his way out to the east-west highway and he got up to a hundred and backed off and Madelaine handed him a cup of bourbon and ice and water. She sipped her pink wine.

"You find everything Du Pré?" she said.

"Yah," said Du Pré.

"Pret' holy place I bet," said Madelaine.

"Gabriel Dumont maybe hide there," said Du Pré. "Someone carve GD eighteen eighty-seven on that wall, a cross."

"We maybe let them alone, eh?"

"Oh, yes?" said Du Pré.

They shot over the top of a hill and saw a big truck lumbering down the far side with a load of posts and poles. Du Pré passed the truck at the bottom and he shot up the hill on the far side and the truck driver honked a long blast on his air horn.

"You see that Benetsee?" said Madelaine.

"No," said Du Pré.

"Him there I bet," said Madelaine. "Him everywhere."

Du Pré didn't say anything.

"You find out who kill that professor?" said Madelaine.

Du Pré nodded.

"What you going to do with that?"

"I don't know," said Du Pré.

"Bart he come in yesterday and he say he is buying two hundred thousand dollars, chain fence, put around Le Doux Springs for a while. He said he will take it down some day."

Du Pré laughed.

"It have electricity?" he said.

"No," said Madelaine, "but once it gets out where them Horned Star People are found he will have plenty reporters, the TV, you bet."

Du Pré rounded a long curve and came up on a slow tractor pulling several giant round bales of hay on a trailer.

Grass is not up yet.

Du Pré shot around the tractor and he pulled back over and a pickup moving nearly as fast as Du Pré went past.

"Someday we hit head-on," said Madelaine. "You drive like a madman."

Du Pré laughed.

"Montana she is ver' big," he said. "Drive slow you never get anywhere."

"Maria call," said Madelaine. "She is on the honors list again. She is a ver' smart girl, I tell her come back here, have babies, she say this rude thing, me."

Du Pré laughed.

"Oh, yes," he said. Maria, my little daughter at that big Eastern school, she is doing well. She will not live poor and Métis in Montana. She will miss it all her life though.

"What you going to do the dead professor?" said Madelaine.

"Don't know," said Du Pré.

"Better do nothing," said Madelaine, "I think that is best."

Du Pré laughed.

The road crested a high hill and they could see it laid out forty miles ahead. Even see the traffic on the north-south highway winding to the west of the Wolf Mountains. Sun glinted on the glass of cars and trucks.

They pulled up to the stop sign where the highways joined twenty minutes later. Du Pré waited for a big truck to pass and he pulled out and shot around it before the truck was a mile from the intersection.

Madelaine finished her pink wine by the time they got to the turnoff to Le Doux Springs. The road in was torn up from heavy truck tires and Du Pré had to pick his way carefully through the ruts. When they got up high enough to look down on the Springs there were several semis laden with rolls of chain-link fence and a dozen workers setting posts in cement and bracing the posts so the wire could be strung without waiting for the concrete to set.

"Looks like a damn prison," said Madelaine.

Bart was standing talking to a man in a blue hard hat. The hard hat pointed off at something and Bart waved, too.

Booger Tom was sitting on the hood of Bart's SUV, drinking something out of a silver flask. The metal glinted in the bright sun.

Burdette was off above the springs, kneeling and staring at a line of gravels in the cut the earthquake had made in the earth.

Du Pré wallowed up through the churned earth and he got on the grass and the tires grabbed and he parked by Booger Tom. The old man nodded at them as they got out.

"A carny park," said Booger Tom. "Maybe I get the job bitin' the heads offen the chickens out back there."

"You be good at that," said Madelaine, "you old goat, drinking chicken blood maybe get that old pecker of yours up."

"Such talk," said Booger Tom.

"Such old pecker," said Madelaine. "Maybe you use it for what God stuck it there for you are not such an old grouch."

"Have a drink," said Booger Tom, *"please."*

The man in the blue hard hat strode off yelling at a crewman who was doing something the hard hat didn't like.

Bart turned and looked for a moment at Du Pré and Madelaine and then he shambled over. His bruised face was getting much better and his smile didn't look so pained.

"Get this sucker fenced," said Bart, "and then Burdette can bring in a crew and do a proper dig here."

Du Pré nodded. He looked at a new power pole and a transformer stuck in the raw earth.

"Need a few metal buildings for processing the finds," said Bart.

"Where them fish ponds going?" said Du Pré.

Bart looked at Du Pré.

"Someplace else," he said.

The workmen yelled. A concrete truck roared up and over the hill and men picked up wheelbarrows and headed to the dump spot.

"What did you find?" said Bart, finally.

"Not much," said Du Pré. "Still don't know who killed that guy."

Bart nodded.

"Maybe we'll never know," he said.

"No," said Du Pré, "I find out, me."

Bart shrugged.

"Where is that Burdette this winter anyway?" said Du Pré.

"Canada, the East Coast," said Bart.

Du Pré nodded.

"You seen that Benetsee?" he said.

"He come by the bar yesterday," said Madelaine. "He ain't wearing them filthy dog skins. I feed him, give him some wine."

Madelaine feed the whole earth, give it wine, Du Pré thought.

"Lots of surprises in this country," said Bart.

Du Pré nodded.

The concrete truck revved its engine and the mixer rotated.

"Greatest find I know of," said Bart. "Think of it. Same people who are buried in Russia and Scandinavia and Keewatin."

"Yah," said Du Pré.

"Madelaine," said Du Pré, "maybe you catch a ride back, Bart, Tom. I got to go down there to that Bozeman."

Madelaine looked at him.

"OK Du Pré," she said. "You be careful though."

❖ CHAPTER 35 ❖

Professor Morgenstern opened the door a few inches and he stared out with his huge watery old eyes at Du Pré for a long time. He slipped the chain out of the lock slide and walked away. Du Pré pushed the door open and he went in and closed it behind him.

The apartment smelled of medicine and death.

Morgenstern had lost a lot of weight and he shuffled bent and marked for death to an easy chair. Pills and potions covered the end table under the fringed shade of a Victorian stained-glass lamp with a cast bronze base. The old man fumbled with a pill bottle and he took a couple out and put them in his mouth and lifted a glass of water to his lips. His hand trembled so badly he had to put his elbow on the arm of the chair to steady it.

Morgenstern started to speak and then he began to cough and cough. Tears dripped from his eyes and a silver thread of drool fell from the corner of his mouth to his stained shirt-front. His hair was awry and the cuffs and collar of his white shirt were yellow-brown.

"I knew . . . you . . . would come," said Morgenstern. He looked resigned.

Du Pré nodded.

"I found that place," he said, "where the dinosaur is, where them Horned Star People are buried under the water. Met them Crow that Benetsee told me some. I am here before you lie to me, yes? You don't lie now. You got them pages, your great-uncle's books, you got them. You cut them out. Nobody else do that. Why?"

Morgenstern coughed again, a deep weak bubbling. He swallowed a few times.

"Brandy . . ." he said, pointing to some crystal decanters on a silver rack sitting on a rosewood sideboard.

Du Pré poured some in a big snifter and he took it to the old man. Morgenstern raised the snifter with both hands and he sipped and coughed and sipped and coughed till it was gone.

"You want more?" said Du Pré.

Morgenstern shook his head.

"I buy my time in minutes these days," said Morgenstern. "A month at most I'll be dead. What would you do then, Mr. Du Pré."

Du Pré shrugged.

"Something," said Morgenstern. "Benetsee said you were smart like a wolf is smart."

Du Pré laughed.

"Me, I much rather be smart like a coyote," said Du Pré. "Them God's dogs, they know everything, even God's jokes."

Morgenstern coughed. He was laughing.

"It is the wolf who ranges far," said Morgenstern. "A coyote lives and dies a few miles from where it was born."

"When you see Benetsee?" said Du Pré.

"While ago," said Morgenstern. "Doesn't matter. I don't talk of my friend much, Mr. Du Pré, for fear I will anger him and he won't come and see me before I die."

"How he get in here anyway?" said Du Pré. "Them security people they see a ragged old man, they throw him out, think he is a wino."

"A stupid question," said Morgenstern. "You know what Benetsee is. I thought perhaps he changed into a yuppie stockbroker till he was at my door. He comes when the building is locked, too. In the night. He is a creature of night, Mr. Du Pré, he lives where our fears are."

Du Pré nodded. He went to the sideboard and found some whiskey and poured himself some. Scotch. Tasted like charcoal and kippered herring.

"Where are them pages?" said Du Pré.

"There's a leather rod case in the back closet of my bedroom," said Morgenstern. "They are in there. Be careful taking them out. Some of the paint has already flaked off."

Du Pré drank his Scotch and he rolled a smoke and lit it and he went back to the bedroom. It stank of sweat and medicine and death. The bedding was all on the floor, awaiting the maid, and more pills and bottles sat on the bedside table.

Du Pré opened the closet. Cedar. It was stuffed with expensive suits in style forty years before. The rod case was leaning in a corner. Old bright tan leather with green straps and heavy brass buckles.

Du Pré unhooked the cap and then he reached in and gently twisted the big vellum pages out. They had taken a curl. He carried the roll out to the worktable.

Morgenstern was standing beside it, a cane in each hand.

"Spray some water on the marble," he said, nodding to a bottle with a pump sticking out of the top. "Use those brass weights to hold it down. A little damp and the curl will come out."

Du Pré wetted the marble top. He slid one page out of the other and he weighted the right margin and then he slowly and carefully unrolled the heavy paper. It had a lot of spring in it. He set the long heavy brass weights top and bottom and then he finished unrolling it and he put three heavy weights on the left margin. Then he unrolled and weighted the other one.

Morgenstern stood wheezing.

Du Pré looked at the pages. Eleven samples of yellow paint on the first one and seven on the second and last page of the huge book. He looked at the three stripes on the last page nearest the bottom. They were spaced farther apart than any others. Spidery script in faded pale brown ink, blotted with water spots in places, filled the blank spots beneath the strips of paint.

Directions.

To the cave that Du Pré had seen.

Wrong directions. Take them and you'd wind up forty miles away.

"He protected his friends the Crows, Mr. Du Pré," wheezed Morgenstern. "It was their last holy place and one not found by the whites. A single Crow family has guarded it ever since. It's a large family and they never have betrayed those secrets, Mr. Du Pré, not in a century."

Du Pré nodded.

"You ever meet that Palmer?" said Du Pré, "The one got killed."

Morgenstern looked at him a long time.

"Yes," he said, "he came here several times. First time twelve years or so ago. I never trusted him. Said he was doing a monograph on Crow paints. He'd figured it out, some of the secret anyway. He moved very slowly and quite cautiously. He wanted money. It was the Tyrannosaurus skeleton he wanted. He must have been in contact with the Japanese then, or perhaps shortly after. His questions were elliptical. I put him off. But he let enough slip so I knew he was on the track. That country was all surveyed during the Second World War and much of the uranium was at least found and mapped. Then richer deposits were found in Canada. They could make bomb-grade uranium or plutonium in breeder reactors easier than they could mine it. The government bought up the claims as the miners realized that nothing was going to be done, for a few dollars."

Du Pré nodded.

"That tooth, the one that was in the museum," said Du Pré, "your uncle or whatever, he find that, it goes there when he dies."

"Apparently," said Morgenstern, "though he never mentioned it in his notes. He took careful notes."

"How long you know Burdette?" Du Pré said. He looked hard at the old man.

"A long time," said Morgenstern. "A brilliant and honorable man, not a usual sort of chap. Never could survive in an academic setting, the dishonesty and backstabbing are constant and unrelenting. Burdette would have probably slaughtered his entire department. No, he found other ways of supporting himself. I gather your Mr. Fascelli helped him often, has for decades. Digs in Russia, Canada, Sweden."

Du Pré nodded.

"He suspected the Red Ochre People had gone a lot farther than anyone knew," said Morgenstern. "Oh, for years archaeologists have known that when the seas were three hundred feet lower the paths from Asia to America went down the beaches, down the littoral. All that evidence is washed away, under fifty fathoms of water. So we won't ever really know. But those Red Ochre People had the sighting tool. It wasn't needed for short trips. It's hard to tell where the waters were here, with the ice dams and so forth. The levels changed constantly, the rivers changed course."

Du Pré nodded.

He pulled a small notebook out of his pocket and he scribbled down some portions of the notes beneath the paint strips.

"You want these back, that rod case?" said Du Pré.

"No," said Morgenstern. "If you could insert them in the book I would appreciate it. I am not long here now. A friend will come here in a few days and take everything my great uncle left me and much of my stuff to boot. The museum may have anything that doesn't matter."

Du Pré pulled the drawer open and he lifted out the giant folio and he opened it and put the pages in the back and carefully shut it and then he stuck it back in the drawer.

"My regards to Benetsee when you see him," said Morgenstern.

"Yah," said Du Pré. He picked up his jacket.

"Just keep their secret," said Morgenstern. "They deserve that."

Du Pré nodded.

"I don't tell no one," he said.

He let himself out while Morgenstern coughed and coughed. The old deep pile carpet felt funny under his boot-soles and his feet itched strangely.

He took the elevator down and he walked past the security desk. There was no one there. Two uniformed guards were laughing in the office, out of sight.

Du Pré went out the front door of the Baxter Hotel and around to his car, past yuppie shops selling nonviolent toys and handmade huckleberry chocolates.

A meter maid was checking clocks.

Du Pré asked her where the police station was.

She pointed east.

✤ CHAPTER 36 ✤

Sorry about that," said the detective. "There hasn't been a cowboy seen in Bozeman since about 1969. Everybody here is from California now. I'm from California. Montanans hate Californians. So we dislike them right back. We're the new Okies, actually, loathed wherever we go."

"OK," said Du Pré.

"You look like you stepped out of a John Ford western," said the detective. "I mean they thought you had a gun."

Du Pré nodded. His forehead hurt where three cops had slammed him up against the wall when he had reached in his shirt pocket for his notes.

"I speak some English," said Du Pré, "I think pret' good but they don't understand me soon enough."

The detective cast an eye out the door toward the hall.

"Sue 'em," he said. "They assaulted you."

"That is all the better they can do, assault," said Du Pré. "I maybe send them some meat. Them soybeans they don't help, you are assaulting somebody. One guy, he hit me, I have been hit harder by wind. Not much wind either."

"OK," the detective sighed, "not only are we all Californians, we are all pussies. The humiliations never let up. Now, in response to your questions, now that I understand them, I went up with my partner to the museum on the fourth of February to investigate the theft of the tooth of a Tyrannosaurus Rex. We questioned the staff and narrowed it down

214

to a few possibles and gave them lie detector tests. They all passed. So it seemed that some strong fellow just picked it up and disguised it somehow and sailed out the front door. It must have been a busy time, it was a Saturday and it was cold and snowy and a lot of parents brought their kids because Saturday is a reduced rate and the students come because it is a cheap date. Some of them have a club, they fuck in the stagecoach. They say 'You laid in Butterfield?' "

Du Pré laughed.

The detective took out a thick plastic folder and he set it down on the desk and he waved to Du Pré.

"Have at it," he said. "We can photocopy anything you want. I have to go for a few minutes, talk over a case with the captain."

Du Pré nodded. He took out his tobacco pouch and absently began to roll a smoke.

"Uh," said the detective, "no smoking. City ordinance."

"Yah," said Du Pré, "that secondhand smoke it is very bad for you Californians."

The detective grinned and he went out.

Du Pré read through the reports, all in neat computer type. Interviews. The results of the lie detector tests.

Case open.

A photo of the empty case. A photo of some scratches near the screw that held the side of the case down, and a photo of the screw and socket on the other side, the socket broken out when the Plexiglas case had been lifted and the tooth taken.

The detective came back.

"So the tooth is in the evidence locker up in that godforsaken one-hole town, Christ I can't even remember the name of it. The museum hasn't complained yet about that."

Du Pré nodded.

"I thank you," he said.

"A question," said the detective. "You're a law enforcement officer. A brand inspector. Not that I know what that is. What are you doing investigating a murder case in another county?"

"We are very short-handed," said Du Pré.

"Gabriel Du Pré," said the detective, "I've heard some stories about you."

"I play the fiddle," said Du Pré.

"One other thing," said the detective. "You smell very strongly of alcohol. It is unlawful to drive under the influence. They may be loose up where you are about that, but here in Bozeman we are tough on it."

Du Pré nodded.

"It is this funny toothpaste my daughter send me, Christmas," said Du Pré, "and you know they are worried, I got this gun, slam me up against the wall out there? I got the gun but it is in the car and me, I take enough crap, one lifetime."

Du Pré scribbled on a small sheet of paper on the detective's desk.

"I drive an old police cruiser," said Du Pré, "that license number, I maybe don't like being fucked with, Californians. Thank you for your help."

"Right," said the detective, "I get it. I am an extremely bright Californian. All those vegetables I eat."

Du Pré left.

He went out to his cruiser and he got in and wheeled around in a U-turn and headed up for the museum. A police car roared up lights flashing and Du Pré put his hand out the window and gave them the finger and then he punched the accelerator when he turned on to the main drag south and the cop followed for three blocks and then turned off his light bar and abruptly turned left.

Du Pré went around the campus and to the parking lot of the museum and he parked and went in. A cheerful young woman took his five dollars. The tepee made of cowhides with the brands on, dyed red-brown, still stood in the foyer. Du Pré went past it. About half-size, but kids could stand up in it in air that smelled like shoes.

Du Pré looked in the window at the plaster-coated Tyrannosaurus. A number of people in lab coats were bent over one or another portion of the fossil, picking at it with dental tools.

Giannini was looking at a clipboard. He made a couple notes and then he looked up and saw Du Pré. He put down the clipboard and he came out.

"Mr. Du Pré!" he said, extending his hand.

Du Pré shook it.

"You got a picture, that tooth?" he said.

"Somewhere," said Giannini, "we have to. All the exhibits are photographed for insurance purposes at least, more often if they are being carefully studied. The front office has those files. Actually, there are two sets, another over at the main Administration building, in case one or another building burns down."

He led Du Pré down a long corridor and into a huge office. A middle-aged woman with a sour expression got up from her desk.

"Lois," said Giannini, "this is Officer Du Pré, he's investigating that murder the T. Rex tooth was involved in. We have a picture of it do we not?"

"Should," said Lois. She looked at Du Pré, not happily.

"She'll help you," said Giannini. "I'll be in the fossil room if you need me."

He went out.

"Prick," said Lois. She turned and went over to some tan filing cabinets and she pulled out three drawers and slid two back and she dug around for a while and then she pulled out a file and she opened it, chewing gum and staring for a long

217

time. She came back to the counter and slid the folder on it and turned and went back to her desk.

Du Pré looked at the photos of the tooth. Some were taken of the tooth in its case and several others of the tooth on a white background.

Du Pré looked at the photos a long time. They had been taken by a camera that produced a print in minutes. He palmed one and slipped it into his jacket pocket.

"Thank you," said Du Pré to Lois.

She didn't look up from her desk.

Du Pré went out to the lobby and he found a pay phone.

He dialed and spoke and waited.

The detective came on the line.

" 'Lo," he said.

"It is me," said Du Pré.

"Oh," said the detective. "Listen, do you have to piss on us? The U-turn, running away from the traffic cop."

"Yes," said Du Pré, "I do. I don't get to smoke, makes me cranky. Now I am up at this museum, you know, and I looked, the insurance file, that tooth."

"Yeah," said the detective, "so did we. Just a rock."

"Uh-huh," said Du Pré. "Anything else it is stolen then?"

"Not that I know of."

"This is a pret' big rock," said Du Pré. "Weighs maybe seventy-five pounds, you know."

"Seventy-eight pounds four ounces," said the detective. "All in the report."

"Had some of that magnetic stuff on it," said Du Pré. "Go out the door it sets off the alarm. Have to fill out a form, call security, you want to move it out of the building."

"There's ways around that," said the detective.

"Sure," said Du Pré. "You cut a hole in the roof, dig a tunnel."

"Oh, God," said the detective, "that was one thing we didn't do."

"Uh-huh," said Du Pré. "The tooth we find, the dead guy, it is not the tooth that was stolen."

"Shit," said the detective.

"They got a lot, rocks here, yes?" said Du Pré.

"Uh-huh," said the detective.

"Get your sorry ass up here I watch that Giannini," said Du Pré. "I see he stay in that room, knock him on his ass I got to."

"Oh, God, don't do that," said the detective.

"Maybe you hurry," said Du Pré, "He is waiting, me to leave."

He hung up.

He walked back to the window that looked into the fossil room.

Giannini looked up and he smiled at Du Pré and then he turned and spoke to a young assistant who laughed. They laughed together and then Giannini came out of the door.

"Anything else I can help you with?" he said.

"Oh not me," said Du Pré, "but that detective he will be here, any time. Then maybe you find him that tooth that is still here."

Giannini smiled again but his eyes weren't.

"We just stand here nice," said Du Pré, "or it gets real western, you know?"

❧ CHAPTER 37 ❧

Ho Du Pré," said Madelaine, "you find it all out, yes?"
She was standing behind the bar in the Toussaint, while
Susan Klein sat on a chair near the cash register. Susan's face
was drawn. Her repaired tendons were shrinking and she had
to stretch them very painfully. It wore her hard.

"Some," said Du Pré. He sighed. "This is one, them things,
maybe I don't want to know too much."

"Knowin' it is OK," said Madelaine. "Got to pray before you
do some things, though, you know. You are hungry Du Pré?
We got that prime rib now, it will be ready, fifteen minutes."

Du Pré slammed the dice cup down on the bar. He'd already rolled and lost the shake for the day.

He looked glumly at the sixes.

Boxcars.

Crap.

The jukebox made noises supposedly Cajun. Du Pré didn't
think so.

He sipped his bourbon.

Bozeman. Jesus.

Maybe I don't go back there, I have to, I have to pret' bad.

"Du Pré," said Benny Klein. He had come in quietly, maybe
through the back door and through the kitchen. "You find out
who shot that guy Palmer yet?"

Du Pré shook his head.

"Maybe we don't know," he said.

"Well," said Benny, "out of my jurisdiction."

Du Pré snorted.

Susan Klein got painfully down from her chair and she came along the bar. She made a drink for herself and one for Benny and she dribbled some more bourbon into Du Pré's glass and then squirted in some water.

"Hurt some, eh?" said Du Pré.

"They're gettin' better," said Susan, "by God."

Du Pré laughed.

Benny went back down the bar and sat near the cash register.

Madelaine brought the prime rib, a thick red slab. Baked potato. Big salad with lots of cucumbers. Du Pré loved cucumbers.

"You stop, see that Benetsee is there?" said Madelaine.

Du Pré shook his head.

"Ah," she said, "tell you what, this dinner rush is over I can go a while we go out there. You need a bath. Ho. Smell you from here. You smell funny. What you drink that Bozeman?"

"Scotch," said Du Pré, "tasted like smoked fish."

"Yah," said Madelaine.

Du Pré finished his supper and he drove over to Madelaine's and he showered and changed into clean clothes and then he went back to the saloon. It was packed with people eating prime rib and laughing and talking and joking. He waited at the bar. They were all ranchers and had to get up early and by eight the bar was almost empty. Susan was still sitting in her chair. She got down and she walked to the front door and went out. Du Pré looked at her go.

She do that so she can walk fast and hard and we don't see her face screw up, pain, Du Pré thought. One tough lady.

This all start a damn earthquake. Even the earth don't sleep good here, no, wind either.

Madelaine came out of the back wearing a wool jacket she had made from a Hudson's Bay four-point blanket, white with red and green and black stripes. It had a hood like the old long capotes of the Métis.

She sat down beside Du Pré.

"That Susan gets back we go," she said.

They waited a few minutes and then Susan came in, sweating furiously from her forehead. She walked grimly to the bar and behind it and she ran cold water on a towel and she held it to her face.

"Go on," she mumbled, "I can handle it. I really am feeling better."

Du Pré and Madelaine went out and got in his old cruiser and Du Pré wheeled around and headed out of town and up the bench road to Benetsee's.

Smoke curled up from the leaning tin chimney.

Du Pré bounced over the deep ruts and he parked on a patch of grass near the porch of the old cabin.

Madelaine got out and she went and pounded on the door.

It opened.

Pelon. Madelaine looked around him.

"Old man!" she shouted. "You are here this is good. We got to talk to you now. Don't be changing into no pillbug, hide under the cabin, eh?"

She motioned to Du Pré.

Benetsee sat at the table, grinning, a few black old teeth showing.

Madelaine went on in and she sat at the rickety table. The old man grinned at her. She pulled a quart of fizzy pink wine from her coat pocket.

"That all you got?" said Benetsee.

"All I got you tell us a few things," said Madelaine. "You got to tell me more than you tell Du Pré, he knows things I don't."

"Hee," said Benetsee, "he don't know much, not much. He maybe got some tobacco, an old man, though."

Du Pré rolled a smoke for Benetsee and one for Pelon. He lit them and handed them over.

"You old goat there," said Madelaine, "my Du Pré he is going around maybe getting shot guys all painted and you sit there drink my wine. You maybe want a fat nose?"

"Hee," said Benetsee, "that Du Pré he look around find things, some of them bite."

"He get bit I rip your ass off shove it down your damn throat," said Madelaine. "Some holy man. What is this? Japanese they want this dinosaur. They say, seven million dollars. Lots of people get killed a hundred bucks. Seven million dollars."

Benetsee nodded.

"That Bart he buy them Le Doux Springs," said Benetsee, "he dig for them Horned Star People. Long time gone. Bart he don't need money. Makes him holy, you know."

"Huh?" said Madelaine.

"Rich men need more money," said Benetsee. "It is like me and wine. Not enough you know."

Du Pré laughed. He went out to his car and he fished a gallon of screwtop pink wine out of the back and he carried it in."

Benetsee was smoking and looking up at the ceiling. Du Pré filled the jam jar he was drinking from.

"Long time gone," said Benetsee softly.

"Them Crows," said Du Pré, "I talk to them, I see that cave. I think maybe Gabriel Dumont he hide, that cave."

"Yes," said Benetsee, "priest betray us and Gabriel he come down here, hide there, his wife, too. Hide there three months."

The Red River Rebellion, the second one, the time the English they hang poor crazy Louis Riel, who talks with Jesus.

"That dinosaur," said Du Pré, "them Horned Star People they find it. They bury their dead there."

"Thunder Horse," said Benetsee. "Sioux call them bones, horses of the Thunder People. Maybe the Horned Star People do too. Thunder Horse carry their dead, the Star Trail."

The Milky Way. We go to the Star Trail, good water, game, enemies to fight, Du Pré thought, it is there right over us in heaven.

Thunder Horse.

Like to see the saddle for that son of a bitch.

Bit for that mouth.

"Who kill that Palmer man?" said Madelaine.

Benetsee coughed.

He shrugged.

"Money kill him," he said.

"OK," said Madelaine, "my fool Du Pré here he will keep digging, he find who kill him you know, he is like that. Somebody kill my Du Pré, maybe, I will be very mad with you."

Benetsee looked sad.

"Don't talk," he said. "It don't help."

"You know," said Madelaine.

Benetsee looked at her. He had a crooked smile on his mouth.

"I be gone someday you have to figure things out yourselves you know," he said, "Pelon, Du Pré, you, my Madelaine."

Madelaine nodded.

"What is this though?"

Benetsee stood up and he shuffled outside and they heard him go round the house to the privy and the door slammed.

"It is all right," said Du Pré.

"Crap it is all right," said Madelaine. "Them Crow about shoot you and we want to help them, Crow fight with us long time, you know."

Du Pré nodded.

"Du Pré," said Madelaine, "what you got you don't tell me."

Du Pré shrugged.

"I think maybe but I don't talk I am sure," he said.

"OK," said Madelaine, "these men they come now, my house, get something to eat."

Pelon laughed.

Benetsee's worn old moccasins flapped on the porch boards. He came in and he drank the last of his wine.

"She want maybe feed you?" said Du Pré.

"She respects old people," said Benetsee. He looked at Du Pré.

Du Pré held up his right fist and he slowly raised his fore-finger.

Then he did the same with his left.

Benetsee laughed and laughed.

He nodded.

✤ CHAPTER 38 ✤

Burdette was bent over the bones, carefully examining something through a thick magnifying glass. He was whistling. Mozart.

Du Pré stood for a moment, looking at the bones of the Horned Star People under a cone of yellow light from a big lamp hung high overhead.

Burdette whistled.

Du Pré padded across the cold concrete floor. Some thick new carpet had been laid in front of the big work table and a metal fireplace with a glass door sat near Burdette's stool. The yellow flames flickered and the stovepipe cracked with heat.

Du Pré pulled up another stool and he sat a little away from the huge man. He was picking at something very carefully with a dental tool.

"Might be there is some DNA in that tooth," he said. He took some big stainless steel tweezers and he put the tooth carefully in a plastic bag and he snapped the zipper lock. He wrote on the bag with a felt-tip pen.

"Bart about got it fenced in?" he said. "Should by now."

"Yah," said Du Pré. "Me, I come maybe ask you about a couple of them dinosaur teeth."

"Um-hum," said Burdette.

"I find the one, where that vertebra come from," said Du Pré, "but there is another one. The tooth, the museum, it is not stolen, that Giannini just hide it in there."

"Tsk, tsk," said Burdette, "how rude."

"There is another, though," said Du Pré.

"Gabriel," said Burdette, "in that country out there there may be five hundred of the damn things. It's the old beach. It was a big beach and a shallow sea. Very little tide and a lot of sand sloughing off the mountains. Maybe sand flats covering hundreds of square miles. I don't know of any more T. Rex skeletons."

"You are a scientist," said Du Pré, "so maybe you mean you don't know you have not seen them, yes?"

Burdette turned and he grinned.

"OK," he said, "I am a scientist and I don't deal in rumors."

"Who set that Palmer up?" said Du Pré. "Somebody tell him and he come here you know."

Burdette shrugged.

"Murder is a serious charge," said Burdette. "I wouldn't care to speculate."

"OK," said Du Pré, "maybe I speculate some you grunt I am right you cough if I am wrong."

Burdette motioned to Du Pré. Gabriel handed him his tobacco and papers.

"Morgenstern he call that Palmer because somebody asks Morgenstern about the paint. The paint is uranium, you know, so maybe it was found, prospectors, fifty years ago. Maybe there is a map. They maybe go each place on that map. One of them dinosaurs is in that cave the Crows watch. The other is out in that country, near, far, something, but this Palmer he gets hold them Japanese."

Burdette nodded. He rolled his smoke and he lit it.

"Palmer comes to Bozeman he tries to steal Morgenstern's paint books but what he wants is hidden. He don't know that, the old man is passed out, he maybe die, so Palmer he panics and calls them ambulance."

Burdette shrugs.

"Palmer come up here. Somebody knows he is looking for that dinosaur and that he knows about the uranium. Maybe he find the cave, the Crows. So this person gets a tooth the other dinosaur and he . . . Palmer gets the damn tooth but he is shot."

"I guess," said Burdette, "he had it with him."

"Palmer he is shot and . . . this I don't know. He is shot, he is on that stolen snowmobile. Goes into the gully. He could not get out of there he is wounded. Collarbone and shoulder are shattered. I can't get out of it one-handed I am not shot."

Burdette nodded. He blew out a long stream of blue smoke.

"You don't kill him. Morgenstern is too old. Somebody goes out there, meet him, has the damn tooth."

Burdette nodded.

"There's nothing out there," said Burdette, "where Palmer is shot, I mean, could have been miles from where he died."

Du Pré nodded.

"Hearsay is a terrible thing," said Burdette.

"I get shot at you don't give me some hearsay I come back here and be pissed off," said Du Pré. "You are bigger than me so I use a damn crowbar you son of a bitch."

Burdette put back his head and he roared.

He laughed and laughed and tears ran down his face.

"God damn," said Burdette, "Bart was right, you are your own self."

"Shit Bart is right," said Du Pré. "Me, what I don't get is why they got to go off, a snowstorm, snowmobiles, fuck around out in that country, damn wind take your skin off them storms. Bullshit. They can go to a nice saloon, warm place, you know, look at the thing in the parking lot, talk inside, a booth."

Burdette nodded.

"Benetsee he does something here," said Du Pré.

Burdette shrugged.

"You don't tell me nothing," said Du Pré.

"Gabriel," said Burdette, "I don't know all of it and I won't tell you things I don't know. I don't know who shot Palmer. And I sure don't know why he was in the middle of fuck-all in a snowstorm riding a stolen snowmobile. Another thing, I don't want to know. You understand. All I want, Gabriel, is to spend the rest of my life with the Horned Star People. There's never been anything like this. Nothing. They came in their boats through Hudson's Bay and up the Red River, they came here before there even was a Missouri River. All the others came down the Great North Trail, probably. Or maybe the Horned Star People were here and they intermarried. Lots of things never explained, Gabriel. Mandans with blue and gray eyes and pale hair. People gone without a trace, people who came long after these folks on this table here. I want to know their story."

Du Pré nodded.

"You been to that cave, the Crows?" said Du Pré.

"No," said Burdette. "I'd like to go, but only if I am invited and only if we can keep it secret. Those poor people had their whole world ripped to pieces. I have plenty here. I have plenty more at Le Doux Springs. I have all I can handle. I have more than I can handle. I don't want to make trouble. Bart . . . Bart would . . ."

"Bart going to buy that, too?" said Du Pré. "That has to be government land."

"They'll trade for other land," said Burdette. "Bart's looking at some private property, very valuable private property the Park Service wants very badly and can't pay for. He buys it, the government gives him those badlands—shit, they're worthless—and there it is. Has to move slowly though."

Du Pré nodded.

"Gabriel," said Burdette, "let it be. Palmer doesn't matter a hill of shit."

"He don't," said Du Pré. "Them Japanese do though. They still got their seven million on the table, that is lots, it will bring on flies."

Burdette nodded.

"Yeah it will," he said.

"Them Crow they keep that, long time," said Du Pré. "But seven million dollars, lots of money. It changes people."

Burdette nodded.

"Ah, shit," said Du Pré. "I maybe should let Madelaine beat on that Benetsee. She maybe get something out of him."

"I were you," said Burdette, "I'd kinda leave old Benetsee alone. He ties fools like me and you in knots."

Du Pré got up and he walked out of the building to his car and he reached under the seat and got the bottle of whiskey and he went back in and he got back on the stool and he had a stiff snort. He offered the bottle to Burdette.

"Ah, shit," he said, "it is right there but me I don't see it."

"Spent my life doing that," said Burdette. "I figure I might have a little clue a decade from now I keep my nose on this burial. Course I expect there is a lot more over at Le Doux Springs. I am going to have all sorts of grant providers and greedy corporations offering help so they can spoon off some glory."

"I know Indians shit they hear 'bout them Horned Star People being white," said Du Pré.

"Yeah, well," said Burdette, "you know, my grandmother found out late in life one of her ancestors was black. I think it killed her. I have always been kinda proud of it myself. A real American, got a little bit of everyone in me. Some Cherokee, too, I think."

Du Pré had another drink.

Burdette joined him. The big man held out his hand and Gabriel gave him the tobacco pouch.

"I feel guilty," said Burdette.

"Oh, yes," said Du Pré.

"I . . . I feel I ought to help you but I don't know what help is," said Burdette. "You know I don't just want to make things worse."

Du Pré looked at him.

The big man's eyes were twinkling.

"I don't know any of this for sure," said Burdette, "but there is a kind of good thing about scientific method. You know, asking one question and finding out and going on to another."

"OK," said Du Pré.

"You keep asking about the tooth," said Burdette, "and who shot Palmer. OK. But maybe there's a better question. Who would be stupid enough to go off on a goddamn snowmobile in a snowstorm with a T. Rex tooth to meet somebody he was going to sell it to?"

Du Pré cursed and he stood up and he stormed out.

✦ CHAPTER 39 ✦

"Not in the head, Du Pré," said Madelaine.

"Yah," said Du Pré.

"You don't put Benny on the spot, that," she said.

"OK," said Du Pré.

"Somebody just shoot the asshole someday," said Madelaine. "Me, I don't want you, jail, because of that fucking Bucky Dassault."

"He is Benjamin Medicine Eagle these days," said Du Pré. "His life is coming up in the world."

"You *got* to do this?" said Madelaine.

"Yah," said Du Pré. "See that prick there? He beat the shit out of Bart and Bart he don't press no charges. Bart is my friend."

They were sitting in Madelaine's car across the street from Benjamin Medicine Eagle's Spiritual Center in Cooper. An Art Deco eagle with spread wings hung over the door. The new brick building was bright with painted wooden circles, cartoons of the shields of Plains warriors.

One of the young thugs who had beaten up Bart was standing outside the front door, glaring stupidly at nothing. He tossed his butt on the grass and he went back in.

"I not be very long," said Du Pré. He got out of the car. He had a baseball bat in his hand and his 9mm in his waistband.

Du Pré walked across the street quickly, his weight on his toes. He was wearing double-soled Cree moccasins with fiberglass cups in the toes. He carried the bat lightly in his right hand and his left was in his pocket wrapped around a small can of pepper spray.

He dodged in the front door. The young thug was laughing with a blonde at the front desk. She looked up in horror as Du Pré ran toward her. The thug didn't turn around. He was staring at her tits.

"Ahhh," said the blonde.

The thug turned and Du Pré swung the bat and crushed his left kneecap and the thug yelped and collapsed.

Du Pré smashed the telephone deck on the desk.

"You," he said to the blonde, who was shaking with fear, "get your dumb white ass out of here."

"What's going on here?" yelled Benjamin Medicine Eagle aka Bucky Dassault, from the office behind the secretary.

Du Pré ran through the door. Another of the thugs who had beaten Bart up was sitting in a chair across the desk from Bucky.

The thug jerked out a knife and Du Pré swung hard overhand and smashed his right collarbone. The man screamed and fell. Du Pré kicked him in the gut and he folded up moaning.

"Jesus!" screamed Bucky Dassault aka Benjamin Medicine Eagle. He tried to run through the wall in the corner. A shelf set full of videos fell over.

Du Pré stalked over to the New Age shaman. He was slapping the bat in his palm.

"You got things to tell me, you stupid fuck," said Du Pré. He picked up a video.

"Ah," said Du Pré, "*Ancient Sioux Sexual Practices*. Very spiritual. They fuck skunks till them whites bring them goats. You are a movie producer. Yes. Tell me about this dinosaur tooth, I maybe don't break every bone in your damn body."

"Oh God," screeched Bucky, "I don't know that guy got killed. I just go out there!"

"Go out there for who?" said Du Pré.

"A woman she call me say it is for someone else I get part of seven million dollars. Meet this guy, give him the tooth he give me half a million then they give the rest later!"

"In a fucking snowstorm," said Du Pré, "on a snowmobile stolen from Red Lodge. Jesus."

"Louis steal it," said Bucky.

"What happens?" said Du Pré. The thug with the sore gut and busted collarbone moaned. "You," said Du Pré, "shut the fuck up." He waved the bat and the thug rolled face down and was quiet.

"I go to the road and I take the snowmobile down and I go up the road I am to meet this guy and when I get there there is no one. I wait ten minutes, then the guy is behind me, pointing this gun. He takes the snowmobile, the tooth is in the back."

"Where you get the fucking tooth?" said Du Pré.

"Somebody leave it, front seat of my car," said Bucky.

"That pink-ass Mercedes?" said Du Pré.

"Yah," said Bucky.

"OK," said Du Pré, "I believe you. Nobody else be dumb enough think they are that James Bond in feathers, you. Asshole. What happens then?"

"Guy roars off I hear a gun open up so I run back, get in the truck with Louis. We leave."

The room stank. Bucky had shit his pants.

Bucky was crumpled in the corner.

Du Pré walked closer.

Bucky whimpered.

He cowered.

"Stand up," said Du Pré.

Bucky straightened, trembling.

"My friend Bart he get bad beaten up," said Du Pré. "Now here is what I maybe do, you know. You, your lousy little fucks you send for that, I maybe see any of you, Montana, again, I kill you. It is a promise. So maybe you go take your videos, you fucking goats, and go someplace. Not them Dakotas, nice people there. Not Wyoming neither."

Bucky was gulping in air.

"OK?" said Du Pré.

Bucky closed his eyes and nodded.

Du Pré slammed the end of the bat into his solar plexus. Bucky let all the air out of him and he folded up.

Du Pré went back out.

The blonde was still sitting at the desk, a gray wad of chewing gum sitting on her front teeth.

"Have a nice day," said Du Pré.

He walked back across the street and got in the car and Madelaine drove away.

"You don't hit them in the head," she said.

"Nah," said Du Pré. "Them head I leave alone."

"Now Bucky have poor Benny Klein arrest you."

"Oh, no," said Du Pré. "He do that all sorts, bad things happen. I explain things, him. Use small words, too."

"What is that thing, your hand?" said Madelaine.

"*Ancient Sioux Sexual Practices,*" said Du Pré. "Dirty movie."

Madelaine laughed.

"You are kidding me," she said.

Du Pré shook his head.

"Jesus," said Madelaine. "How dumb people get."

"I got this one more place to go," said Du Pré. "You maybe come so she does not maybe shoot so much."

Madelaine looked at Du Pré.

"Sure, Du Pré. Where we go?"

Du Pré pointed west.

He threw the video out the window.

It began to snow, wet big flakes, not very many of them.

Madelaine sang some old meat-making songs. Hunting songs. Du Pré joined in.

They stopped at a roadhouse and got some pink wine and some whiskey and cups and ice, some cheese and potato chips.

They sang. They didn't talk.

They crossed the county line and they began to wind back to the little town. The sheriff's car was parked out in front of the courthouse.

Du Pré filled the gas tank at the grocery store and he got a sack of tobacco. He smoked and Madelaine had one, too.

The sheriff's little ranch was lit. The arc light blazed on its pole and house was bright with the light of kerosene lamps, and the dogs barked and barked and then put their paws up on the windows tails wagging.

Du Pré and Madelaine got out and they stood in the light of the pole lamp with the big flakes whirling down.

The sheriff's wife slipped out of the shadows of the barn. She was carrying an assault rifle.

"Du Pré," she said, "it is good to see you."

Cree. Good Cree, too, Du Pré thought.

"I am not here, make trouble," said Du Pré. "I know things and I need to know the others. Maybe somebody ask me I send them south when it is west that they really want to go."

The sheriff's wife laughed.

"This is Madelaine," she said. "I am glad you brought her." She waved the rifle.

"You don't be shooting my Du Pré," said Madelaine.

"Not now," said the sheriff's wife.

They went inside. The house smelled delicious, spices and baking and meat.

236

The sheriff's wife got plates of food for them and for herself and they sat at a lovely old simple oak table and they ate.

"So," she said, "what do you need to know."

"You know about the cave?" said Du Pré.

"Oh, yes," said the sheriff's wife, "my grandmother was half Crow. I first went to the cave as a child. The last place, you know. They will have that, if I have anything to do with it."

Du Pré nodded.

"Palmer was getting close," said Du Pré.

She nodded. "Yes he was."

"There is this other dinosaur."

She laughed.

"Two more, actually," she said. "We will give one up slowly now. And your friend Bart may help us."

"What about the Japanese?" said Du Pré.

"All they had to do was offer all that money," said the sheriff's wife. "It was sufficient to start all this. Just the money. Other than that, they did nothing and they know even less."

"Benjamin Medicine Eagle," said Du Pré.

"Him," said the sheriff's wife. "Oh, I had him in my sights. But then who would we have to laugh at?"

✦ CHAPTER 40 ✦

How much do I want to know," said Bart.
Du Pré shrugged:

"You know enough," he said.

"Good," said Bart. "I hang around you I find out things I would much rather see asleep."

"Yah," said Du Pré. "All of us that, you know."

The cyclone fencing was up and there were floodlights on poles on the perimeter of the property. Crews were erecting several big metal buildings and grading and readying the roadbed and a parking lot for paving.

"Trout ponds," said Booger Tom. "Now that would have been a damn shame. You know, I know an old cowboy song about Le Doux Springs."

Du Pré nodded. He'd heard it. It was ribald. A cowboy out riding came on a wagonload of whores bathing in the spring. And so forth.

The day was bright and there were only a few high fleecy clouds scudding across the bright blue. It was too early in the year for the dust to dull the sky.

The Wolf Mountains rose up to the east, white peaks lined up here and there. Up there it was still snowing and would till the middle of June.

"Christ," said Booger Tom, "there's more of them shits of reporters." He spat in the dirt and he walked over to his SUV and he got in and drove off down to the gate, which was manned by a couple of uniformed security guards.

"Booger Tom is the press relations officer for the dig," said Bart.

Du Pré roared with laughter.

"You don't let him carry a gun, yes?" said Du Pré.

"Nope," said Bart, "his cussing will have to do."

"He listen to you?" said Madelaine.

Bart paused and he looked up at the sky.

"Of course not," he said. "But I can hope."

An armored truck lumbered up the roadway, deforming the careful grading. The crews jabbered at each other and the man on the dozer threw his hard hat at the ground.

"Uh-oh," said Bart, "I better go tell the boys there's a bonus." He walked off toward the men.

The armored truck paused a moment. Burdette got out and he walked to the smallest metal building, still plenty big enough, and the truck turned and began to back up to the tall sliding doors. Burdette went into the building and then the doors opened and he pushed first one and then the other aside on their tracks and the truck backed right up to the concrete pad and stopped.

"They coming home," said Madelaine. She looked up at the high ridge over the fence behind the springs. A black figure was trotting alone along the top.

She poked Du Pré.

"Our friend the Coyote Master," she said. She shaded her eyes with her hand.

Du Pré snorted.

Benetsee dropped down from the ridgetop and he went behind a stand of aspens filling a small draw and disappeared.

Boooger Tom was standing out in front of the gate. The reporters had backed up.

Bart saw what was happening and he ran flat out toward the old man, who was waving something in his hand.

"Maybe he find another press guy," said Du Pré. "Booger Tom he is a simple cowboy. Cowboys got good manners, they just shoot rude people. It is not the best job, Booger Tom."

"We maybe go see them Horned Star People," said Madelaine, and she had her rosary in her hand. They walked toward the armored truck and the metal shed and her lips moved and her hands rubbed the beads.

The metal building smelled of new concrete and electricity and pitch. The frame was of pine posts and beams and the roof strips of wood with metal sheeting screwed down tight. Light still showed at the bottom of the walls, the outside needed to be sealed and bermed.

Burdette was on a forklift, carrying a pallet with some of the bones in their plaster piled on it. He set the pallet down on a huge metal worktable and he slipped the forks out from under and went back for the other. When he slipped the second pallet out the driver and guard from the truck closed the doors and they stood waiting, the driver with a clipboard in his hand.

Burdette stopped the forklift and he got down and went to the armored truck guards and he signed the form on the clipboard and they got in the truck and left. Burdette slipped the doors closed and he pinned them in the center and latched the edges with spring clamps.

The huge man came back. He was smiling and whistling.

"Oh boy oh boy oh boy," said Burdette. "I never thought in my life that my dreams would come true. You know I first heard about the Horned Star People, saw it in a Russian archaeology journal, they called them the Red Sailors, of course, when I was still in high school. I don't know why but I was just sure that they made it all over the North. I used to dream about it and then . . . here they are and here I am. Not many men can see their entire life's work in front of them and be happy about it. I am. Oh, yes, I am."

He got on the forklift and he set the second pallet down on the huge worktable and slipped out the forks.

"Come on, Du Pré," said Burdette. "Help me slip them off the wood. There's a secret up there, too."

The bones and molds were heavy and Du Pré and Burdette grunted as they rocked them off the oak pallets.

Du Pré looked down at the tabletop. It was filled with holes, an eighth of an inch or so across, and an inch apart. The whole table was a grid.

They tossed the pallets off and Burdette got down and so did Du Pré and Burdette grinned and looked at Du Pré and Madelaine.

"Toys toys toys," he said. He reached under the table and switched something on. A compressor far off boomed and thumped.

The table hissed fiercely.

Burdette reached over and he grabbed one of the heavy chunks of plaster and skeletons and gravel and he drew it to him easily and then he spun it. The mass moved easily. Burdette positioned it and then he pulled the other over and he reached under the table and shut off the air and the huge chunks of plaster and bones settled down slowly.

"Bart, Bart," said Burdette, "and all his lovely money. That's what us scientists really like. Money, money, money."

He laughed and so did Du Pré.

Madelaine walked over to the ochred bones and she bent her head and her lips moved. Burdette bowed his head, too, and so did Du Pré.

Long time gone, Du Pré thought, long time gone.

Red River. I wonder how many Red Rivers there have been, this world, how many voyageurs gone up them. How many buffalo dressed out for winter meat, Le Doux Springs. How many happy people dancing, got the full bellies and that winter is not so terrible coming, they have good meat, they will live.

Leather whispered on the concrete floor.

Du Pré turned and looked and there was Benetsee. There was no way the old man could have come all that distance down the mountain and around the fence and through the gate. The guards would not have let him in without calling.

Du Pré laughed.

Raven shit on the roof, another glob on the ground outside the door.

Burdette looked up and he smiled.

Benetsee came and he stood by Du Pré and Madelaine. She was still praying and he bent his head, too, and his old eyes slid closed.

She raised her head and she kissed her rosary and put it in her pocket. She turned and looked at Benetsee.

"Old man," she said, "you come here, pray?"

"Oh no," said Benetsee, laughing, "I need a smoke."

Du Pré laughed and he rolled one for the old man. He lit it and he handed it over.

Benetsee drew the smoke in his lungs and then he blew a thin blue stream out. East. He turned slowly and blew six more times and then he pinched the coal from the end of the cigarette and he grinned at Du Pré and Madelaine and Burdette.

"Come," he said. And he walked toward the door.

They followed him outside. He walked down the low hill to the springs. They were shimmering with the silver heart of moving water. A raven sat on the cyclone fence, motionless.

Benetsee took off his jacket and pants and moccasins and he pulled off the old stained riverman's shirt he wore and he walked down to the water.

"You come," he said to Du Pré and Madelaine and Burdette.

They stripped down to underwear.

Benetsee laughed.

"Plenty cold so we don't stay long," he said. He went to the edge of the spring and he slipped into the water smooth as an otter.

Du Pré dove in and the cold crushed him. Madelaine and Burdette followed.

Benetsee was down a few feet, right over the deep golden cone of the spring where it was cutting through the gravels.

He pointed down where the water shimmered.

A red skull looked up, the eyepits deep and black with time.

The skull moved a little.

Du Pré looked until he had to breathe. He swam up and his head broke the water, and he saw Burdette and Madelaine and Benetsee.

They laughed and laughed and then they made for shore.

Du Pré and Madelaine stood at the back of the crowd. The auctioneer rattled the bid and the carved walnut sideboard went for fourteen hundred dollars. The buyer was a cold-eyed woman in designer expedition gear. Her Mercedes-Benz SUV had Bozeman license plates. The sideboard would go to her store and grow greatly in price.

A couple college kids backed a rental truck around and they put the sideboard in the back.

It was a raw March day with snow promised in the wind's scent.

The auctioneer offered three more pieces of furniture, and they all went to the woman from Bozeman, too. The college boys loaded the pieces and they slid down the door and locked it and got in and drove off. The woman was counting out hundred-dollar bills to the lawyer who was taking the cash and checks.

"It is very sad," said Madelaine, "I don't know the Messmers but they are here a long time and this place is gone, too."

One more old family ranch ended, five or six generations of people who had made a living here, working in the wind.

The Messmer place was forty miles west of Toussaint. The Wolf Mountains shoved storms right at it. The weather was rough but the weather brought water.

The Messmers had bought a motor home, to go south for the cold months. They went. Down on the border the motor home blew a front tire and the top-heavy vehicle went over. Mr. and Mrs. Messmer both died.

"They have a daughter, eh?" said Madelaine. "She is killed but they never find out who?"

Du Pré nodded.

She is found along the highway, behind a gravel pile put there by the Highway Department, one bullet in her head. Bullet blows up in her head, Du Pré remembered, little pieces, can't even tell what it was. Nothing. Nobody caught.

Long time gone, 1980, '82, something like that.

"They have son, too," said Du Pré. "Bad kid. He is in some trouble, he is sent away, he don't come back here. I don't know what happen, him. I think he is sent to that Boy's Town or something."

Beat a horse to death, that was it, rope the horse up it can't move and beat its head in, a sledgehammer. Mean little shit, Catfoot tell me about it.

Du Pré looked over at the farm machinery ranked in rows. All you needed to raise wheat. Big tractors, plows, drills, sprayers, even a combine. Pretty good ranch afford its own combine. Most people they contract it out.

Nothing for that hay, though, they are not selling the cutters and rakes and balers.

Du Pré looked off toward the old white ranch house. The house was shabby, paint peeling, shingles mangy. On a ranch the animals and equipment usually had better buildings than the people who owned them.

A man came out of the house. He was about forty, dark, six feet tall. He wore a three-piece suit and irrigation boots. No hat. Dark glasses.

"That is him?" said Madelaine.

Du Pré couldn't remember what the mean little shit looked like, or if he had ever seen him.

Catfoot and Mama they are killed 1983, Catfoot is drunk, the train hit them.

Son of a bitch, life, just like that.

Du Pré shrugged.

"We get somethin' to eat," said Madelaine, "They auction

the china and stuff after the guns and the tools. That take an hour maybe."

Du Pré nodded. They walked back to his old cruiser and got in and Madelaine took some sandwiches out of a cooler in the back seat and a plastic tub of the good crabapple sauce she made. They ate. Madelaine had some pink wine and Du Pré sipped whiskey and they smoked, the big handrolled cigarettes for after eating. Hand-rolling meant you could build the smoke the size you wanted.

"This guy he maybe come back and run this ranch?" said Madelaine.

Du Pré shrugged.

"I hate it when them places go," said Madelaine, "All the stories are gone, too."

My Madelaine, Du Pré thought, she got this cheap old oak table maybe cost three dollars, Sears & Roebuck, hundred years ago, she love that table. Got burns on it, some drunk carve his initials in it, she love that table.

Think, Du Pré she say, all the things got said around this table.

Old piece of shit, I spend about two weeks fixing it, so it don't fall to splinters.

"My oak table is not a piece of shit, Du Pré," said Madelaine.

Du Pré looked at her.

"You thinking pret' loud there," said Madelaine. "We go now, maybe buy that china."

Madelaine had her heart set on some gold-rimmed flowered china that she said was old and very valuable.

I pay for it, I eat off of it, I don't care, Du Pré thought.

When the china set finally came up for bids Du Pré got the whole set, minus a few broken over the decades, for eighty dollars. He paid the lawyer the money and then he picked up two boxes and Madelaine the third and they walked back to the old cruiser and slid them into the back seat.

"Anything else you want?" said Du Pré.

Madelaine shook her head.

Du Pré got in the car.

"Where you know, this china?" he said.

"Susan Klein hear about it think I maybe like it," said Madelaine.

Women, Du Pré thought, know about everything.

He started the car. He turned around and he headed down the long drive toward the bench road.

A couple of hands were hazing some cows toward the barn. The cows were huge in the belly and ready to calve.

"Bet you are glad you don't do that no more," said Madelaine.

"Yah," said Du Pré. Pulling calves was hard work, and it usually went on day and night for weeks. He'd been kicked once so hard his left femur snapped and he heard it break, like a stick on a knee.

They got close to the gate and the cattle guard. Du Pré looked over. There was a cow there already calving, and the calf's rear legs were out. It was stuck. The cow bawled in pain.

Du Pré backed up until he could turn around and he drove up to the ranch buildings. The hands were moving the cows very slowly. Du Pré went through the fence and trotted toward the riders.

A cow lay dead in a little hollow.

Blood seeped from a hole in her skull. She had a live calf partway out, too.

Du Pré stopped and waited. He waved at the riders.

They didn't move any faster and it was ten minutes before the lead rider got to him.

The man was an ordinary hand, middle-aged, weathered, bent. His face was dark with sun and his clothes filthy.

"You got a cow in trouble, the gate," said Du Pré.

The hand nodded.

"Thanks," he said, "I knew that."

Du Pré looked at him. That cow was a lot of money and her calf would die soon without help.

The hand looked at him.

"The boss said do the easy ones and shoot the others."

Du Pré looked at him.

"He's gettin' out of the cow business," said the hand. "It don't make any sense to me either."

"Who is your boss?" asked Du Pré.

"That son of a bitch Larry Messmer," said the hand. "I worked here ten years for his folks. Soon as the calves are in, we get paid off. Got to be gone by the end of the month."

Du Pré shook his head.

"Say, mister," said the hand, "you know anybody lookin' for good hands?"

Du Pré shook his head.

There were very few jobs any more in the cattle country.

The hand looked past Du Pré. He put heels to his horse and trotted after the cows and his partner.

Du Pré turned.

Larry Messmer was standing at the fence, feet apart, looking out at Du Pré.

Du Pré waved.

Messmer didn't take his hands out of his pockets.

Messmer was looking at something far away.

Du Pré walked back to the fence and stepped through, and he went to his car and got in.

"It is him," said Du Pré, "that Larry Messmer."

"What is with his cows?" said Madelaine.

Du Pré shook his head and started the engine.

248